STRIPPED BARE

'This isn't for your pleasure,' he said. 'Turn around and bend over the trolley.'

She considered trying to resist, but gave up and did as he asked, then gasped as he roughly tugged the back of the uniform up, exposing her bum. She blushed as she realised that he'd be looking at her best knickers, selected specially to impress him.

'We'll take these off,' he said, pulling them down and waiting for her to step out of them.

She let out a little sob as her sex was exposed, sure that he'd see the moist pinkness and realise that she was aroused, but if he did notice he didn't say anything. She heard a snapping sound, then her bum cheeks were being parted, her sex opening with a wet sound, and a gloved finger was rubbing something cold over her bumhole.

STRIPPED BARE

Angel Blake

This book is a work of fiction.
In real life, make sure you practise safe, sane and consensual sex.

First published in 2005 by
Nexus
Thames Wharf Studios
Rainville Road
London W6 9HA

www.nexus-books.co.uk

Typeset by TW Typesetting, Plymouth, Devon

Printed and bound by
Clays Ltd, St Ives PLC

ISBN 0 352 33971 3

Contents

1   Shop Girl   1
2   Doctors and Nurses   29
3   Filly   57
4   The Chalet   80
5   The Stewardess   101
6   School Disco   117
7   This Little Piggy   142
8   Ballet School   156
9   Up the Aisle   192
10   The Waves   215

You'll notice that we have introduced a set of symbols onto our book jackets, so that you can tell at a glance what fetishes each of our brand new novels contains. Here's the key – enjoy!

cp (traditional)

cp (modern)

spanking

restraint/bondage

rope bondage/hojojutsu

latex/rubber/leather/enclosure

fem dom

willing captivity

medical

period setting

uniforms

sex rituals

1

Shop Girl

I'd never been bullied before. I'd got on well with my colleagues at my last job, but I didn't want to work in the suburbs all my life. I'd been working in a department store in Kingston, where I'd grown up, but it was deathly dull and I fancied something more cosmopolitan and sophisticated: the West End beckoned. Annie, my boss, had written me a great reference, and I started to apply for all the jobs which looked right. But the one I ended up getting was the one I'd wanted most of all: working on a cosmetics stand in one of the big department stores on Oxford Street. The interview had been difficult, with a very stern woman, Miss Caldicott, who oversaw all of the cosmetics stands in the shop, and I thought I'd failed it – but that's always the way, isn't it? When I found out I'd got it, my colleagues were really happy for me, and told me how much they'd miss me; I said I'd miss them, too, but in truth I was far too excited at having landed the job to look back, and as I worked out my month's notice I could barely contain myself, full of enthusiasm for a new start in life.

I had to turn up extra early on my first day so that some of the other girls could show me round before the shop opened. We had to wear long white lab-coats, helping to maintain the illusion of scientific exactitude in cosmetics, and so that we didn't soil them on our way into work – they had to be absolutely pristine – there was a small changing room that the girls on all the cosmetics stands used.

Our stand itself was more like a room, except that it was missing a ceiling and two walls – more, then, like a stage set, or a cutaway designed to show off a particular style of furnishings. There was a counter running along the longer wall, a few chairs and a table with some magazines and cosmetics bumf scattered along the top, a water dispenser and a till. We'd be working in rotation, either behind the till, behind the counter offering product-oriented advice or sitting down with clients on the chairs for informal chats about beauty and skincare. It was a far smarter set-up than the one I'd been used to, but in its essentials it didn't differ that much, and I was confident that I'd be able to cope.

But it's always tough starting in a new job, a bit like the first few days at a new school, when you don't really know your way around and have to rely on a friendly face or two to help you out. I was lucky and not at the same time here, with Lindsey, one of the other girls on the stand, taking the time to explain everything to me and make sure that I was fitting in OK. And then there was Fiona. She basically just ignored me for the first few days, but the first things she did say to me made me realise that this wasn't going to be an easy relationship.

It happened on my third day at work, just as I was getting ready in the changing room. We each had a locker, and some of the girls kidded about a bit – just like school really, all the more so this time when Fiona eyed me critically as I stripped down to bra and panties. They were pretty sheer – my tits are small, and don't need much support – so she didn't need to look too hard, but still I was shocked by what she said.

'Bit thin down there, aren't you?'

It took a couple of seconds before I worked out what she meant. We barely knew each other, and already she was making comments about my pubic hair! I just stared back at her, but she continued blithely on.

'Looks like a comb-over! Bet the boys don't like it much.'

And she zipped up her coat and walked through on to the shop floor. Fiona had more or less ignored me up to that point, and I'd imagined that I'd get to know her over the weeks to come. But now I felt humiliated. I've never had much hair there, it's true – it just never grew. But boys I'd known hadn't seemed to mind; I know most don't go for a thick thatch anyway. You just need to look at the magazines to find out; they're all shaved or waxed, with little razor streaks or V-shapes. Who wants to rummage through thick curls? But Fiona's self-assurance seemed to mean more than any of that.

I carried on dressing and went out to the stand. I hoped that Fiona's behaviour in the changing room was a blip; she'd been rude to me, but I could forgive her. I didn't want to get off on the wrong foot with any of my colleagues; I was far too anxious to succeed in this job for that.

But, after she'd made her scathing comments, it looked like she had it in for me. She seemed to delight in everything I did wrong, and even cut me off as soon as I started talking to customers, taking the clients for her own.

And the way she looked only made it worse. She was immaculate, with her dark-brown hair all pulled back in a tight ponytail, her makeup perfect. She was statuesque, too – tall and full-bodied, with boobs she was only too happy to show off, leaning down for male customers to catch a glimpse of her cleavage, or looking disdainfully at my thin chest. Men stared admiringly at her as they walked past, and I could have sworn some came to the stand just to be near her; they weren't interested in cosmetics at all. Her accent was pure home counties, cut-glass and precise. She was perfect.

I just couldn't compare; my hair was mousy and all over the place, and, while I don't normally feel short and thin, Fiona made me feel like a second-class citizen, as though she couldn't believe I had the gall to work on a cosmetics stand. Every time I opened my mouth I could see her flinch, clearly aghast at the common new employee.

I was desperate for us to get on, though, and persevered with her, trying to crack jokes and chat with her, but she would ignore me, turning her back and flicking her hair in my face.

It got worse, too. Every few days we'd need to replace the water bottles on the dispenser. I'd been told how to do it: the bottles themselves were very expensive, and the fixture at the top should never be removed. But since I'd started on the job, there had been one bottle next to the dispenser with the top removed, and while replacing an empty bottle on the dispenser one day I absent-mindedly took the top off it. I swear I'd only done it because there was that other bottle lying next to the dispenser with its top off, but I had a sick feeling when I realised what I'd done, and knew that the cost would probably be docked from my pay.

Fiona, always on the lookout for a moment of weakness on my part, spotted it instantly, and made the most of my blushes and guilty expression. She came over, incredulous.

'Did you just take the top off that bottle?'

'I – yes, it was a mistake, I –' I flushed an even deeper red, and bit my lip to stop myself from crying.

'You did the other one too, didn't you?'

'No! That's been there since I started!' I could barely believe the injustice of such an accusation; she knew full well it had been there before I started work. Just my luck, then, to have Miss Caldicott, who was doing her afternoon rounds of the stands, walk towards us. I looked at Fiona, and implored her silently not to tell on me. But my vulnerability seemed to spark off something cruel in her, and with a curt shake of the head she walked towards Miss Caldicott.

Miserably, I turned back towards the stand, and took up my position behind the counter, fighting to keep back the tears and trying to pay no attention to the conversation Fiona was having with Miss Caldicott, just out of earshot. But I could tell they were talking about me; once I glanced up to see Miss Caldicott staring at me with a peculiarly severe expression, and I actually shuddered, frozen for a second like a terrified rabbit, before being able to look away. They didn't talk for long, and when Fiona came back to the stand she had a self-satisfied smirk on her face. I tried to ignore her, and wanted to get Lindsey's attention, but she was busy with a client.

Five minutes later a call for me came over the PA. I had to go and see Miss Caldicott. That got Lindsey's attention, and she looked alarmed when she saw the expression on my face. But I knew I had to get it over and done with, and smiled weakly at Lindsey then walked across the shop floor to the staff lift up to Miss Caldicott's office.

Her secretary glanced up at me from a letter she was typing as I murmured my name, then turned her attention back to her screen as she told me to go in.

I hadn't been here before; the interview had taken place in more neutral surroundings. Miss Caldicott's office was like an extension of her personality, all prim reserve and obsessive neatness: there wasn't a paper out of place. I closed the door behind me quietly and stood in front of the desk.

'Sit down, please, Joanne.' Miss Caldicott gave a brief, professional smile as I took my seat. 'Tell me – how are you settling in?'

This could be a chance to tell her about the bullying. But she seemed to get on well with Fiona, and she might just think that I was weak, not up to the job. I didn't want to rock the boat.

'Fine, thank you, Miss Caldicott.'

'Coping with the duties OK?'

'Yes, thank you.'

'Fiona tells me that you've broken two of the water bottles.'

'That's not true! I admit that I broke one, but the other one was already broken when I arrived.' I'd gone bright pink again, I could feel it.

'Are you calling Fiona a liar?'

'No – but it's not true. I only broke one of them.'

'Well –' Miss Caldicott studied a sheet of paper in front of her '– two have been broken, and somebody's going to have to pay for them. They're thirty pounds each.' She raised her eyes and fixed me again with her glare. 'Do you wish to continue working here, Joanne?'

'I – yes, of course, Miss Caldicott.'

'Then I suggest you stop accusing your colleagues of lying and pay for your mistakes. Is that clear?'

'But I didn't –'

'Is that clear?' she asked again, in a firmer voice.

And that was it. I knew I couldn't argue any more, that she could have me sacked if I did. I couldn't face going back to Kingston, couldn't face losing this job so soon after getting it. I lowered my eyes to the ground, and tried to control the wobble in my voice. 'Yes, Miss Caldicott.'

'Good. Then I'll arrange for the costs to be taken off your next paycheque. Good day.'

I got up, almost shaking with rage and resentment, nodded to Miss Caldicott and left the room. Then my eyes filled and my mascara started to run, and I barely made it to the Ladies before I burst out crying. More than anything I needed a good cry. I knew that things like that – unfairness, being picked on – could happen at any job. I also knew, in theory at least, how I should be dealing with Fiona. I should pretend it wasn't happening – a bully needs a victim, and I was determined not to be hers. But it took a long time to gather my resolve.

When I left the Ladies and returned to the shop floor, the lights were dimmed and the cleaners had already started to move around. I hadn't realised it was so late. I was embarrassed to have spent so long away from the stand, but relieved that at least my day was over. The changing room should have been pretty much empty by then. But it wasn't – not quite.

When I saw Fiona there, her back to the door, unzipping her labcoat, I almost turned tail and fled. But she'd already spotted me in the mirror, and I had to go in. She didn't say anything for a while, and you could have cut the silence with a knife. She just stared, as I exposed my body to her withering gaze. She'd stopped undressing by now and was sitting on the bench, dressed only in her bra and panties, watching me as I changed. I couldn't face mentioning the water bottles – I was worried that I might go crazy and try to claw her eyes out.

'Almost bald,' she murmured.

'What?' I couldn't believe she was starting on this again, not after what she'd already made me go through that day.

'You're like a child down there! Not like me.' She smirked and leaned forwards, pressing the sides of her arms against her breasts, as if to show off her cleavage. Then she did something astonishing. She held my gaze as she opened her legs, slowly spread them and exposed the front of her knickers to my view.

I couldn't help but look down, all thoughts of the day's traumas put to one side, and was mesmerised as she tugged the crotch to one side, slowly, revealing a beautiful glossy mess of curls, auburn and shiny. I couldn't believe she was showing it to me, and stared, transfixed, as she stroked the curls with one hand, as if to show off their perfect condition. But that wasn't all I could see. Her sex lips were poking out too, and beyond their paleness I could see a flash of pink, and the glistening of something damp inside. I think I might have licked my lips.

'What are you, a lezzer?' she spat out, breaking the spell.

My eyes shot up to meet hers. I didn't know what to say.

'Keep your eyes to yourself.'

I couldn't help looking down again as she released the crotch of her knickers and pulled them tight against her crease; then she turned away, swishing her ponytail over her shoulder, and started to step into a pair of jeans. Almost conversationally, she spoke again. 'I don't like girls myself. My boyfriend's called Johnny.'

She sat down again and ran her fingernails absently down the front of her knickers, saying dreamily as she gazed at the wall, 'He likes me all bushy.' Then she stood, pulled up her jeans and fixed me with a steely glare. 'You're probably only a lezzer because you're so bald down there. Johnny wouldn't even look at you.'

My mind was whirling, and I could barely move as she finished dressing. She left without another word, although she did turn back to smirk before she closed the door. I just sat there in my bra and knickers, thinking about what she had said. I didn't like other girls either. I was normal – I liked having sex with boys. There was only that one time at school, but that was normal too; most people tried that kind of thing when they were younger, just to see what it felt like.

I couldn't believe her cheek. She was definitely the rudest person I'd ever had to work with. Not only bullying me in the workplace, but making wild comments about my body – there was nothing wrong with my pubic hair! And the way she'd displayed herself like that! It wasn't my fault if I looked. Anyone would have done it. I pulled myself together and got dressed. But I couldn't get the image out of my head of her sitting there, her legs spread, holding her knickers to the side for me to get a good look. I could have sworn her bum had slipped forwards a bit as she'd done it, pushing it all closer towards me. How dare she accuse me of being a lesbian, behaving like that? I bet she'd made it all up about Johnny.

The worst thing about it all was that I was a little damp myself.

The next day wasn't any better. She was in the changing room when I arrived, almost as though she'd been waiting for me, and she made another snide comment about my pubic hair, while running her fingers down the skin each side of her knickers.

'Almost time for another waxing. Even Johnny doesn't like it *too* thick. What do *you* use?' She turned to me, stifled a giggle and looked away. I could feel myself blushing.

And all that day she seemed to be flirting with me. Not in a way so that I could accuse her of doing it, though; she just flashed her cleavage a few times, making me look, then smirking. Her nipples were stiff when she did it, too. She also squeezed past me more times than was really necessary, and I was sure she was pushing her arse cheeks against me when she did it. The rustle of starched cotton as she rubbed against me sounded so loud in my ears I was sure everyone would hear it. But nothing changed. My other colleagues seemed oblivious, and the shoppers just kept on shopping. Only Fiona smiling slyly to herself gave me any idea that I wasn't just making this up.

It was almost as if she knew what I'd done the night before. When I got back I was feeling upset, so I ran a bath and had a glass of wine. In the bath I thought I'd give myself a rub just to feel better; I didn't want to admit to myself that my pussy had been swollen and aching dully since I'd seen Fiona in the changing room. I tried to think about other things while I rubbed it – Frank, my last boyfriend, grabbing me by the neck as he pumped his thick cock into me; sucking men off in alleyways like a dirty whore; the kind of things I'd made myself come to recently – but the image of Fiona leering at me as she showed it all off came back into my head again and again.

Finally, I gave into it – I couldn't help myself – and rubbed hard at my clit as I thought about her thick bush, all moist inside, and the rudeness of her showing it to me in the changing room. I stuck a soapy finger up my bum, pushing it in and out as I frigged myself to a climax, coming hard with the picture of her slumped lewdly against the wall, legs splayed and her pussy all open and juicy, burned in my mind.

The way she behaved during the next day kept the image alive, and by the time it came to close up shop my panties were damp and I knew it would show. I dreaded having to go to the changing room, but there was nothing for it. I tried to undress with my back to her, and to keep my thighs pressed together so that she wouldn't see the damp patch, but she didn't miss it. I think she might even have smelled it.

My eyes caught hers, and a look of impossible superiority passed between us before she arched an eyebrow and returned to her own dressing. My cheeks burned. She didn't say anything, and she left while there were still other girls in the changing room. I wasn't sure whether to feel glad or not. Part of me wanted her there, wanted her to acknowledge what had happened and respond to it; the rest of me hated her, and wanted to pull her hair and scratch her, to take revenge on the bitch for having made me feel so small. Both parts of me wanted her to pay attention.

I first met Gemma a few days later. I was coming back to work from having had my lunch sandwiches in the park – I'd tried the canteen a couple of times but the girls from the other stands hadn't been particularly friendly – when I saw Fiona and another girl talking outside the shop. The other girl was just as striking as Fiona: tall, with cropped blonde hair and a lithe body. It looked like they were arguing, and I hoped they'd ignore me when I walked past, even though I'd seen them both nod to Lindsey when she went back in; but it didn't work. As I tried to squeeze past, making myself as inconspicuous as possible, the girl Fiona was talking to looked up and caught my eyes. I managed a brief smile then walked to the changing room to put my labcoat back on.

She was waiting for me outside after work. I didn't even notice until she called out.

'Joanne?'

I whirled round, alarmed. She stepped up behind me, smiling apologetically, and held out a hand. I took it, but the confusion must have shown in my face, as she laughed.

'Sorry. I'm Gemma. I used to work on the stand.'

'Oh?' I still wasn't sure what she wanted.

'Look, do you have time to go for a coffee? There are some things I want to talk over with you.'

I must have looked undecided, as then she played her trump card. 'It's about Fiona.'

Fifteen minutes later it was as though we'd known each other for years. Gemma was friendly, frank and seemed genuine, her conversation a breath of fresh air after the snide remarks I'd had to put up with from Fiona. She broached the subject of my colleague delicately, sounding me out slowly before revealing that she'd left the company after having been bullied by Fiona.

And then it all came out. I hadn't told any of my friends about Fiona – I was sure it would have sounded whiny, self-pitying, and I didn't want to dump on them – and I hadn't realised how much I'd bottled up. I didn't mention any of the stuff about the pubic hair – not at first, anyway – and I certainly didn't mention what I'd done in the bath a few nights before, but I told her how Fiona constantly put me down, how she made me feel as though I were seven again and what had happened with the water bottles.

Gemma was so sympathetic that when she suggested that we move on to a pub I was delighted. And after a couple of drinks, and a few hints that she'd suffered something similar, I told her about my problem. The pubic hair, I mean. Not that I'd considered *it* a problem; just the way that Fiona used it to put me down. Gemma's eyes widened when I told her that Fiona had showed her thatch to me, and they gleamed when I talked about what a vindictive little bitch she was.

She chose her moment well. 'I think we should do something to get back at her.'

I giggled. The idea sounded hilarious. 'What kind of thing do you have in mind?'

'Oh, I don't know. But something big. She made me so upset when I was working there, and I can't bear to think that she's doing the same to someone else. Someone so nice.'

I basked in the warm glow of wine and revenge-fuelled bonhomie, and tried to come up with some ideas. 'We could try and do something about this . . . Johnny.'

She looked confused, so I explained to her that Fiona's boyfriend was called Johnny.

'Oh! Of course.' She smiled to herself, then looked back at me, her eyes sparkling as she took my hand in hers. 'That might work,' she said doubtfully. 'But I'm sure you can come up with something better. Just keep your eyes open.'

We exchanged mobile numbers and promised to catch up in a few days. I felt happier already, as though talking about taking revenge on Fiona was just as good as actually doing it. On the tube on the way home I drunkenly turned the situation over in my mind again and again, before I knew what I wanted to do. It had to be something to do with her pubic hair. She was obviously so proud of it, and I wanted to hit her where it hurt.

* * *

The idea came to me a few days later. Fiona's behaviour hadn't changed; she was still dropping hints about her thatch and general attractiveness to men; still looking disdainfully at me even as she flaunted herself; still boasting about Johnny and how much he worshipped her. I hated him already and I hadn't even met him.

I was still finding my way around the stall, and would ask one of my colleagues for information when I found a product I hadn't dealt with before. It was while I was looking for a foaming cleanser one of our regular customers wanted that I found them: long, thin boxes containing strips, like plasters, only thinner. I waited until I'd served the customer then asked Lindsey what they were. She glanced over and saw what I meant.

'Oh, they're depilatories. Most people use cream or wax nowadays, as those strips hurt a bit, but they're very effective. Some of our customers with –' she lowered her tone '– *thicker* hair use these. Can't imagine it myself, though.' She frowned. 'Must hurt to hell when you take them off.'

A plan had already presented itself to me. 'So . . . how long do you have to leave them on for?'

'Oh, they're instant. You just put them on, smooth them down then tear them off. But we don't sell many of them; that's why they're hidden away down there. There are just a couple of customers who ask for them; you'll get to know them soon.'

I'd turned away to put them back when Fiona, having just finished batting her eyelashes at a male customer, noticed and slid over. She knew exactly what they were.

'Oh!' she tittered. 'I don't think you'll be needing those. No!' She shook her head, laughed and flounced away, my eyes boring holes in her back.

And that decided me. It could go horribly wrong; I could get the sack, and she might even involve the police. But I had to do it. And I had a friend who would help me.

That evening I called Gemma and told her about the idea. She was delighted, and we spurred each other on to make more and more outlandish suggestions about what we could do with our victim. The date was set for Friday, and I giggled as I put the phone down. I could hardly wait.

Every Friday there was a new delivery of cosmetics out at the back of the store, and a couple of us had to go through to collect it; Lindsey had shown me where on the first day, and had told me to ask any of the other girls to help with the next delivery. She'd also warned me to be careful out there. The food for the canteen was delivered and the rubbish taken away from the same courtyard, and there were tall wire bins filled to overflowing with food waste out there. Needless to say, nobody wanted a splash of grease on their labcoats, so we had to take extra care. I'd gone out there a few times myself earlier, to get an idea of where everything was, and the setting was perfect. Gemma knew it well too, and had arranged to leave her job early so that she could help.

In the end it was easy. The other girls were busy with customers, and Fiona was preening herself in front of a mirror, checking her lipstick.

'There's a new Clinique delivery out back,' I told her. 'Can you help me bring it in?'

She scowled, and looked around, only to find the other girls tied up. With barely disguised annoyance, she nodded and stalked off towards the deliveries yard, swishing across the shop floor. I was right behind her.

She stopped outside and peered around, then turned to face me, her expression changing from confusion to triumph. 'You screwed up! There's nothing out here.'

'There is – it's over there.' I indicated the area near the bins.

Scowling again, she turned and walked towards them.

'I'd better not get any stains on this. And there'd better not be any of those kitchen staff around,' she said. 'But I don't see any –'

Gemma slid out of the shadows to her left, and we took an arm each.

'What the fuck?' she shrieked as we dragged her, half-pushing, half-pulling, to the bins. We'd chosen the right one before; only half-full with rubbish for the compost, orange peels, eggshells and tea bags, nothing that could hurt her but plenty that would leave a nasty stain all over her labcoat. I wasn't sure we were going to get her in, as she was thrashing around so much, but Gemma was stronger than she looked. And more vicious, too.

'You're going in the bin, you bitch,' she hissed.

This was no joke to her, and for a second I wondered what I'd let us in for. But there was no turning back now. As Fiona wailed and sobbed, we shoved her headfirst into the bin, wedging her arms in so that she wouldn't be able to pull herself out. I could see her face, red and swollen from being upside down, through the wire mesh, already slimy from cabbage leaves and potato peel. She looked furious, panic-stricken and not a little scared. And that rid me of my doubts: scared was how I wanted her. I grabbed her legs before she could start kicking and overturn the bin.

Gemma peeled her labcoat down over her knickers,

all the while muttering obscenities. 'You deserve this, you fucking bitch, head down in the bin.'

I could make out the sound of Fiona sobbing, but my eyes were fixed on the knickers, imagining the plump sex inside and what was about to happen to it.

Gemma slapped her arse cheeks a couple of times before tugging at her knickers, and I had to hold her legs extra hard when she started to kick again. I could hear a muffled 'No!' then a cough as Fiona inadvertently let something rotten into her mouth.

I was transfixed as Gemma pulled the knickers down, exposing all that glorious hair. And then we had our first surprise. Right in the middle of her silky white knickers was a brown streak.

'A skiddy! The bitch has been scratching her arse!' Gemma could hardly contain herself, and ripped the knickers off the rest of the way before dangling them in front of Fiona's face.

I just kept on staring at her pussy, all ripe and inviting. It was a struggle not to touch it.

And then Gemma was hurrying me along. 'Go on, then, get them out.'

With one arm circled around Fiona's thighs, I reached into one of my coat pockets and fished out the depilatory strips, then handed them to Gemma. Her eyes gleamed as she took them, an incredulous smile playing about her lips, then she was squatting in front of Fiona's face.

'Look what we've got for you! *Johnny* won't like you much when we've got rid of all of this, will he?' Gemma spat the name out so ferociously that I was surprised. The bullying must have really got to her.

Then she carefully and methodically peeled the back off the strips and laid them down all over Fiona's rich bush. Fiona's arse was twitching as she felt Gemma smooth the strips down, and I had to hold her legs open wide so that we got all of it. And there was a lot of it to get. We used all the strips I'd brought out.

I knew it had been my idea, and I knew that I wanted it to happen, but still I thought Gemma took too much pleasure in it. She took the edge of the first strip and peeled it back ever so slightly, her eyes shining demonically as she listened to Fiona whimper, then she ripped it off. Fiona gave a yowl that had me looking over my shoulder, petrified that all of the kitchen staff must have just heard us. I knew they listened to the radio in there, but still, she'd been so loud. And the struggle she put up now! It was all I could do to hang on to her legs.

I'd thought of doing them all at once, but Gemma seemed determined to torture her, and waited until her sobbing had died down before pulling off the next strip. This time the yowl was even louder, and her struggle just as fierce. But now you could see the difference: half of her pussy was naked, and all red and puffy where the hairs had been pulled out.

Gemma didn't look at me once while she pulled off the other strips, the only sounds the tearing, the yowling and the whimpering. But, when it was done, she turned and smiled at me. I'll never forget that face. She had a ferocious gleam in her eye, but she didn't look unhappy. Anything but. Her pupils were dilated and her lips slightly parted, as though she were high on drugs.

I stared as Fiona's pussy moved to her racking sobs. Despite myself, I had been a little worried that it would look ugly without any hair – and, while I wanted revenge, that wasn't all I was after, if I was absolutely honest with myself – but now, all red, swollen and naked, it looked better than ever. I touched the skin, experimentally, and felt her flinch.

'Oh, God.' I could just make out her muffled moan. The depilatories had done a fantastic job. I'd never seen someone look so exposed. You could see everything, every crease of her sex lips, her arsehole all rudely out in the open. Her pussy was almost totally hairless now, apart from a few wispy hairs along the edge of her lips. Just to check how many were left, I ran a finger along the length of her crease, parting the lips just a little. Her hips wiggled a little underneath me. I touched the rest of the skin where the hair had been, enjoying the feel of the smoothness, revelling in our triumph, and staring at the pink slit in the centre, which before my eyes seemed to open up and glisten.

'What are you doing?'

I snapped out of my reverie to find Gemma staring at me, a curious expression on her face.

'That's not what she needs. Hold her legs again.' Gemma moved behind me and started to slap the cheeks. '*That's* what she needs.' Then she was talking to Fiona, her victim's eyes puffy from crying. '*That's* what a little slut needs. A good spanking to take her down a peg or two.'

I was stunned. Gemma hadn't mentioned this before. I thought we'd just take off the hair then let Fiona sob her heart out in the courtyard. And, if she'd started with a few light slaps, that wasn't how it was now. She was really putting all her strength into it, landing her open hand with a solid meaty thwack, and making the cheeks glow redder and redder. With each slap the naked pussy winked lewdly at me, and I could see that it was juicy inside. I couldn't believe that she was actually enjoying this. But then again, I was too. Despite myself, I could feel my knickers getting damp as I watched Fiona's arse wobbling each time Gemma's hand landed. It just looked so rude, exposing her like that. But I had to protest. This was too much.

'Gemma, I –'

'Shut up.' Then she spoke to Fiona again. 'That's what you need, isn't it, you little fuck-slut.'

And now she built up to a good rhythm, slapping both cheeks hard, then occasionally landing one right in the middle, so it squashed her sex lips out with a wet noise. Fiona wasn't begging any more, just making a high-pitched keening noise, which went up in tone each time a cheek was spanked. Then the wail was fixed on a high note as Gemma's hand spanked away furiously, harder and faster than ever, raining blows all over the pink cheeks.

Finally she stopped, and I breathed a sigh of relief. Fiona's arse was a mess, all red and blotchy. I touched it, and drew my fingers back with a gasp. It was hot. Gemma watched me, then smirked, and pinched some of the red arse flesh between her fingernails.

'Ow! You bitch!' came the muffled reply. Then her legs started kicking again. 'Fucking let me out of here!'

I thought this would be the end of it, and mixed in with my relief was a little disappointment. But Gemma had even more planned. 'Hold her legs. I'm just going to get someone.'

'But who –' I was too late. She was already walking determinedly round to the kitchens. I was tempted to run there and then – I definitely did not want anyone else to see me like this. But the sight of Fiona's pussy there, all open and juicy, ready for me, was too much to resist. I ran a finger down the middle, and it opened wetly. I could see her clit, all stiff and out of its hood, and pinched it lightly between my fingers. I was rewarded with a low purr.

I didn't care now: I had to do it. Bending my head down, I smelled her juice. She was soaking now, and

I could see it running down and pooling around her arsehole. I stuck out my tongue tentatively, just for a taste. But I'd wanted to do this for so long – now that I had the chance, I wasn't going to throw it away. I started to lick, long slow licks from her clit to her arsehole and back again. She sighed, and ground her pussy against my face as I sucked on her clit. Then I used her own juices to worm the end of a carrot, part of the rubbish that had spilled into the courtyard, into her arsehole. She squealed, then relaxed, and I had it in all the way, sliding it in and out as I nibbled on her clit. I was in bliss, pushing my tongue as far as it would go into her, when I heard a clatter behind me.

I whirled round, my chin wet with Fiona's juices. Her arsehole closed on the carrot, and it slid out with an audible plop, then traced a lewd, slow trail down her crease before finally falling to the ground. I stood up, ludicrously trying to look innocent when I'd been caught in the act. But they didn't care.

Standing by the other bins were Gemma and one of the kitchen workers. I'd seen him a few times before, a burly middle-aged man, muscle running to fat, who helped to shift boxes. He looked confused, half-excited and half-convinced that he hadn't fully understood the situation. I could see that Gemma had a strong grip on his arm, to stop him from running away.

'Look at that lovely little pussy. All ready for you to fuck. Do you want it?' She gave his crotch a squeeze. I could see that it was stiffening down there. But he wasn't convinced.

'Uh – I don't think I should. I should get back now,' he stuttered. But his eyes were fixed on the red and juicy pussy, the freshly spanked arse, and he involuntarily took a step forwards.

Gemma's hand had found the shaft of his cock now, and was rubbing it through his pants. 'Yes, you want it. You're all stiff. You want to fuck that little slut's juicy hole, don't you?' She tugged on his cock, leading him towards it. I could see that he was mesmerised by the sight of it.

She glanced at me, and pointed with her head to one of the other bins. I knew what she meant. We had to knock one of them over and roll it under Fiona, so that he could get the right angle. His eyes darted nervously back and forth between me, Gemma and Fiona's arse as I pushed another bin over and moved it into position.

'It'll be all right, won't it? I mean, nobody will find out, will they?' He was staring at her juicy hole. 'This isn't a trick, is it?'

'It'll be fine,' Gemma cooed, unzipping him.

We took one side of Fiona's bin each and lowered it until it was at the right angle. I could see her looking back at Gemma with a mixture of fear and expectation in her eyes. Then Gemma was back with the man, tugging his cock into full thickness. She'd chosen well. It was thick and veiny, with a huge purple head, and his heavy balls looked obscene hanging down. She massaged them with one hand as she eased the head of his cock into Fiona's hole. And that convinced him.

With a groan he slid it all the way in, his balls nestling against Fiona's clit. He grabbed her blotched arse cheeks then and pulled it almost all the way out before ramming it back in. Fiona moaned. I didn't know what to do with myself. I stole a glance at Gemma, who was staring at his cock as it pounded into Fiona. She had slipped one hand into her shirt and was stroking her nipples, almost absent-mindedly, as she watched.

He carried on fucking her, his thick cock stretching her hole and filling her completely. Occasionally he pulled it out and smeared her juices all up and down her crease before shoving it back in and pounding hard again. It was obvious that he wasn't going to be able to hold out for long.

'I'm going to spunk in her hole,' he said breathlessly.

'No!' Gemma was next to him in a flash, pushing him away from Fiona and taking his cock in her hand. She whispered something in his ear. His eyes widened and he shook his head.

'No, I can't do that. It'd get all messy.'

Gemma smiled. 'It'll be fine. Take my word for it.'

I didn't know what they were talking about, until Gemma started to smear Fiona's juices around her arsehole. She eased one finger in, then another, and started to move them slowly up and down, oblivious to Fiona's squeals. The man stared at what she was doing, pumping his own cock to the same rhythm. While nobody was watching, I stole a hand under my labcoat and felt my knickers. They were soaking, and I scraped a fingernail under them, along the swollen lips. When Gemma looked at me knowingly, I gave a guilty start and pulled my finger out, wiping it on my labcoat before I knew what I was doing. She smiled, and shook her head slightly. I wasn't sure what she meant – that I shouldn't be touching myself, or that she couldn't understand why I was stopping.

In any case, it was ready now. Gemma called me over. 'I want you to kneel next to her and rub it while he's in her.'

Watching was more than enough for me. 'Can't you do it?' I asked.

She shook her head and smiled slightly. 'I have something else to do.'

So I kneeled, and held Fiona's lips open as Gemma helped the man to ease his cock into her arse. It must have been tight. He slid it in slowly, half an inch at a time, and I stroked her clit each time he pushed. And then, with a sigh, she relaxed, and the rest of it slid in. Now it was his turn to groan.

'I'm not going to be able to hold it for long,' he told Gemma.

'That doesn't matter. But when you do, pull it out and spunk all over her arse. I want to see you do it.' And then she said to me, 'Rub her hard.'

So I did. I watched him push his huge cock into her tiny arsehole then pull it out, the little ring of muscle pulling and pushing on it as he shoved it in and out. I'd never had it done to me; it looked painful, like it wouldn't fit. But in her it looked just right, and really dirty, and I could feel her getting juicier and juicier with the sensation. I circled her clit with my finger then started to flick it to the rhythm of his thrusts.

Meanwhile, Gemma had squatted over the end of the bin, by Fiona's face, which was turned to see as much as she could of the man whose cock was filling her bum. Gemma had pulled her skirt up so she could play with herself, and I could see her fingers wriggling away under her knickers, which were damp at the front, as she stared at the man.

Finally, it was too much for him. 'I can't –'

He pulled it out and it was spurting all over her open arsehole. I strummed her clit even harder as I watched his cock pumping its seed over her, some of it trickling down into her pink slit and some of it running down the walls of her bumhole.

'Put it back in,' I heard her whimper.

Gemma heard her and spat it at the man, rubbing herself hard. 'Go on, put it back in.'

He did it, shuddering as he eased his purple cock head back into her bottom, his shaft still stiff. And then I saw her bumhole clench on it, spasming as she came on my finger. I gave her clit one last hard flick as she squealed, higher than before, her pussy opening and closing in rhythmic contractions as her arse squeezed his cock out again, glistening with come.

But still that wasn't enough for Gemma. She squatted down further, hooked a finger round the front of her knickers and spread her legs over Fiona's face, just in time to let a spray of pee jet out over her as she came. Fiona's mouth had been open, and now she spluttered as the pee soaked her face.

The man pulled away, confused, muttering 'What the fuck?', and I got up and ran, shame burning my cheeks, the picture of Gemma squatting, her eyes closed in bliss, indelibly etched on my mind. She'd gone too far this time, and my mind was in a whirl as I pushed open the doors back on to the shop floor.

I didn't know what I was doing; all I wanted was privacy, and I pushed blindly past the shoppers, almost in tears at what I'd seen, until I found a cubicle in the Ladies. I'd just wanted to get away, to collect my thoughts – it had been too powerful – and I didn't want to admit to myself how turned on I was. But there was nothing for it. I opened my labcoat, pulled my bra cup down, exposing my nipples to the air, and pinched them hard. Then I pulled my knickers halfway down my thighs and slumped down on the seat, jamming my feet against the door as I started to rub myself with one hand, the other stroking my arsehole.

Images raced through my mind – Fiona's pussy all red and puffy after we'd got rid of the hair; Gemma spanking her hard; her hole getting wetter and wetter; the man's cock easing into her arse, and the thrill as it slid all the way in; and Gemma peeing over Fiona's face, letting it all spray out.

That was it. It hardly took me any time before I was gasping out my own come, a finger and thumb pinched on my clit while I had another finger rammed into my bum up to the knuckle. My legs shook against the cubicle door, the force of it leaving me trembling, and I waited, one finger still jammed inside me and another on my clit, until I felt the contractions fade away.

My damp knickers felt cool against my burning pussy when I pulled them back on, and I knew that I had to look a mess. Some of Gemma's pee had spattered on to my labcoat, and I must have reeked of sex. There was no way I was going to go back to work. But my mind was so fixed on how to leave the building without going past the stand that I didn't even check to see if anyone else was in the Ladies, and got an open-mouthed look from a teenager washing her hands in the sink. My cheeks on fire, I fled for the safety of home.

I didn't come in for the next few days. I just couldn't face it, and called in sick. It always sounds better when you take a few days off rather than just one – like you really have been ill – and I could use it as an excuse for why I'd taken off so abruptly on the Friday. It had given me time to have the labcoat dry-cleaned, too, and I'd ignored the raised eyebrows at the dry-cleaners when I'd taken it in. I could ignore the man from the kitchens easily enough, too. All I had to do was to avoid the kitchens, which wasn't really a problem; if that man had told any of his friends about what had happened, there's no way they would have believed him.

But Fiona was a bit more of a problem. What was I going to say when I saw her? 'Gemma and I decided to play a trick on you, but it went a bit too far'? I'd even tried calling Gemma to go over what our story should be, but there was no reply. I couldn't even leave a message.

When I went in on Wednesday, there was no sign of Fiona, and the other girls acted like nothing had happened. I asked Lindsey where Fiona was, trying to make it sound like a casual question.

'Oh! She's left.'

'What do you mean? Doesn't she have to work out her notice?'

'No – she's freelance, and apparently she'd told them she was planning to leave. They've known for weeks.'

'Are they going to give Gemma her job back, then?' It was all I could think of to say.

'Who?' Lindsey looked puzzled.

'You know, the girl who used to work here before me.'

'But there wasn't anyone here before you.'

'Come on, Lindsey, you know the girl I mean. I know you saw her arguing with Fiona the other day. Outside, at lunchtime.'

Now Lindsey's eyes widened; she knew who I meant. 'But she never worked here.'

'Well, who is she, then?'

'I'm not sure. I've seen her with Fiona a few times.' She lowered her voice to a whisper. 'I think it might be her girlfriend.' Then she looked quizzically at me. 'Didn't you know?'

'No!' I could feel my face flushing. 'But – but what about Johnny?'

'Who's Johnny?'

'Fiona told me about . . .' I trailed off, utterly confused, and turned away.

Lindsey hadn't finished with me yet, though. 'I almost forgot. She left something for you.'

'For me?'

Lindsey nodded, and pointed to a package on top of one of the cabinets. Then she caught a customer's eye, and turned on her best sales smile as she approached her.

There was no card on the gift. I didn't dare to open it then. I had no idea what might be in there. Anyway, there was work to do. They hadn't replaced Fiona, and they'd been badly short-staffed while I'd been away. Even now it was busy, and I didn't get another chance to talk to Lindsey that day. But I kept on stealing glances at the package, dying to rush home and open it.

Finally, it was six. I changed quickly and was one of the first of the shop-floor girls out of the building. I didn't open the package on the tube, either, as I was too scared that it might be Fiona's revenge on me, although I couldn't imagine how bad a long, thin box could be.

I poured myself a glass of wine back at the flat and took a deep breath before opening the package, my heart pounding. But there was nothing sinister, just a box of Belgian chocolates. Relieved, but a little confused by the anticlimax, I opened the lid. There it was, a note. The message I'd been looking for.

'You were great. Thanks for a lovely time.
XXX
Fi and Gem'

2

Doctors and Nurses

Getting hold of the uniform hadn't been a problem at all. She'd been around the hospital a couple of times, and made a careful note of what the nurses wore, then visited a medical outfitters in the West End, set back a little from the mayhem of most of the shopping streets.

She'd been excited as soon as she went in, looking at the rows of uniforms, surgical masks and caps on disembodied heads, starter packs of stethoscopes, and shiny metal pincers and curved tubes whose purpose she could only take wild guesses at.

She was almost sorry that she'd gone for one of the easier options here, and a crazy notion of trying to pass herself off as a surgeon leaped into her head, but was just as swiftly crushed. She wanted to have fun, not get into anything too heavy.

The outfit was easy to find, hanging with thirty others just like it on a rack. She slid it off and held it against herself, looking into the mirror, seeing how the crisp white material would look against her long black waves of hair and full, curvy figure, then saw in the reflection as the assistant, a pretty girl of about Beth's age, moved behind her.

'Can I try this on?'

'Sure – they're pretty standard sizes, but you're welcome to. The fitting rooms are over here.' The assistant gestured to a row of curtained cubicles set back from the main displays.

Beth draped the outfit over her arm, mouthed a thank you to the girl and stepped into the cubicle. She stripped down to her underwear then paused to watch herself in the mirror. She wouldn't need these. After unclipping her bra and letting her full breasts spill out, she slid her knickers down and stepped out of the heap on the floor. She put an arm through the thick white cotton of the nurse's uniform and shivered at the touch of the material. She waited for a second, feeling her nipples stiffen at the unfamiliar feel, then felt a warm glow run through her as her excitement quickened.

It wasn't just the getting away with it, convincing people you were something you weren't – it was the outfits as well. They'd all excited her: the nun's habit she'd worn around a few churches, flashing herself to a couple of astonished tourists on a pew; or the policewoman's uniform she'd used to wander around some Soho sex shops, enjoying the looks of panic on the faces of the men there, their confusion as they wondered whether she was genuine or just liked dressing up, watching open-mouthed as she stroked her truncheon suggestively, enjoying both their un-ease and their arousal; and the barrister's outfit she'd worn around Temple, showing far too much cleavage to do anything but impress a lecherous judge.

This would be the same, she realised – or even better. She'd always fancied doctors, and had been turned on even in her teens by medical inspections, once even making up an imaginary complaint so that the curly-haired young doctor at her clinic would snap on his rubber gloves, spread her thighs gently but firmly and try to ignore the clear signs of excitement between her legs as he greased his finger entirely redundantly with lube.

30

She shuddered with pleasure as she remembered his touch, and the satisfaction she'd felt at seeing the bulge in his pants at the end of the examination, when he'd looked at her with a curious expression in his eyes. She watched her pupils dilate in the mirror as she fastened the final button on the outfit.

She squeezed her upper arms against her chest, seeing how much cleavage she could display, then undid another button, keenly aware of how sluttish she looked now, how entirely unprofessional. Then she pulled the curtain back.

The assistant was a couple of racks away, busying herself with a set of straitjackets, but had clearly been waiting for her to come out, as she turned with a professional smile ready on her lips, only to flush deep red when Beth came out.

'What do you think?' She did a little twirl for the girl. She hadn't expected her to be shocked, and Beth realised that she'd misjudged her age; she was probably only seventeen, working in one of her first jobs.

'Well, it looks like it's the right size. Is it –' she gulped visibly '– for a fancy-dress party?'

Beth laughed. 'No, it's for my new job. Why do you ask?'

She teased the girl by bending over near her, making the tops of her soft breasts bulge out even further. The girl's eyes flashed down, widening as she took in the expanse of bared skin – the material was open almost to Beth's nipples, and she knew the top of the brown disc of one was probably visible – then back up to meet Beth's gaze.

'It's just –' she looked helplessly around, starting to panic '– most of the nurses don't wear them so – so low cut.'

Beth put her head back and laughed. 'Well, I bet

the doctors won't mind; and probably the patients won't kick up too much of a fuss either.'

The girl just looked confused, but Beth wasn't finished with her yet. She turned, sure that the girl was following her every move, and pulled aside the curtain to her cubicle.

She heard the girl gasp as she saw the knickers in a pile on the floor, and bent over, keeping her legs straight and feeling the starched cotton slide up over her bum, baring the bottom of the cheeks and displaying the dark furry pouch between them as she pretended to rummage around in the pocket of her jeans.

There was a sob behind her, and a clatter of heels as the girl fled. Beth stood up and pulled the outfit back down, chuckling. She peered around the shop floor, slightly disappointed that nobody else had seen her little display. Still, there was plenty of time for that when she got to the hospital, and she felt another rush of excitement as she pulled the curtain to behind her and changed out of the uniform.

It had been even easier than she'd expected to get in. Nobody had even batted an eyelid as she came out of the tube station and walked down the busy road, choked with exhaust fumes and overflowing bins. The hospital was big, one of London's largest, so she imagined everyone was used to seeing nurses, but still she hadn't expected to be so roundly ignored.

It was the same even once she was in. She'd paused just outside, making sure she was ready for it, mentally rehearsing the lines she'd say if anyone confronted her, but she shouldn't have worried: the guy at the security desk didn't even look up as she sauntered past.

Not that she blamed him: the bustle was extraordinary, medical staff everywhere she looked, some walking purposefully with clipboards, some wheeling trolleys and others standing around chatting. She had a good idea of where she was going, and knew that if she looked as busy as most of these people nobody would stop her, and it didn't take long before she was pushing open the swing doors into the outpatients department.

Nothing beat this thrill, for her. For a couple of hours she could become someone entirely different, play at being someone who had nothing at all to do with her old life, and better still she could get other people to join in, never knowing that she was tricking them all. Jauntily confident now, she approached the duty nurse and waited for her phone call to finish before leaning over and addressing her.

'Hi – I've got a spare half-hour, if there's anyone here who needs to see a nurse rather than a doctor.' She gave the duty nurse, a huge, matronly black woman with thick glasses, a winning smile.

The nurse looked doubtfully at her, then at the list of entries in front of her. 'I don't know, Nurse –' She looked at Beth's outfit, scanning it for a name tag or ID card.

'It's Malory – I think I lost my card on the tube.' Beth gave a little laugh, trying to hide a sudden attack of nerves – if the plan was going to fall down, this would be it. But the duty nurse just nodded and scanned the list again.

'Well, it's irregular, but I suppose it'll take the pressure off Dr Taylor. You can take him –' she gestured towards a young man, probably in his mid-twenties, leafing through a copy of *Country Life* with a bored expression on his face '– Justin Moss. He's just here to have a knee dressing taken off; you can't do him much harm.' Her massive bulk heaved with silent laughter as she pressed the button to activate

33

the room's PA. 'Mr Moss, please come forwards.' Then she turned to Beth again and handed her a slim folder. 'Here are his notes. You can use Room Three, nobody in there.'

The young man stood up and limped towards them, and Beth turned to him with a bright smile. 'Mr Moss? Follow me, please.'

She held the passage door open for him and he limped past, colouring slightly as he brushed against her, then he waited in the corridor while she opened the door to the empty room.

'Just the dressing needs taking off on your knee, is it, Mr Moss?'

Justin cleared his throat. 'Yeah, that's all. I would have done it myself, but the doctor said I should come back here just to have it checked. Anything that stops me going to work is OK, but I'm pretty sure it's fine.'

Beth pointed to a chair. 'Sit down please, Mr Moss.' When he was seated, with his leg stretched out, she asked, 'Would you take your shoes and socks off for me, please, then remove the trousers.'

Justin flushed again. 'I think I'll roll them up; that'll be OK, won't it?'

Beth gave him a hard, professional smile. 'Come now, Mr Moss. There's no need to be shy. I'm a nurse, and I'm sure you don't have anything down there I haven't seen before.'

Now he was scarlet, and bent down to busy himself with taking his shoes off so he didn't have to meet Beth's gaze. She kept watching him as he pulled down his trousers, then she tried to take her eyes off the impressive bulge in his pants and focus on the dressing on his knee.

She winced in sympathy, then squatted down to take a closer look. 'Looks nasty. How did you do that?'

'Skateboarding. I was going down a hill and slid on some gravel, then –'

'Skateboarding?' She looked up at him, smiling. 'You look a bit old for that, Mr Moss.'

She was pleased to see him colour again, and noticed him trying to look up her skirt. He saw that she'd caught him, and turned away, clearly embarrassed.

She didn't mind him having a look – she wasn't wearing any knickers there, so he'd get a bit of a shock, but he'd get a shock anyway with what she was about to do. She positioned herself so that she was squatting over his foot, then, as she reached for the dressing to peel away the edge, she lowered herself slowly on to his big toe.

He gasped as he felt first the coarse hairs then a warm, soft wetness on his toe, and Beth started to peel the dressing back.

'Now be brave, Mr Moss. I'll try not to hurt you,' she said, rocking back and forth on his toe, feeling herself open out.

The scab on his knee looked healthy enough – she'd told herself that if she was involved with anything she couldn't handle, she'd get someone else straight away, and she'd read up enough about first aid and nursing to see that it was healing fine.

Justin was staring at her, open-mouthed, as she rubbed herself against him, and she was delighted to see the bulge in his pants thickening and lengthening. He shifted in the chair, one hand covering his crotch, but he made no attempt to pull his leg back, and just asked, 'What are you doing, nurse?'

She pretended to misunderstand him. 'I'm just taking the dressing off, doctor's orders. You don't need another one now; this will heal fine in the air. Just try not to get it wet,' she said, as she sank further on to his toe.

His cock was fully hard now, and his hand couldn't cover it up. He looked confused, and she leaned forwards to push his thighs apart, moving her hands up along the inside of his legs towards his crotch.

'You've been a very brave boy, Mr Moss,' she said, 'and I think you deserve a little reward.'

She could see anxiety and lust battling in his eyes, then lust won, and with a groan he took his hand away from his crotch, leaving the tight outline of his hard cock and balls standing to attention. She reached under the material, and he gasped as her cold hands stroked his tight balls.

'There now,' she said. 'We can't let you go like this, can we?' She pulled down the material, exposing the engorged head, and took it in one hand, feeling the weight and thickness of it before she leaned over and licked the drop of pre-come from the tip.

'Oh, God,' he said, as she started to suck him, alternating quick bobs of her head with slow, languid caresses with her tongue.

His foot was wriggling under her, but it wasn't enough, and she moved closer to him, still squatting, and opened her legs to show him her wet sex, peeling the greasy lips open with one hand then rubbing slowly from side to side as she felt his balls tighten and his cockhead swell even larger.

He didn't last long, the unexpected attention and the sight of his nurse stroking her pussy too much for him, but he tried to warn her. 'Oh, nurse, I'm going to come. I can't stop –'

She held her head down, keeping the pulsing cock in her mouth and squeezing his balls as spurt after spurt of come hit the back of her throat, making her gag, more oozing out on to her tongue and some spilling out of the sides of her mouth and running down his cock, now starting to soften. She pulled her mouth up and kept it open to show him the pool of come on her tongue, then, keeping her eyes locked on his, she swallowed it, still stroking her pussy.

But she knew they'd been in there long enough, and that someone might come in – taking a dressing off only took a few minutes. He seemed unsure of what to do, so she told him to get dressed and leave, and, when he asked her out, gulping, his face still crimson, she smiled gently and told him that it wasn't possible, that he should just treasure the memory; privately, she wouldn't have minded, but she knew that mixing her nurse character with her private life would have been disastrous.

He left, looking slightly regretful but still pleased, and she wrote up his notes. She knew what to do, and also knew that, if she gave the same kind of nondescript swirl for a signature that most of the doctors gave, nobody would look at it twice. She cleaned herself in the sink, wiping the rest of the come off her lips and rearranging her hair, before leaving the room. The duty nurse was on the phone when she put the folder back on her desk and barely noticed Beth.

Flushed with the success of her first encounter, Beth decided to call it a day; back home she could run through everything that had happened without any fear of being caught. She called a lift and waited with a gathering group of doctors, nurses and cleaning staff. It was going to be busy, she realised, and she was on the verge of walking down the stairs when the lift doors opened. It was too late now; people behind her were pushing her in, and anyway she'd seen a man there who reminded her of the doctor she'd fantasised about when she was younger, with a similarly slim build, curly hair and glasses.

The lift was rammed, and it wasn't hard to position

herself so that her back was facing the man. She could feel his breath on her neck, and looked around. Everyone was facing forwards, their eyes locked on the slow-moving set of floor numbers, so, still high from getting away with sucking off Justin, she slowly arched her back until her bottom was pressed against him. She heard his breathing quicken, and this made her bolder, so she swung her hips from side to side, rubbing the bulging cotton against him. It could have been the motion of the lift – she didn't want to be too obvious, although she was tempted to reach back – but he was responding; she could feel it. His crotch was against her bottom now, and she could sense something hard pressing insistently against her, so she slowly shifted her cheeks from one side to the other, feeling the bulge of his cock scraping against her.

When the lift finally arrived at the ground floor she moved away quickly, not wanting to prolong the contact any longer, and walked out towards the exit, ignoring a soft 'hey' behind her. But he ran after her, then grabbed her arm with one hand while he adjusted his crotch with the other.

He smiled apologetically and held a hand out. 'I'm Dr Blunt. Who are you? I haven't seen you here before,' he began, steering her away from the exit and towards one of the waiting areas.

She tried to pull away from him, anxious now in case her cover was blown. 'I'm – Nurse Malory. June Malory. I just started here,' she stammered.

But as she tried to escape from his grip, he suddenly let go and her bag fell to the ground, spilling her belongings out on the floor.

'Let me get that for you,' he said, bending over, and she realised aghast that her business cards and driving licence had fallen out of her wallet.

She bent down as well, trying to kick them out of the way, but it was too late: he'd seen them, and was studying the card.

'Beth Jameson, Estate Agent,' he read out, then looked at her. 'I thought you said your name was June Malory?'

She made a grab for the card, but he pulled it out of reach.

'That – that belongs to my estate agent. I'm looking for a flat, you see.'

She put out her hand again, but now he was looking at her driving licence.

'So she gave you her driving licence as well, did she?' He stared at her, the ghost of a smile playing around his lips. 'You're not a nurse at all, are you?' When Beth didn't reply but just looked down, biting her lip, he carried on. 'You know you can get in a lot of trouble for this. I thought something was up in the lift. Some of the nurses are a bit forward, but –' he laughed and swept a hand through his hair '– I've never seen anything like that before. So what's the story?'

Beth, horrified, didn't know what to say. 'It's nothing. I – I'm training to be a nurse, I just wanted to see what it felt like to be in an actual hospital,' she babbled. 'You won't tell anyone, please, will you?' Suddenly aware of the possible repercussions if the truth of her position should come out, she begged him. 'Please? I'll do anything for you.' She searched his eyes, but a steely glint had come into them.

'Anything?' He pocketed her driving licence, ignoring her shocked gasp. 'Meet me back here tomorrow at one. You can do a few things for me, then you can have this back.' Beth started to protest, but he stopped her with a finger to his lips. 'I'm sure you can get out of work, Miss Jameson. Be here, or –'

he smiled '– who knows what your employers might find out?'

As Beth turned to leave, he called her back, and loudly pronounced, 'Oh, and make sure you wear a bra and knickers next time. White, preferably.'

A few of the people sitting in the waiting room heard this, and looked from him to Beth and back again. She fled, hating the rush of pink that showed her body's embarrassed reaction.

That night she debated what to do. It would be easy enough to turn up – she could just say she was showing prospective buyers around a property, and she had such a good track record that nobody would think of checking up on her. But she didn't entirely trust the man, either to give her driving licence back or to be fair in the tasks he set her. At least he fancied her, she thought, and she consoled herself with the idea before settling down to a sleepless night punctuated by strange medical nightmares.

The next day he was there, waiting for her with a grin on his face. He gestured towards the water dispenser. 'Have a drink.'

She shook her head. 'It's OK. I'm not thirsty.'

His smile stayed fixed, but his voice took on a harder edge. 'Have a drink.'

She complied, then, when he nodded his head to the dispenser again, had another. His eyes softened, and he patted her on the rear, ignoring the inquisitive glances from the few visitors scattered around on the chairs. 'That's good. And I can tell you're wearing underwear today.'

She nodded.

'Fine. I'm going to send you to see Andy, a patient of mine. He's in a private room on the third floor, so you don't need to worry about being disturbed, but you're to do everything he tells you. I've told him all about you, and he's looking forward to meeting you.'

'Are you going to –' she managed, biting her lip, before being cut off by his laugh.

'Am I going to be there? What, to watch? Good lord, no. This will be just between you and Andy. When you're done, you can meet me back down here, and I'll give you your stuff back, OK?'

She was confused – didn't he like her? Why was he sending her off to another man? She'd been excited that morning, dressing up specially in her carefully chosen white underwear, not wanting anything to show under her uniform; she'd imagined being made to put on a display for him, taking everything off slowly, and now he wasn't even going to watch. But she took the room number and set off, apprehensive but still intrigued by whatever he'd prepared for her.

She found the room in the private ward. The atmosphere here was very different, the light less harsh and the acoustics softer too; the floor was even carpeted, rather than the shabby lino of the rest of the building. After one final check of the door number, she knocked and entered.

An old man was lying on the bed, grinning from ear to ear, his eyes bright with excitement. Beth suppressed a shudder: he must have been at least eighty, the skin on his scrawny neck loose and hanging in folds to either side, his head dotted with liver spots, with only a few wispy strands of hair remaining.

'Andy?' she asked tentatively, hoping that she'd made some kind of mistake, but already knowing that this was exactly where she was meant to be.

The man nodded and her heart sank. He raised a hand and made a circling movement with one finger.

'Come closer, and turn around for me, my dear. Let me have a good look at you,' he croaked.

She did as he asked, unable to stop herself flinching when he reached out a hand to pull up her skirt.

'Good, good,' he mumbled to himself.

When she'd turned full circle, she waited for further instructions.

'Dance for me – take your clothes off.'

His hands were already rummaging around under the covers, but she was relieved. This was easy, nothing she hadn't done before, and she swayed to an imaginary beat, shifting her weight from one side to the other as she slowly undid the buttons of her top and leaned towards him, showing him a full cleavage. If she was going to put on a show, she might as well put on a good one.

He was laughing now, his mouth open in glee, and she could see a tenting in the bedclothes, where his hand must have been wrapped around his ancient cock. Despite herself, she was flattered that she could have such an effect on someone so old, and she shimmied around the room, excited herself now by her own power, her own sexuality, as she slid out of the nurse's outfit to stand before him clad only in her underwear.

With her back to him she unclasped the bra, then turned to face him, holding her arms over the cups as the straps fell from her shoulders, and moved closer to let the heavy globes spill out. She dropped the bra to the floor and moved her hands back up her sides to cup the firm flesh; she pushed the nipples of one, then the other, to her mouth, licking them as she watched Andy's hand go into a frenzied pumping under the covers.

She moved away again, ready for the coup de grace, and stuck her bum out towards him, hiking a finger over each side of the pants and pushing them down slowly, exposing the creamy whiteness of her bottom cheeks. She heard a choking sound, but put it down to excitement and continued, only for a frantic 'No, no!' to come from Andy. Confused, she straightened, her hands still on the sides of the knickers, and looked at him.

He'd gone red, and was gesturing with his free hand. 'No, you stupid girl! Leave them on; pull them back up!'

She coloured and pulled the knickers back on.

'Now sit down over there.' He pointed towards a chair facing his bed, and she sat down. 'Spread your legs.'

She did as she was told, feeling the material of her knickers stretch until it was just covering her, a few stray hairs peeping out from either side.

'Rub it.' The order came without preamble, and she was about to pull the knickers to one side to give herself better access, when he said in an annoyed voice, 'No! Put your hand under your knickers.'

She licked her fingers and ran a hand down to her crotch, already damp from showing herself off earlier and from the anticipation of what the doctor had had in store. She closed her eyes and tried to block out thoughts of the decrepit old man in the bed, and think about the doctor instead, or the doctor from her youth; even Justin, the man from the day before. If any of those had been watching, she'd have enjoyed putting on a show, flashing some pink to get them excited, rubbing against the bulges in their pants, maybe sucking them off. They might order her to dance for them, just like she had for the old man, but they'd probably want more, maybe making her put something inside herself, something ridiculous like a banana, or maybe something a little dangerous, like

43

a lit candle, making her rub herself but stay stock still, so that none of the hot wax dripped on to her skin.

She was juicing up well now, and she gathered some of the pooling liquid to rub over her clit, hard now and erect, when Andy's voice broke the spell.

'Piss your pants.'

The order came as a shock, but she suddenly realised why the doctor had made her drink so much water earlier. She could have done it easily, she realised, if there was nobody watching, but she wasn't sure if she could manage with a stranger there. Still, she didn't want to give the doctor any excuse for not giving her driving licence back, and so she squeezed her bladder, her hand now still between her legs.

'Keep rubbing! Don't stop!'

She started to stroke her slit again, trying to relax, imagining herself in a toilet cubicle, imagining the relief of letting go, and she felt the first spurt, a couple of warm drops on her hand. She heard Andy hiss 'Yes', then it all came out, spattering hot pee on to her hand and soaking through her knickers, and she felt a dirty sense of satisfaction as she kept on rubbing herself, flicking her clit as the warm liquid spilled out over her busy hand, running down into her sex and out the sides of her knickers to pool down around her bumhole. The thought of what she'd done hit her suddenly, and she felt her bumhole clench at the touch of the pee, her pussy hot and aching, and with a couple of last, hard flicks she was coming, her legs stretched out and shaking and her pussy contracting as the wave of her orgasm flowed through her.

Dimly she heard the old man crow with delight, then shame and embarrassment quickly followed arousal, and she got to her feet, feeling the sticky mess between her thighs.

'Can I –?' she gestured towards the bathroom.

'Yes, yes, clean yourself up,' he said, gesturing irritably with one hand.

She found a flannel there, and patted herself down, wiping away most of the pee, then towelled herself dry. Her knickers were soaked, and she wasn't sure how she was going to carry them out – she certainly wasn't going to wear them again – but when she went back into the room Andy solved that problem for her, reaching out for them, saying, 'I'll take those. Souvenir, my dear. You wouldn't begrudge an old man his wish, would you?'

Beth shook her head, then turned away to pull on her nurse's outfit again as he cackled.

Dr Blunt was nowhere to be seen when she returned to the waiting area, and after standing waiting for him for a few minutes she resignedly sat down to leaf through a magazine. She felt pleasantly relaxed after her little show, and, although it hadn't been her ideal fantasy scenario, she knew she'd probably use it in the future. She was surprised by how successful her nurse ruse had been, how easy it had been to use it for sex, and almost regretted that Dr Blunt wouldn't be able to make her do anything else for him; she'd have to find a new hospital, and start all over again.

When he appeared she'd gone through two copies of *Cosmopolitan* and was halfway through reading a recent *Heat*. She was engrossed, and didn't notice him when he suddenly loomed over her, with a stern expression on his face.

Slightly flustered, she put the magazine down, stood up and smiled at him, holding a hand out. 'My driving licence, please.'

The doctor raised an eyebrow, and folded his arms in front of his chest. 'I don't think I can give it back to you yet. You didn't do quite what Andy said, did you?'

She felt the colour rising in her cheeks as it dawned on her what he was saying. 'What? I did everything to the letter!'

He was shaking his head. 'You started to take your knickers off, which wasn't what he wanted, not at all. Almost ruined it for him, it did.'

He'd made no effort to quieten his voice at all, and Beth looked round anxiously, acutely aware of her naked sex under her uniform and suddenly feeling vulnerable. She looked at him with a pleading expression, one that she'd honed on boyfriends over the years, but he returned a stony glare.

'You'd better come back tomorrow. This time I'll be dealing with you. Don't be late.' And with that he turned on his heels and walked off, Beth staring after him.

If she was honest with herself, it wasn't entirely unexpected. She'd known she had no guarantee that he would give the licence back, and had already considered reporting it lost and getting a new one, and just taking her chances with whatever he told the authorities. But she knew that it wouldn't just be his word against hers – there were cameras everywhere, and she'd be on film, in clear view, on any number of tapes. She was still intrigued, too, and excited by the idea of what he had in store for her. With his tousled locks and youthful frame he presented a far more attractive proposition than the decrepit old man, and she went to bed that night wet with excitement, only just resisting the temptation to rub herself, to keep herself at fever pitch until the next day.

In the morning she surprised herself by fretting over what she should wear. He hadn't specified whether she should be in underwear or not, and she searched through her drawers to find something suitable – something that would show him she had class, that she wasn't just some tart in off the street. Despite herself, she liked him, fancied him, and wanted to make a good impression. She finally decided on a pair of creamy silk knickers and a matching bra, shivering as she imagined the touch of his firm fingers on the sheer material. After a couple of phone calls covering herself at the office and a small lunch – she was too nervous to eat very much – she set off.

He was waiting for her again in the same place, grinning as though he'd just heard a particularly rude joke. She smiled falteringly at him, and he nodded. 'Good. Follow me.' He turned and pushed through a pair of swing doors, to lead her along an overlit green corridor.

After going up a flight of stairs, and a couple of twists and turns down other corridors, they arrived at a sign to the staff canteen. For a second she thought they might have a coffee together, but then he suddenly opened a door and ushered her inside. There had been no sign on the door, no warning of what it held, but as she looked around her heart sank, and she realised her idea of coffee had been the height of naiveté.

The room contained a trolley fitted with a rubber mattress, and a contraption by its side with a funnel on a stand leading into a tube that rested coiled at a point halfway down the stand. On the other side of the room there was a door, which she presumed led into a toilet. She was horrified by the room, clearly dedicated to colonic irrigation and enemas, but at least, she was faintly relieved to realise, there'd be somewhere to go afterwards.

Still, she'd been expecting sex, and she knew that she was damp down there. She bit her lip, then addressed the doctor. 'You don't have to do this.' She gestured to the equipment. 'This doesn't really turn me on. But I can do other stuff for you, if you like.' She licked her lips, trying on her most sultry expression, but he seemed indifferent to her advances.

'This isn't for your pleasure. Turn around and bend over the trolley.'

She considered trying to resist, but gave up and did as he asked, then gasped as he roughly tugged the back of the uniform up, exposing her bum. She blushed as she realised that he'd be looking at her best knickers, selected specially to impress him, but he didn't even seem to realise.

'We'll take these off,' he said, pulling them down and waiting for her to step out of them.

She let out a little sob as her sex was exposed, sure that he'd see the moist pinkness and realise that she was aroused, but if he noticed he didn't say anything. She heard a snapping sound, then her bum cheeks were being parted, her sex opening with a wet sound, and a gloved finger was rubbing something cold over her bumhole. He did it slowly, rubbing the cream all around the crinkled edges before dipping a finger in, up to the first knuckle then further. She felt her ring contract around him, and pushed her pussy up towards his hand, desperate for it to be touched, played with, but, apart from a graze from his hand as he removed his finger, he ignored it completely.

Suddenly she was filled with something cold and hard, and knew that the nozzle was inside her.

'So, Miss Jameson, have you had one of these before?'

She shook her head, then managed a strangled 'No.'

'But you know what it is?'

She nodded.

'Well, as you're a beginner, I'll be kind and not give you too much. Just a pint, which shouldn't be too difficult for you. The tricky bit will come next.' He chuckled to himself, and, as she wondered what he meant, she felt the first trickle of it running into her.

It was cold and she could smell the carbolic in it, stinging her when it hit her tender rectum. As she filled up, she shifted her weight from one foot to the other, then stretched up on tiptoes, the pressure building up into an irresistible urge to go to the toilet.

'Is it finished?' she managed.

'Nearly there now,' he replied, and she heard the funnel being tugged from side to side.

Then the nozzle was being pulled out of her, and she barely stopped herself from spraying the contents of her bottom out. She clenched her bum cheeks hard.

'Can I go to the toilet now?'

He chuckled. 'I don't think so. There are some on the other side of the staff canteen,' he continued breezily. 'They're easy enough to find. I'll follow you, in case you get lost.'

'But I'm desperate! I can't wait! Please, you've got to let me go now.' She was hopping from one foot to the other now, doing a dance to try and hold it all in, but already she suspected that a trickle had escaped. She didn't have the courage to look, and she could have screamed when he just chuckled.

Tenderly, she swung herself off the trolley, then pulled the back of the outfit down. She briefly considered making a break for the toilet here, but realised that he'd stop her, and that she'd make a mess all over the floor here, and he'd probably leave her in it, with no fresh clothes and no way of cleaning up. She had no choice – she had to try and cross the staff canteen.

She took the first teetering steps towards the door, mincing carefully, her belly feeling huge and bloated. Behind her she heard him saying appreciatively, 'Well done! That's right.' Then she was out of the door and walking slowly down the corridor towards the staff room.

She heard him follow behind, walking just as slowly, then tried to concentrate on where she was going. She knew she'd never make it if she thought about the whole distance; but if she just took it one step at a time she might be OK. It was like being at school, trying to finish one of the punishing long-distance runs they were made to do, and she almost smiled at the thought of the wholesome jolly hockey-sticks mentality there and the sordid filth she was being made to indulge in here.

But it was painful now, more uncomfortable than a minute ago, and she gritted her teeth, tears already starting to well up behind her eyes, as she made it to the door of the staff canteen. It was bigger than she'd imagined, a long stretch of varnished floor leading from the food all the way to a smoking area on the other side, and she could see the door he meant. It looked like it was a mile away, and she sobbed, almost breaking down in tears at the thought of the distance she had to cross.

But she'd started, and she carried on, her eyes fixed on the floor, feeling her heart leap whenever any medical staff passed holding their trays, dreading what might happen if they should bump into her, spill some hot drink on her sleeve, sure Dr Blunt would just turn and leave her to it, the whole canteen up and watching, with sounds of disgust and accusing fingers pointing all around her.

No, it wasn't going to happen. She was going to make it. With renewed determination, she pressed on, only to be stopped by an orderly when she was halfway across the floor. With the shock of it her bumhole relaxed for an instant before she clenched it tightly shut again, and she could feel a trickle starting to roll down her thigh as he spoke to her.

He put a hand on her shoulder, and tried to look into her eyes. 'Are you OK? You look upset. Is there anything I can do to help?'

She looked up, barely holding back the tears, and tried to smile at him and move on. 'No, it's OK. It's nothing, really.'

But he wasn't letting her go. 'It's just – I look after staff welfare here, and I'm always keen to hear about any cases of staff harassment.'

She almost smiled as she thought of the harassment she'd had at the hands of the doctor, and he misinterpreted her expression.

'No, you don't need to worry. Everything's confidential; you can speak to me and you won't get into trouble.' His eyes flicked over her uniform. 'Why aren't you wearing your name badge, Nurse –'

'Malory,' she sobbed, pushing against him. 'I lost my badge, and – oh please, you've got to let me go. I've got to get to the toilet!'

He fell back, clearly horrified, and she started to trot, almost running but unable to with her bloated fullness. She could hear a laugh behind her, and felt the trickle on her thigh reach her knee. She thought another had started too, and felt herself blush deep red as she imagined the eyes on her, the man who'd stopped her changing his expression from concern to disgust, the other nurses pointing and laughing, and then she was through the door at the other end, trying to blink the stinging tears out of her eyes and find the sign for the toilet.

She barely got there in time, spraying the contents of her gut all over the bowl then sitting down and sobbing, half in relief and half in humiliation, at what she'd been made to go through, at what she'd *agreed* to do. The worst thing about it was that she was still wet, still open and ready for attention, her hole aching, and as her sobs died down she touched it, her humiliation becoming a turn-on now, now that she was safe, and she started to rub herself, her clit a hard nub crying out for contact, then she stopped. Dr Blunt would be waiting for her. She could get her driving licence back; she could get out of here.

She cleaned herself up as best she could with tissues, then washed in the handbasin and tried to put the cubicle back in order. Her ring felt sore as she walked, from the soapy water and the invasion of the nozzle, but it was nothing compared to the agony of before, and she was almost happy when she returned to the waiting area.

The doctor looked happy too, and this time he had the driving licence in his hand. 'Well done,' he said, as he offered it to her, looking slightly apologetic.

She snatched it out of his hand and gave him a foul look. He'd gone too far. She'd expected sex, and what she'd got was abject humiliation. She knew she was kinky, but he was just sick.

He was still smiling. 'We could still – uh – see each other, if you like?'

She glowered at him, barely able to believe he'd made such a suggestion, and put the licence in her bag then stood up. 'In your dreams, pal,' she said, almost relenting when she saw his face crumple, but then her resolve returned and she stormed out, ignoring his pathetic attempts to calm her down.

That night she relaxed with a long, warm bath full of bubbles, and opened a fresh bottle of wine. There had definitely been something good about it, but she didn't regret having told him where to get off. After all, if he thought he could get away with that, what wouldn't he try? Still, she knew she'd rub herself later, and felt a tingle of anticipation between her legs.

There was no hurry, though, and she poured herself another glass and sat in front of the TV. When she turned it on she realised it was the news, and almost switched over, but something stopped her.

There were images of a hospital, somewhere in the Midlands, and the newscaster's portentous voice was droning on about someone having skipped bail. Her interest perked up when she heard the words 'bogus doctor', and then she was glued to the screen. A young man, whose only actual job had been delivering pizzas, had been arrested by the police on suspicion of having passed himself off as a doctor in a Birmingham hospital. There had been a number of complaints by patients who'd had inept operations performed, and he hadn't been hard to track down, but soon after being arrested he'd skipped police bail.

She started to laugh at the sheer audacity of it, then dissolved in tears of mirth when a police spokesman came on and talked about his suspected involvement in impersonating police officers, priests and judges. This man was like some bungling version of herself, she realised, and then they flashed his photo up on the screen. The hair was shorter, and he wasn't wearing glasses, but she recognised it instantly, and her mood changed from hilarity through bemusement to rage, then back to renewed hilarity, in an instant. There was no mistaking him – Dr Blunt wasn't a doctor at all, any more than she was a nurse.

Her first impulse was to call the police, but that was easily resisted: he was only doing what she did, after all, even if she drew the line at giving operations. Maybe she'd go back there and blackmail him a little, see how he liked it. She sank back into the sofa, ignoring the news now, having switched to a new story, and cradled her wine in her hands as she started to hatch new schemes.

She hadn't seen it coming at all. In the ambulance, she'd recognise that it could have been worse: at least it had happened to her and not the prospective buyer. The company could easily have been sued – negligence claims were all the rage now, and it wouldn't have been difficult for the buyer to make a case. It might even have been possible for her as well, but she wasn't about to do something like that: she treasured her position at the firm, and knew it would have done her no favours in the industry if she got a reputation as a litigious employee.

Still, such thoughts were far from her mind as she sat dazed at the bottom of the stairs; all she could think of then was to wonder what on earth had happened. For an instant she had no idea where she was, then the buyers, man and wife, were fussing around her, and it all came back.

She'd slipped, of course, on some stupid mat left at the top of the stairs, and had banged her head on the wall before sliding down to the bottom. Her head pounded uncomfortably, and she groaned. The man was holding up fingers, gripping her shoulder and asking, 'How many?'

'Four,' she replied irritably.

He tried to smile, then reached up with a tissue to dab at something on her forehead.

'My God, Henry, she's bleeding!'

She could see the wife standing up pale and trembling, and tried to smile at her. She'd feel a lot better without wifey there panicking. It wasn't anything serious; she'd stand up and show them.

'It's nothing, just –' But she hadn't expected her legs to be so wobbly, and sat down again almost immediately.

Henry turned to his wife. 'Call an ambulance, darling.'

She tried to wave him away, but the effort made her head spin.

Henry took her hand and spoke slowly to her, as though addressing a small child. 'You've had a nasty fall, Beth. I've called an ambulance; they'll get you checked out. I'm sure you've just got some concussion and you'll be fine, but we don't want to take any chances, do we?' He loomed over her, smiling considerately, and she closed her eyes. 'Do you want me to call the office?'

She managed a nod, and heard the man stand up and walk away. All she really wanted was to be in a darkened room, left alone for a while, until the throbbing in her head stopped.

The couple fussed around her until the ambulance came, and she was aware even through her daze of how quickly it had arrived, and how little time it took them to get there. They must be close to the hospital, she thought, but it wasn't until the doors opened and she was wheeled out, having been put in a chair against her protestations that she was fine, that she realised that she'd been taken back to the hospital where she had posed as a nurse.

She almost started laughing to herself: her private life had finally caught up with her job, or was it the other way around? The paramedics left her at the A & E desk, and it wasn't long before a nurse wheeled her into a room and shone a torch in her eyes.

She straightened. 'Hmm. Maybe some mild concussion, nothing special. You didn't really need to come here in an ambulance,' she said in a half-accusing tone.

'I told them I was fine!' Beth fired back, feeling less groggy now, but the nurse had turned away, and was busying herself with her notes.

Then she turned back, and peered at the cut on Beth's head. 'You'll need a couple of stitches for that, though. I'll just see if any of the doctors are around.'

She swished out of the room, and Beth put a finger to the cut. It didn't feel that serious, but she knew that even small cuts could scar badly unless they were dealt with properly.

She was still touching it, tenderly fingering the sides, when the nurse brought in the doctor. And just before Beth fainted, she heard his voice, which seemed so familiar now, the face, too, with its curly hair, gleeful grin and homely glasses, saying, 'Ah, yes. Pass me the needle and thread, please, nurse. This one shouldn't be too difficult.'

3

Filly

'What on earth are you wearing?'

This was not the greeting I'd been expecting. I pushed past Paul and into the hallway. 'No "Hello, darling, lovely to see you"? No kiss for poor little me?' I leaned over and gave him a peck on the cheek.

'Yes, of course, but still –' Paul pushed the door closed behind me and looked me over slowly from head to foot, consternation clouding his face.

I gave him an icy smile. 'This is perfectly adequate country wear, I'll have you know.'

Actually I was a little hurt. I'd taken real time and effort over choosing these clothes. I'd never been to a point to point before, but I had a pretty good idea of what people wore, all horsy stuff. So I'd got hold of a pair of jodhpurs, some riding boots, a short cropped jacket and a white shirt unbuttoned just enough to show a bit of cleavage. The shoes aside, I'd gone for everything a bit small, as I knew Paul liked me to show off my curves. And the colours all went well with my blonde hair – natural, of course – which I'd been brushing all morning, so that the curls were bouncing on my shoulders. After all, I'd be meeting some of Paul's friends for the first time, and I was keen to impress.

'But, for Christ's sake, Sophie, it looks like you're going to be competing!'

I bristled and turned away, angry now with him. 'It's stylish, Paul. And, anyway, who's to know whether I'm riding or not?'

Paul just stared at me, then took his coat off a hook. 'Come on, then, let's go.'

He hardly spoke to me on the way to the course, so of course I sulked, staring out of my window at the endless, boring fields. I couldn't understand why anyone would want to live in the country. There was simply nothing to do, unless you wanted to waste your time gardening, or become some chapped-faced farmer's wife and get up every morning at four to milk some cows. I knew that Paul, for all that he worked in London, viewed himself as having country roots, and often grumbled about the smells and noises of the city, but, if he wanted to call this deathly dull landscape home, he was welcome to it. Putney was leafy enough for me – and it had more than enough bars and restaurants to keep a girl about town occupied. What was there to do for fun here? Chase down some poor defenceless animal, or maybe kill your own chickens? No thanks.

'This is it.'

Paul turned off into a field, where I could see an assortment of Land Rovers and estate cars lined up in rows next to a few small marquees. Paul handed some money to a smirking urchin and received a couple of programmes, one of which he handed to me as he was ushered to a space. I glanced around. The people here even looked like horses; I could imagine them braying and snorting. I stifled a giggle, and turned my attention to the programme, as Paul pulled in. It was black and white, and full of incomprehensible details, as well as ludicrous adverts for hunting jackets, fertiliser and farm equipment.

'Paul, I don't understand this.' I indicated the race listings.

'Which bit don't you understand, dear?' I could see a muscle working in his jaw, but chose to ignore it.

'Well – all of it, really. What does this number here mean? And these phrases? "Going good to heavy", and all the rest of them.'

Paul sighed. 'Come on, let's get out of the car. I'll explain everything to you on the way to the track.'

Ten minutes later I was really none the wiser, but I have to admit that it wasn't all Paul's fault, as I'd seen some lovely jewellery in a shop that I just had to have. I hadn't realised they'd have shops here – well, not really shops, just stalls really, but it was still shopping. And they had clothes: jackets, fleeces, boots and hats. I tried on all kinds of things, and passed the ones I liked back to Paul, who was a darling and paid for them for me. I could see that he was getting a little bit bored, but it was only fair that he should be nice to me now, after treating me so horribly when I arrived at his house.

Eventually I'd had enough, and told Paul that I wanted to see a race.

'Well, the first one starts in about ten minutes. You can see the horses before the race down there –' he pointed towards a fenced-off paddock, around which I could already see horses being led '– and you can bet over there.'

A crowd was forming in front of a line of boards, each of which was flanked by men writing numbers on it, or rubbing them out. Paul had explained something about these odds to me, but I didn't really get it. I wanted to know more.

'Paul, I –'

'I'd better take these things back to the car,' he interrupted, lifting up the bags of shopping. 'They'll just be in the way here.' I suppose he had a point, and he was carrying them, after all. 'I'll see you back here in a little bit.'

Suddenly it dawned on me: the best way to learn would be through experience. And I was feeling lucky too. 'Paul, I don't have any money. Can you –?'

A flicker passed over his face, then he put the bags down and took out his wallet. 'Sure thing, darling. How much do you need? Twenty? Forty?'

I spotted a fifty-pound note in his wallet, which the cheeky boy had tried to hide behind tens and twenties. 'Can I have the fifty, please?' I asked in my best girly voice, my hands clasped before me and my head cocked to one side; he couldn't refuse me like this.

Paul blinked. 'Of course.'

As Paul waddled off with the shopping, I walked down to the enclosure to look at the horses, as well as the other punters. It was a weird bunch of people there: a mixture of posh older sorts in tweeds, a younger contingent divided between ruddy-faced, vigorous-looking youths with straw hair and horsy faces and their pasty, spotty counterparts, clad in sportswear and Burberry caps, who looked a bit more like rats. I was also shocked to see some rougher-looking groups wandering around like they owned the place, all leering at each other menacingly. Paul hadn't told me that these kinds of people would be there. Instinctively I patted my pocket to make sure that Paul's – or rather *my* money was still there.

I watched the horses being led around the track. I had to admit to myself that they were pretty impressive, all neatly groomed, some with plaits in their mane and two-tone colour schemes through the way their coats had been trimmed. One in particular caught my attention, and I opened my programme to see what it was called. 'Voice that Thunders' – it sounded impressive, better than those ridiculous names some of these horses had.

I turned to the bookies and scanned the boards. Most of them were offering the same kinds of odds – sixteen to one – and I went for the one with the shortest queue.

'Fifty pounds on "Voice that Thunders", please,' I told the wrinkled man by the board, proffering the note. I felt good about this one, and anyway fifty pounds wasn't a lot of money – I knew that Paul would have more with him.

'To win or each way?' he asked, not unkindly.

This had me stumped. 'What's each way?' I asked, but there was some jostling behind me, and a muffled 'Come on!'

I turned to stare at whoever had tried to rush me, but was met with a sea of faces ignoring me and holding money out to the bookie. I turned back to him, but he just looked at me for a second, then took the note from my hand and said something to the man next to him, who was writing things down in a big book. Then he gave me a ticket, and turned to the man behind me.

I was dreadfully excited, and couldn't wait to tell Paul. I looked around for him, and finally saw him with a few other men by the enclosure. He saw me too, and waved. As I walked over to him, I realised that the people he was with weren't at all the kinds of people I'd expected would be his country friends. There was one jolly-looking chap with a huge beer belly and a thick mop of curly hair, and one rather stern and dignified-looking country gent, who I could imagine in full military get-up overseeing some kind of parade. I slowed my pace, aware that they were both staring at me.

'Ah, Sophie, there you are.' Paul beamed and started to introduce me around. 'This is Bernard –' he indicated the chubby chap, who was staring at my cleavage '– and this is John.' He nodded towards the country gent, whose heels clicked together as he gave a small bow.

'Paul, I've had a bet!' I exclaimed delightedly.

He smiled, a slightly pained expression in his eyes. 'So what have you gone for?'

'Um – "Voice that Thunders"!'

John coughed, and Bernard opened his programme.

Paul turned to the bookies' boards. 'Oh. I don't know the horse, but –' then he turned back to me '– what odds did you get?'

'Sixteen to one.'

'Well, they've gone up quite a bit now.'

'What do you mean?'

Paul turned back to the bookies' boards. 'Most are now giving forty to one.'

I blanched, realising that this was not a good sign. Paul looked ashen, but the other two had sympathetic expressions on their faces.

'You could still get lucky!' Bernard pointed out.

'Well, anyway, the race is about to start. Let's go and watch,' said Paul, and reached out for my hand.

It wasn't my fault the horse was pulled up halfway through the race. It had looked fine to me in the enclosure. But when Paul asked me how much I'd put on it I had to tell him the truth, as otherwise he wouldn't have given me any more money. I don't know why he got upset – it wasn't like he didn't have more money, and his friends seemed to see the funny side of it – but I only managed to get another thirty out of him now, with a warning not to spend it all on the same horse. Well, I wasn't likely to make *that* mistake again, was I? Then he and his friends started talking about country stuff, people they knew and that kind of thing, so I got bored.

I was thirsty, too, and needed a drink to cheer myself up after Paul's rude behaviour. The main tent was a bit too full, but I remembered seeing a cider stand. I'd always had a bit of a soft spot for cider, having drunk it on family holidays to Normandy, but I hadn't had much of it in the past few years, what with being in London.

The man at the stall was friendly enough, and even let me taste each of the different types before I bought a pint of the extra dry, which was also the strongest. He looked a bit doubtful as he poured it for me, warning me that it packed a punch, but I just grinned, told him I could handle it and paid. After all, if I had to be somewhere like this I might as well have a bit of fun.

I went back down to the enclosure to pick another horse. I kept some money for drinks now, and just put twenty on it, 'on the nose', as the bookie put it. The cider had started to work, and I was feeling confident again, sure I'd picked a winner.

I went to find Paul again, and sure enough they were down at the track, waiting for the race to start. I didn't tell him what I'd put my money on this time, just giving him a smile when he asked, but couldn't hide the disappointment on my face when the race was over. My horse had come in fifth, which at least was better than it not having come in at all, but still I hadn't made any money on it. What made it worse was that Bernard and John had, and were looking very smug and self-satisfied as they made their way to the bookies.

'So, did you lose on that one, too?' asked Paul, looking half-sympathetic and half-angry.

I pouted and shook my head. 'Not going to tell you.'

He sighed. 'Anyway, I'm hungry, and I'm going to get some food. Shall I get something for you?'

I was hungry too, and this cider was going right to my head on an empty stomach. 'Yes, please.'

We arranged to meet back by the enclosure and, as Paul walked off, I scanned the programme, trying to work out what would be a safe bet for the next race.

By the time Paul had come back, I'd joined his friends. Bernard was complimenting me on my outfit, which made a welcome change from Paul's complaints, and I was starting to enjoy the attention. I didn't even mind when he stared at my cleavage, sometimes leaning over a bit to give him a bigger flash, the cider having made me feel a bit cheeky.

But when Paul put some kind of bap in my hands, I was outraged. 'What's this?'

'Pork and apple bap, best food here. Actually, pretty much the only food here, if you don't want a burger.'

I'd been expecting a punnet of strawberries, or perhaps a smoked salmon sandwich. I unwrapped the bap, sniffed at it then took a tentative bite, which I quickly spat out. It was dry and horrible, all pork fat, margarine and floury bread.

'I'm not eating this shit,' I announced, and threw it on to the ground, the wrapping opening in the air to leave a trail of bread and pork behind it. A few people turned to look.

Paul's face had gone beetroot red. 'Pick it up,' he hissed in a low tone.

'I will not!'

Paul's eye twitched, and he grabbed me by the upper arm, painfully hard.

'Ow! Get off me!'

'You will clean it up, now,' he said, shaking me.

Bernard stepped over. 'Now steady on, Paul –'

'Bernard, leave it. This has nothing to do with you.' And then he asked me again. 'Will you clear it up?'

'No, I fucking will not. Now let go of me!' I cried, raising my voice.

More people turned, and Paul released me, realising that he was making a scene.

I turned and walked away, infuriated with him for embarrassing me like that. The last thing I saw of Paul as I walked back towards the cider stall was him bending down to pick up the horrible bap himself, gathering all the pieces to put in the bin.

After another two pints and a sympathetic ear from the cider man, who nodded and was indignant in all the right places when I told him about Paul, I'd run out of money. But that wasn't my main concern now. I also needed badly to pee.

There was a line of blue portakabins over near the main beer tent, but when I got there I found that there were queues for all of the cubicles, some four deep. I stood at the end of one for a while, hopping from foot to foot and crossing my legs before I realised I was making a fool of myself and that, in any case, I just couldn't wait.

I looked around, starting to panic now, but saw a gap in a hedge just thirty yards away. There was a stile, and on the other side I'd be free from prying eyes. It wasn't ideal, but it would have to do. It was hard to stop myself from running to get there, and once I was over the stile I didn't go five metres before pulling down my jodhpurs and pants and squatting by the hedge.

Letting it all out was such a relief, and I giggled as I thought to myself of what my jodhpurs would have looked like if I'd had an accident, a big dark stain spreading all over my front and rear. This was better than doing it in a Portakabin, anyway – it felt cheeky, the cool air on my bum and pussy, and more natural than the plastic cubicles, which were no doubt overflowing with all kinds of unsavoury waste.

I had some tissues with me, and when I'd finally finished I took one in my hand and started to dab at myself to dry it up. But the rudeness of being outdoors like this had got to me, on top of my cider high, and it felt so good just touching it, so I carried on, rubbing the damp tissue up and down my slit, until it was slick and juicy from something else. I leaned back, one hand behind me to balance, and spread myself open to the air, closing my eyes and teasing my clit out with the other hand.

'What you think you're doing?' A gruff voice shattered my reverie.

Shocked, I opened my eyes and saw a stocky man, looking like some kind of farmhand, in front of me. I tried to stand up, but he was already beside me, and kept me down with a hand on my shoulder. I closed my thighs and tried to pull up my pants and jodhpurs, but he caught my hand too.

I struggled against his grip. 'Let me up!'

'What you doing here? Pissing? Then rubbing yourself?' He forced a hand in between my legs, to feel the slick wetness there. 'Reckon so.'

I couldn't believe he'd taken such a liberty, touching me like that down there. 'Let me go!' I squealed.

He laughed. 'You shouldn't be pissin' here. This here's private land. I could have you up for trespassin'.'

This was ludicrous. 'Look, I didn't know the field was private. I've just come for the races, and all the Portakabins were being used, OK? Now will you please let me go?'

He smirked. 'Way I see it, I either take you down the farmhouse and you try an' tell them you was trespassin', pissin' in their field, or you give me a little treat now.' He leered, and put a hand down the front of his pants, adjusting what I could already see was a pretty impressive bulge.

At first the thought repelled me, but then some of the cider-fuelled cheekiness came back. Why not? He wasn't good-looking, but it looked like he had a good-sized cock, and nobody would ever find out. Anyway, it would be a way of getting back at Paul.

I was going to offer him a suck, but then I didn't need to: he took one anyway, unzipping himself and holding his thick cock out towards my face. I hesitated, looking at it, and he grabbed the back of my head, bunched up some of my hair in a painful grip then shoved his cock into my mouth.

I squealed in alarm, my mouth suddenly full of cock, but then the masculine taste and smell got to me, and I started sucking. I've always loved sucking cock, even more than full sex sometimes. I'd even sucked off one of Paul's city friends in the toilet in a Soho bar, which I was sure he didn't know about, not long after we'd started going out.

With his cock stuffed in my face, my pussy started to ache, and I spread my legs, slowly letting him see it, all open and wet. I was rewarded with a groan, then he ripped my shirt open, a couple of buttons flying off, before cupping my tits and pulling them up and over the top of my bra. I was too far gone by this stage to care, and started to stroke my pussy while I sucked harder on his cock and he rolled my nipples between his thick fingers.

With my other hand I reached up and felt his balls, all thick and pulled tight against the base of his cock. He was going to come soon, but I wanted to do it before he did, so I rubbed harder, pinching my clit and slapping on it, which seemed to get him going. Finally it hit me, the taste of his cock, the feel of his balls and the shame of being caught rubbing myself outside too strong to resist, as I trembled with the first waves of my orgasm.

He must have been feeling the same way, as when I hit my peak I felt his cock start to pulse. I pulled my mouth away – I may have liked sucking cock, but I didn't like the taste of come – but it was too late: he'd already started to spurt it out, thick ropes jetting out on to my face and some going in my mouth. But the feeling of it, my face covered in gobs of slimy come, my hand still stroking my hot, swollen pussy, drove me to a second peak, and I was about to scream when he shoved the edge of his hand in my mouth, saying, 'Hush, now.'

I bit down on it as my whole body shook with the force of my come, and I heard him chuckle as the waves died down and I slumped back, suddenly acutely aware of the sight I must have looked. I reached down to pull up my panties, cool against the swollen heat of my pussy, and reached into my jodhpur pockets for more tissues, to wipe the come off my face.

The man just grinned, zipping himself up. 'Thanks, miss, you did a grand job. It's true what they say about posh birds, then.' And he turned away and walked back over the stile, leaving me to clean myself up, my head spinning, my face flushed with indignation and arousal.

He'd made a mess of my shirt, but I tried as best I could to make myself presentable again before going back into the main field. I had the taste of his come in my mouth, though, which was really unpleasant, and I'd have to ask Paul for some more money so that I could buy something to drink. Surely he'd be over our little spat by now?

As I made my way through the crowds, looking for Paul and his friends, I was aware that people were watching me. Some seemed to be smirking, or laughing outright, but I ignored them. After all, they were country bumpkins; they'd probably never been to London in their lives. Why should I care what they thought? All the same, I tried to walk in a straighter line, aware that I might have been weaving slightly.

Finally, I spotted Paul talking to Bernard, and raised my arm. 'Paul!'

He looked up, and the smile on his lips faded as he looked at me walking towards him. 'What the hell happened to you?'

I admit it: I must have looked a bit of a mess. My jodhpurs had got a bit muddy from where I'd slumped back after coming into the pool where I'd peed earlier, and the top of my bra was showing from where the shirt had been ripped open, but the only thing for it was to brazen it out. 'What do you mean? I've had a few drinks,' I said airily, running a hand through my hair.

But it stuck on something slimy, and when I pulled my hand away it was covered in come.

'What the fuck is that in your hair?' Paul demanded angrily.

'What? Nothing!' I protested, hiding the soiled hand behind my back.

Paul grabbed me and pulled me towards him, then sniffed at my hair. 'You've got someone's jiz in your hair!'

I could see Bernard, who was watching, stifle a giggle, and glared at him.

'How do you explain this? What the fuck have you been doing?' Paul demanded, shaking me.

'It's nothing, Paul. It's not what you think.'

He stared at me in disbelief. I put on my best girly smile, cocked my head to one side and batted my eyelashes at him. 'Do you have any more money? I've run out and I need a drink.'

But this time it didn't work. Paul looked fit to burst – I'd never seen him so angry – and took me by the wrist. 'Right, it's time you were taught a lesson.'

It was dingy and musty in the stables. Paul had been deaf to my protestations as he dragged me there, past families having picnics and stalls blaring out lines like 'Hunting is a way of life'. I'd briefly considered calling for help, but didn't think it would work – it looked like a man's world here, and I wouldn't have trusted any of the tweedy women we'd seen to take my side. Half of me was slightly afraid at being taken here – I really didn't know what Paul wanted – but the other half was happy that we were hidden. After all, you never knew who was watching, and I didn't want to appear in the society pages with my hair in such a state.

Once we were there he made me strip off, peeling off my pee-stained knickers and jodhpurs and noting the burst buttons on my shirt, then he pushed me down on my hands and knees in the filthy straw. He inspected my pussy, which was still all oily from before, and snorted derisively. I thought he was going to have me there, like that, with my bum sticking up in the air, and my pussy pulsed in anticipation, but instead he took something from the wall and I felt a greasy finger rubbing around my ring. Before I could protest, he'd slid a finger up inside me.

'Paul! You're not going to –'

I'd let him put it up my bum before once or twice, but I liked to keep it for special occasions, and at the very least liked to be able to have a wash afterwards. I twisted round to see if he was unbuttoning his trousers, then gasped as something else, something long and thin and cold, was pushed inside me.

'What are you doing to me?' I craned my head around and could see the end of a black rod, with hairs jutting out, sticking out of my bum. He'd put some kind of whisk inside me! 'Paul, take that thing out this minute. You've had your little game now, and it's time to go back to the races.'

If he didn't want to have sex with me, we'd just go back again; I wasn't interested in this kinky stuff. I might enjoy sex, but I wasn't about to let myself be treated like some kind of slut.

'You're going nowhere. Did you really think you could humiliate me in front of my friends and get away with it?' Paul had his back to me, and was unstrapping something else from the wall. He turned, holding a saddle. 'This should do.'

I was aghast. I'd never seen this side of Paul before, beyond a little light spanking and watching porno films together. He was hard, too; I could tell from the bulge in his pants, and I realised that he was getting off on this, treating a woman like an animal. What a pervert! Hardly boyfriend material, let alone anything else. I tried to stand up, feeling the slimy whisk move uncomfortably inside me, but he clamped a hand round the back of my neck then hoisted the saddle on to my back, where it pressed heavily against me.

As he fastened the straps around my chest, pinching my boobs and making them bulge out, his hands brushed against my nipples and I realised they were embarrassingly stiff.

'Right, Paul, that's enough. I don't know what you think you're doing, but if you don't let me go right now I'll scream!'

71

I wasn't sure if I'd go that far – the sheer indignity of being caught in this position was too much, and God knows who'd hear me – but I had to get him to stop somehow.

Instead, he reached down, grabbed a handful of filthy straw and forced it against my mouth. I squealed, keeping my eyes and lips firmly shut as he rubbed the bristly stalks against my face, but then he pinched my nose, and when I opened my mouth to breathe he stuffed the handful in. It tasted foul, covered in dirt from the stable and God knows what other kind of muck, and I tried to spit it out, only to have him wrap some kind of rag around my mouth and over the back of my head, where he tied it.

I stared wide-eyed at him, squealing behind the rag. I couldn't believe how far he'd gone. He crouched down and looked into my eyes. 'I like you, Sophie, and I want you to know I'm doing this for your own good. You're a stuck-up little brat,' he said, as I struggled against his grip, 'and you need to be taken down a peg or two.'

He reached back and slapped one cheek of my bum, making me move the whisk from side to side, then slid his finger along the length of my oily slit, pausing to pinch the clit between his fingertips. I couldn't help shuddering at the exposure. I could feel my pussy all juicy and open, and hated my body for betraying me like this.

Paul just grinned. 'Just like I thought. Your slut hole's all juicy. Needs attention, does it? Well, I've got just the thing.'

He stood up and reached down to his pocket. I thought for a second he'd get his cock out, let me suck it and get this foul straw out of my mouth, or maybe stuff it in my pussy, all slick and creamy; I wouldn't have minded even if he'd buggered me with it, easing it in and out slowly while rubbing on my clit. But he took out his phone, placed one foot on the saddle to keep me down and said a few things I couldn't quite catch, then he laughed and put the phone away.

It didn't take long for them to arrive. Bernard looked a bit out of breath, red-faced and sweaty; and John looked as stern as ever, but with a twinkle in his eye. I definitely wasn't up for being paraded around in front of Paul's friends, even in my best lingerie, let alone got up like a horse, and I stared daggers at him. But when I tried to squeal again the men just laughed.

'This young filly, fresh and unbroken, is up for auction for this select band of buyers. Would anyone care to inspect her?' Paul was flushed as he spoke, and I looked at the others, willing them not to join in his stupid game, but they both looked excited, and advanced towards me.

'One at a time, please, gentlemen,' Paul admonished them.

I groaned and hung my head as Bernard's thick hands began to prod and probe me. He took hold of the whisk and pulled it out all the way then eased it back in, laughing at the way my ring was closing on it. 'Nice tight arse, Paul. So you haven't broken her in that way yet, eh?' He chuckled to himself.

'Actually she has been used there, but as you can see it's got a nice tight grip. Just the thing when she's oiling up too much. Test the other hole to see what I mean.'

Bernard's stubby fingers left the whisk and brushed against my pussy, tugging on the hairs. I could feel him crouching down under me, peeling back my pussy lips and inspecting my hole. Suddenly, unexpectedly, he gave it a little lick, then pushed two fingers up inside me. I gasped at the feeling of

73

fullness, and tried not to let myself push back as he started to fuck me with his fingers, all the while rubbing my clit with his thumb. But it felt too good, and I gave a little sob as my head sank to the ground, my eyes closed in bliss as I pushed my bum up towards him, feeling my juices trickle down through my pubic hair and on to my belly, clenching my bumhole against the whisk.

Bernard pulled his fingers out with an audible plop. 'Very responsive,' he said matter-of-factly. 'Care to inspect the merchandise, John?'

Another set of hands replaced his, stroking my boobs and tugging hard on my nipples. He pulled my bum cheeks apart, then removed the whisk. I felt something hairy rubbing against my slit, tickling me as it moved up and down along the juicy wetness, and realised he was stroking me with the whisk. Then it stopped, and I could hear him stand up and move away.

'How's she take discipline?' John asked in a gruff voice.

Paul snorted. 'Well, as I say, she hasn't been fully broken in yet. But I don't doubt your abilities in that department.'

I watched in horror as he moved to the wall and looked at the crops. After trying a couple, weighing them on his palm, he selected one and passed it to John.

'Jolly good! Now, filly, no squealing, and stay right where you are.'

I heard John move into position behind me. My mind was in a whirl. Part of me was outraged that they dared to treat me like this – like some common tart, or toy, to be dressed up and beaten for their amusement. I'd never felt a crop before, or anything more than a hand spanking me, and couldn't quite believe it was about to happen to me: pain was pain, as far as I was concerned. And yet I was still juicy; my pussy still ached, and deep down part of me was enjoying this, enjoying being used and humiliated, displayed in front of strangers, my hot slit ready for attention, for a finger or even a cock to go up my other hole, even dirtier . . .

A line of pure white pain jerked me out of my reverie. I'd hardly even heard the swish of the crop, or John stepping up, but now the agony filled my head. My bottom was on fire, and the mark the crop must have made felt huge, and throbbed insistently. My immediate reaction was to reach back, to try and touch it, to calm the pain, cool it down and protect it, but John just tutted and forced my hands back to the floor. My eyes were suddenly full of tears, and I could feel a lump in my throat. I couldn't believe that some people actually got off on this.

A second stroke followed, almost exactly along the line of the first, and my whole body jumped. Then he laid the strokes on with regular cracks, criss-crossing my bum until the whole thing felt hugely swollen. I could imagine it, purple and inflamed, white welts marking my beautiful skin, and those perverts getting stiff at the sight of a woman being punished, rubbing themselves through their trousers as my bum danced and jerked under the strokes. But, just when I thought the pain too much, and was starting to panic, sucking in straw, the white agony hit some other level, and I could feel myself soaring, pushing my pussy lips back so they'd take some impact from the crop too. I'd never felt anything so intensely, never lost my dignity so completely. Until the next moment, when all at once I realised I had to pee and that it was happening, spurting out between the strokes of the crop, trickling down to mix with my other juices.

I could hear them laughing as John held my pussy open with the tip of the crop, and flicked it against my clit. It felt huge, impossibly sensitive, and I jerked at the contact, swallowing my sobs of shame.

'Not much control, this one, eh?' I could make out John's voice.

'No, sadly not,' sighed Paul. 'You can't really take her anywhere.'

'Well, that knocks the price down a bit, doesn't it? I'll give you a pound for her.'

Even through my pain and tears I couldn't believe what I was hearing, and even less when Paul replied, 'Sounds fair. Any raise from you, Bernard?'

'Hmm – maybe one ten. Look at her now!'

I couldn't help it – I had to push it back at them, for attention to my poor aching pussy, some cold cream on my burning bum. Surely I'd had enough punishment now? Surely they'd tend to me, rub my clit, make me bring them off now?

'Let's get the straw out of her mouth and take a look at her teeth. I never make a proper bid without a good look at the teeth.'

Bernard moved towards my head and undid the rag.

I spluttered on the straw and spat it all out, then started to babble, 'Thank you. My bottom . . .'

'Of course, dear, how thoughtless. John?'

As Bernard unzipped himself, kneeled down and brought his cock to my mouth, I could feel Paul move behind me and lie down.

'Just move back a little, then.'

Paul kissed my pussy as I moved over his face, then he grabbed my hips and pulled me down to slide on to his cock, the saddle heavy on my back, the straps bunching painfully around my breasts, squeezing the flesh out until it was tight and swollen. Bernard chuckled and shifted position, taking my hair and stuffing his cock into my face again. I closed my eyes as they rocked me back and forth, Paul sometimes pulling all the way out and rubbing the end of his cock up and down along my slit, flicking it against my clit and making me groan.

Then a cold, slimy hand was on my bum, and I could feel John rubbing some kind of cold cream over the burning globes. It felt so good to have it cooled down, to have all the heat from the raised welts drawn out, that I gasped, pulling my head away from Bernard's cock, only to have him shove it in again.

John's hands started to move towards the centre of my bum, sliding in and out of my hole, slightly sore now from the whisk. He rocked a finger back and forth, joining in with the rhythm of the others, then pushed another in, and twisted the two around. It felt impossibly rude, dirtier than anything I'd felt before, with a cock in my mouth, one pounding in my juicy sex and John playing with my bumhole. He must have given the others a look, as they paused while he crouched over my bum and pushed the head of his cock against it.

It wasn't going to go in – it was too big. But Paul started to rub my clit, and I pushed out on it, like going to the toilet, and felt the head pop in, just like it did when Paul used me like that. I heard John groan, and pushed back on it more, feeling it slide in millimetre by millimetre, feeling it huge stuffed up there, all the while with Paul flicking my clit, his cock twitching inside me, and Bernard's cock pulsing in my mouth.

And then they all started to rock together, pushing back and forth, stuffing me full of cock, plugging every hole with it, and Paul was still rubbing my clit, giving it sharp little flicks with his thumb, and I thought about everything they'd done to me: making me give such a rude display to them; how I'd lost all my dignity in front of them; let them play with my holes; let them take a crop to me; how I'd wet myself in front of them; and how I deserved it all; how I was a bratty slut who got what was coming to her, and how I'd never felt so deliciously full . . .

And then it was on me, a full head exploding, my pussy and bumhole contracting around their cocks as I came hard. I could feel Bernard's cock pushing at my lips, trying to get back in my mouth as I cried out, all control totally gone, my back bucking and arching, the saddle shaking from side to side and pulling painfully at my chest, then my face was covered in hot come, splashing all over my cheeks and running down over my chin, and the thought of how slutty I must look – like a tart from some cheap magazine a lorry driver might pull himself off to – drove me to another high, another hit as I frantically pushed back on the men's fat cocks.

Then, as I came down, my whole body shaking, I could feel John pull out, and the cool air inside my arse as the ring closed slowly on nothing; then Paul pulled out too, pushing me back so that I was sitting up. When my vision cleared I could see the two of them standing in front of me, tugging on angry red cocks, Bernard in the background nursing his for its last few drops.

'Open wide,' Paul rasped, and I did it, even though I knew what he planned to do. I wanted to be a good slut for him, to show him how dirty I was, to take all of it in there, and then I felt it, first one jet of come spurting into my mouth, then another hitting my cheek and dribbling down, the men groaning as they pumped themselves into my mouth, covering my face with jet after jet of come.

I could feel it all in my mouth, slightly salty and thick. Half of me wanted to spit it out, disgusting stuff, and rinse my mouth out, but I didn't. I swallowed it, watching the men's reactions, licking my lips to get every last drop of it; then I got down on my hands and knees again, and licked up the drops of come where they'd fallen on the straw, my stomach tightening, but I didn't care. Then I lay back, my head soaring in bliss, playing gently with my nipples, one hand still stroking my hot, swollen slit.

'Jesus, Paul.' I could hear Bernard faintly in the background. 'One fifty?'

4

The Chalet

Rob surveyed the damage. City boys were the worst. Bottles everywhere, half-full cans of beer now overflowing with ash, a couple of wine stains on the carpet and a pan in the kitchen stuck fast with burned noodles, the remains of some drunken attempt at cooking that would be murder to clear up. And he hadn't even checked out the bedrooms yet. He peered around hopefully, paying particular attention to the surfaces, looking for an envelope, preferably with a telltale bulge. Nothing, not even a note.

Still, the snow was good and he should be able to get the mess all cleared up by lunchtime, leaving the rest of the day free, with maybe even enough time to check out the glacier, before he had to meet and greet the next lot. He took another look at the folder. That's right, all women this time, which should make a nice change. He didn't think he could handle another bestial group of boys on the piss. His nose wrinkled as he spotted something light pink and shiny just under the sofa. Christ, not another used rubber . . .

The bus was late coming in, and he shivered in the cold and breathed on his hands to keep them warm. The later the guests arrived, the later he'd have to start cooking, and the later he'd finally be able to leave. There was a mirror in the station and he wandered over to make any last-minute adjustments before the new arrivals. The icy chill added to the spiky gelled look of his black hair, and he teased a couple of strands out then breathed in deeply, puffed out his chest and stared at himself side-on, only to slump again self-consciously as he heard the dull roar of the bus engine, finally arriving.

He would've liked to have more upper-body strength, not least to help his skiing – he was one of the skinniest of the reps – but he could never be bothered with putting in the hours in a gym. He gave an involuntary shudder, and took another look at his clipboard, trying to memorise the names and details of his new guests. Christy Anderson, 27, Louise Taylor, 29, and Becky Sharp, 31. They were lucky to have the whole chalet to themselves, but they'd probably planned it that way, he thought, waiting to the end of the season. Risky business – a few years back the snow had pretty much gone by then, except on the peaks and the glacier – but this time it would be OK. And three meant less cooking, less cleaning, less hassle all round.

He could see them now, moving down the aisle of the bus, and he prepared his best smile and checked his name badge, making sure they'd be able to see it when they got off.

When the first of them came down the steps the first thing he noticed was her shoes. She was wearing heels, a strange choice here, hardly ideal in the snow and ice, and – his eyes travelled up her legs – a short skirt. When he looked up at her face, he found her glaring at him, and holding her bags out.

'You're the boy from Ruskins?'

He flinched at the 'boy', but nodded and tried out his smile. He'd seen something flashing in her mouth,

81

like she had a piercing in her tongue. She didn't smile back, but just pushed the bags out again.

'Take my bags, will you? They're heavy.'

She looked pretty, an impeccably groomed blonde, but haughty, like she was used to having things her own way. Spoiled public-school kid, daddy's favourite, Rob thought to himself – he knew the type. He took the bags. She pulled her furs around herself – they had to be real; there was no way a girl like this would wear fake furs – and turned to the others.

They'd got out by now too, and Rob tried to introduce himself. 'Hi, I'm Rob. I'm from Ruskins. Welcome to Verbier! Hope you had a good journey.'

The blonde hadn't even turned around while he'd started his spiel, but was muttering something to one of the others, a brunette who looked similar, beautiful but bitchy. Rob groaned inwardly – maybe these girls would be more of a handful than he'd hoped – but then realised that the third girl, a redhead, with long, beautiful hair, was smiling at him.

Wordlessly he took the bags from the brunette, who'd just flicked her head towards them when she'd caught Rob's eye, and he put them with the blonde's cases in the shuttle bus. As he laid the last bag on the pile he heard something clink, and the brunette clawed her way past him, shouting, 'You stupid boy! It isn't a fucking backpack. Take care of my bags.'

Rob bristled, shocked by the language as much as the tone, and turned back as the blonde joined the brunette on the shuttle.

The redhead still stood by the bus doors, smiling apologetically. 'I'm sorry about Louise. We've had a long journey and she's a bit highly strung. My name's Becky, and that's –' she indicated the blonde on the shuttle, who turned her head away huffily '– Christy. I'm sure we'll all be friends.'

She picked up her bags and moved towards the shuttle, but, as Rob reached towards them, grinning sympathetically now, ready to help, she slipped, her feet flying out from under her as she landed with a sickening crack.

Luckily the ambulance hadn't taken long to arrive. Rob could tell that the leg was broken from the start, just from the way Becky was lying, tears in her eyes as she tried to get up. Her friends had just stared from the window, like this was just some inconvenience slowing them down, and Rob had been appalled at their callousness. He'd had to stay with Becky on the way to the hospital, and called Billy, who he knew had a night off, to let the girls into the chalet and cook them something. He'd done favours for Billy before, and knew it was OK to call them in, but he didn't envy him having to deal with the girls, who sneered in disgust as their bags were taken off the shuttle and they were asked to wait in the bus station for the other representative, almost ignoring their friend lying on the ice, with Rob's jacket wrapped around her and her own bag used as a makeshift pillow.

He'd stayed with her until the results of the x-ray were through, and the doctor said that they might have to keep her in for a few days. She'd asked him to take some books and clothes out of her bag, and had smiled so bravely at him that he'd felt his heart in his throat when he said goodbye to her.

It was quiet when he got back to the chalet. Billy's duties hadn't run to doing the washing-up, he saw, and he busied himself with soaking and scraping pans as he wondered where the other two girls were. Wherever it was, they'd be pissed up – there were three empty bottles of wine on the table, and he doubted whether Billy would've drunk much of it.

When he'd finished drying up the last of the cutlery, it was gone midnight, and he left a note on the kitchen table: he'd be in at eight the following morning, and breakfast would be served until nine. Lunch was their own responsibility, but he'd be in again at six to start preparing the dinner. He was sure Billy would've filled them in on everything, but he didn't want to give them any cause for complaint.

It was clear the next morning, another beautiful day, and Rob grinned as he wondered whether hangovers would improve the girls' moods. He'd go and see Becky today – her leg was being put in a cast first thing this morning – whether the girls wanted to go or not.

He wasn't prepared for the scene of total devastation that greeted him inside. There were more bottles littering the floor, plus half-crushed beer cans and overflowing ashtrays; but the mess was worse than that. The sofa cushions were all over the place; one of the paintings had come off the wall; a candle had pooled its melted wax all over one of the tables and clothes lay strewn everywhere. He could see a pair of heels, one still upright, under the kitchen table, and one of the girls' skirts on what was left of the sofa. There was also a frilly pile of pink, and he picked it up, only to put it down again with a start as he realised it was a pair of knickers.

Used knickers. He picked them up again and felt them. The gusset was damp, and he sniffed at it, tentatively at first. He recognised the sharp tang of girl juice, and took a longer sniff, holding them to his face, then heard a door swing open behind him, and swung round guiltily.

Christy stood there, her hair mussed up and her makeup still on, wearing a long T-shirt. 'What are you doing?'

Rob realised he was still holding the knickers, and dropped them. 'I've got to tidy up in here. Do you want some breakfast?'

She just stared at him. 'Are you a pervert? What's your name again? Rich? Maybe I should tell Ruskins that you like creeping around the chalets sniffing girls' knickers?'

He held his hands up and tried to laugh, to calm her down, although inwardly he was horrified. The merest whisper of anything sexual with the clients was enough to get you sacked; he'd known it happen to one of the other reps.

'No! You've got it all wrong – how can I tidy up if I don't pick these things up?' He laughed again, then moved through to the kitchen, aware that she was still glaring at him. 'Shall I make you some coffee?'

He heard a snort, and when he turned back to face her she'd gone. He put the coffee on anyway and started to pick up the pieces of their night, putting the picture back on the wall, rearranging the sofas and plumping up the cushions, binning the detritus of booze and fags, and laying the knickers delicately on the arm of the sofa.

He wasn't going to put the eggs on or make any toast until he saw that they weren't going to go to waste, but poured himself a coffee as he waited, sitting at the kitchen table. There were footsteps above his head, and a toilet flushed. A short while later he heard a creaking noise, and murmuring voices. He checked his watch – there was only another ten minutes to go of the breakfast time, and he decided to go upstairs and warn them. He knew Christy was up anyway – all he'd have to do would be to call out in the corridor that time was nearly up.

But the creaking noise got louder as he climbed the stairs, and something made him tiptoe. The first bedroom door he came to was closed, but the second was halfway open, and the creaking noises were coming from this room. He moved closer to it, trying to stay in the shadows, then peered in.

It was dark in the room, and it took his eyes a couple of seconds to adjust to the gloom. But he'd already worked out from the sounds what was going on. The room stank of sex. He could see a man's arse pounding away between two splayed legs, and could dimly make out a wrist tied to the bedframe. The man was grunting as he shoved himself in, and Louise was cooing, her eyes closed as he mauled her breasts. He gazed at her face, watching her gasp with every stroke, then stumbled back as she opened her eyes and stared back at him.

She didn't say anything, just stared at him as she let the man fuck her. He couldn't pretend he hadn't been watching, and didn't know what to do – if there was anything he *could* do. Her lip curled into a sneer as she saw his confusion, and she closed her eyes again, ground her hips against the man's pumping crotch, pulled at her bonds and let out a long moan.

Rob walked slowly back down the stairs, uncomfortably stiff now, took the coffee off the heat and left the chalet.

His friends had been able to tell something was up during the day – normally they all traded stories about their guests, vying with each other to tell the most appalling anecdotes, but Rob was quiet. They knew he had three girls with him as well – Billy had even described Christy and Louise to the others, although he hadn't seemed keen to tell Rob what had happened last night when he'd made them dinner – and started to tease him about having fallen for one of them.

The teasing masked a serious concern – the reps did occasionally sleep with guests, but Ruskins frowned upon it, and routinely sacked anyone found crossing the line. It was partly because they forgot their other duties – Caroline, one of the girls that Rob had started with, had lost her job after being caught sitting on one of the guests by a rep leader doing a spot check of the chalets. All kinds of rumours circulated about what she'd actually been doing, but the most popular one was that she'd been wanking herself off, his cock in her bum, and had been pouring champagne from a glass on to her slit. Rob suspected that this bit was made up, but he wouldn't have put it past her, and she'd probably been drinking a fair bit anyway, as she'd sworn at the rep leader to get out; but however she'd acted at this point it wouldn't have made any difference – she was out.

But he'd told them about Becky's leg, which diverted the tone of the conversation as everyone agreed it was one of the worst things that could happen on your shift. Rob couldn't believe how selfish some of them sounded – what about Becky? Wasn't it worst for her? – but kept his mouth shut, unwilling to expose himself to his friends' jeers.

He'd left the chalet earlier without picking up Becky's clothes and books, and realised he'd have to go back in the middle of the day. They'd probably be out skiing, he knew, but he still felt anxious about returning. He couldn't get the image out of his mind of Louise staring at him as she was fucked, and he wondered if she'd told Christy. The blonde would definitely have told her friend about the knicker-sniffing incident; he was sure of it.

The door was unlocked, and he knocked before going in. Guests often neglected to lock their doors, so it didn't mean that they were there, but he waited, listening, out on the porch. Not a whisper. The lounge was in disarray again, with shards of broken glass all over the floor of the dining area, and there was an awful smell of burning from the kitchen. The coffee pot had been left on the heat, and a thick oily smoke was rising from the charred blackness at the bottom. He took it off, and surveyed the kitchen. As he'd feared, they'd tried to make breakfast after he'd gone, and there were eggshells on the floor, toast crusts and crumbs everywhere. The sink had been piled high with plates and greasy pans.

Taking a mental note of what needed to be done, he realised it would take too long to wash everything now and still have time to visit Becky. Still, he couldn't leave the mess in the dining area, so he fetched the dustpan and brush to clear it up. At least they'd be billed for these damages, he thought with satisfaction, as he reached out to scrape the glass into a pile, and the thought was so distracting he didn't even hear the girl until she was on his back.

He let out a little yelp as the unexpected weight sank on to him, thighs gripping his upper arms and furs tickling his skin. But, above all, he was aware of the unmistakable smell of girl juice.

'Well, if it isn't the pervert again! Come to clear up our mess! You're not meant to come now, are you?'

He tried to crane his head back, and was rewarded with a glimpse of her open thighs with a strip of sheer silky material between them, before she swept the furs back to cover herself up. He looked up and saw Christy grinning at him, a cruel gleam in her eyes.

'Naughty, naughty! No peeking now. Louise, see what I've found!'

He started to wriggle under her, trying to shake her off, and mumbling at the same time, 'Please – get off.' As he pulled back, she slid forwards, until for a second her thighs clamped his neck, and her smell was sharper still as her crotch rubbed against his skin;

then she was off, standing above him, and he let the furs slide over his head, staring up for another view of her knickers fitted snugly over her sex, noting with an intake of breath the dark dividing slit under the sheer material before standing up himself.

He was blushing, he could feel it. 'I've just come to fetch some of Becky's belongings. She asked me to bring her some new clothes and books.'

Louise had joined Christy now, dressed in a long black leather coat, and whispered something in her ear.

Christy grinned again. 'We'll help you get something together. But I'm not sure if that's why you're really here, is it? Maybe you've come to sniff our knickers again?'

'Or spy on us,' said Louise, glaring at him.

'Maybe you'd like to see who's got the dirtiest knickers? Come on, Lou, let him have a sniff.'

When Rob started to back away, his hands up, Christy stopped him. 'If you don't, we'll tell Ruskins that you've been prowling around, sniffing our knickers like a dirty pervert.'

He felt himself blush again. 'I wasn't – you've got me all wrong, please –'

'Pervert,' Louise said.

'Prowler.'

'He's probably been wanking in our clothes. Have you checked yours, Lou?'

'No, but, oh God! You can't get the staff now, can you?'

'Well, we'll let the little pervert have a sniff, and he can tell us which one's the dirtiest. I bet it's you, Lou, you little tart.'

They giggled.

'We want this to be like the Pepsi challenge. Put one of those eyemasks on him, will you, Lou?'

Christy said. 'We don't want him peeking while we take them off.'

He was stunned; quite apart from how inappropriate this game seemed, he'd thought they'd be yesterday's knickers, richly soiled like the pair he'd found earlier, but they were taking off their own now.

She turned to him. 'And you've already been peeking at mine, haven't you?'

As Louise left the room and ran upstairs, Christy started to pull the front of her furs up, slowly exposing more of her thighs until he could see the mound between her legs. Rob stared, transfixed, and was painfully aware of a growing bulge in his crotch. It hadn't escaped Christy's notice, either, and when Louise came back Christy dropped her furs and flashed her eyes to it, a broad smile on her lips.

'Look, the boy's got a hard-on! Just like we said, a pervert.'

Louise sniggered, and came forwards to put the eyemask over his head. He could feel the swell of her breast through the thick leather as she pressed her chest against him, then everything was dark. He could hear the girls muttering to each other, and a couple of teetering steps, then Christy's voice was in his ear and something flimsy and damp was being pressed into his hand.

'Try these. We'll call them A.'

He heard another giggle, then raised them to his face and sniffed at them.

'Not like that!' Louise's voice now filled his ear. 'Give them a proper sniff; put your back into it!'

So he did it, holding them tight against his nose as he took a long, hard drag, savouring their rich, fresh tanginess. His cock twitched, and he hoped the girls hadn't noticed, but a giggle and mutter told him they probably had, and he felt his face flush with blood

90

again. It wasn't just girl juice that he could smell; there was also a sharper hint of pee, and a background of perfume, as though whichever one it was was used to perfuming her crotch.

'That's enough! Try not to get so excited this time.'

He held the knickers out, and another pair was pressed into his hand. This time he needed no encouragement, but held them close to his face and sniffed deeply, imagining them held snug against the crotch of Louise, then Christy, imagining their slits, their trim and neat bushes, their greasy holes, and he realised with a pang this was probably as close as they'd let him get to them. This one smelled slightly different from the other, darker somehow, and it took him a second before he realised what it was.

'It's these – these are dirtier,' he said, holding them out.

Christy shrieked with laughter. 'I knew you were the dirty bitch!'

He pulled the eyemask up, and looked at the knickers, pale yellow cotton with a delicate lacy frill; and, just as he'd thought, there was a telltale thin brown mark on one side. Louise looked embarrassed, and snatched them off him.

'You'll do the washing for us, won't you, Rob?' she spat.

'That's standard – comes with the package,' he stuttered. But he suddenly felt guilty for letting himself be drawn into their game while Becky was waiting for a visit and for her clothes, and he tried to regain some authority, make a joke of everything that had happened. 'Well, we've had some fun here – we've found out who's got the dirtiest knickers –' he laughed, and tried to ignore Christy and Louise's stony stares '– but I've got to take a package to Becky.'

The girls exchanged glances, then Christy spoke. 'Come on, let's fix him up. Can you walk OK?' she asked, and gave his crotch a squeeze, wrapping her long scarlet nails around the bulge.

He gasped, half in pain and half in excitement, and Louise snorted and walked up the stairs.

Christy turned and walked up behind her and Rob followed, aware that neither of the girls was wearing any knickers, and wanting to try and catch a glimpse but reluctant to be caught in the act. But Christy was holding her furs close around her now, and Louise's coat was as buttoned up as her scowl.

Becky's room was at the end of the corridor, and one case was sitting on top of the bed. He could have sworn she'd had more luggage, but maybe he'd been mistaken. He'd glimpsed into the chaos of the other rooms on the way here, but this was just as he'd left it.

Louise opened the bag, and started to pull out the clothes, draping a flimsy negligee over herself.

'Would you like to see Becky in this, Rob?'

He dropped his eyes, embarrassed.

'Or maybe you'd like to wear it yourself?'

The girls giggled.

Louise did the same with the other clothes she pulled out, holding thongs up to her crotch and looking at him with a suggestive expression. But there weren't many clothes there, which surprised him, and no books at all, and he was wondering what had happened to the rest of Becky's belongings when, with a 'Ta-da!' of triumph, Louise pulled something long and black out of the bottom of the bag and held it up in front of him.

'What do you think this is?'

Rob could tell very well what it was. It looked obscene, sculpted with veins along the side and a thick, bulbous glans. She passed it to Christy, who weighed it in her hand, then asked, 'Is yours as big as this?'

He stared wildly from one girl to the other, and tried to take the dildo from Christy, embarrassed for Becky, wanting to hide it, his face burning with shame on her behalf. 'Stop it! You don't have any right!'

Christy stared at him and brought the black rubber to her lips, opening her lips and trying to fit the monstrous head inside. It was too big, and she gave up and licked it instead, still looking at Rob.

'I've got a confession to make, Rob,' Louise said with a straight face, with Christy giggling as she rifled through the remains of Becky's belongings. 'We've already been to see Becky, and we've taken her all the stuff she needs.'

'Except this!' Christy put in, and the girls burst out laughing.

Bewildered, Rob asked, 'But when's she getting out?'

'Tomorrow, at about lunchtime. I'm sure she'd like to see you, too.'

The girls sniggered again.

When Christy walked downstairs with him, leaving Louise to rearrange Becky's bag, she seemed a little sweeter, almost apologetic. She and Louise would be eating out tonight, she said, so there was no reason for him to make any dinner; and they wouldn't be up in time for breakfast, so he needn't come in the morning either.

He begged off skiing the next day, telling his friends that he was feeling a little under the weather. Billy gave him a curious look, but the others didn't seem to mind, and a couple agreed that he looked a bit peaky. He hadn't slept much, images from the previous day's events whirling round his mind, and he'd kept coming back to a picture of Becky smiling sweetly at him. She seemed so different from the others – kinder, somehow – and he couldn't understand why she'd go on holiday with them, or why she had that grotesque thing in her bag. Despite himself, he thought of her using it, rubbing herself with it and stuffing it slowly inside herself.

He wasn't able to eat much for breakfast, and only managed a couple of slices of toast for lunch. He wanted to see Becky again – in fact, it was pretty much his duty as her rep to make sure she settled in OK – but he was afraid of the two other girls, who were sure to be there when she arrived.

He finally decided that three was a good time to go. The chalet looked deserted, and was locked. He knocked, and there was no reply, so he went in. Just as he'd expected, the lounge area was a mess, plates of half-eaten food with cigarettes stubbed out on them on the table, a packet of condoms on the floor and a heady smell of cigarette smoke, stale alcohol and sex. He opened the windows to air the room then started up the stairs.

The door to Louise's room was open, and he peered in to check there was nobody in there before walking in, his heart racing. The ropes were still around the head of the frame, with the sheets half off the bed. They were stained with something greasy and clear, and he saw the open bottle under the bed and picked it up, only to drop it again when he saw what it was, what it boasted in bold letters: lubricant 'specially designed for anal play'. Her knickers were on the floor too – the same pair he'd sniffed yesterday – and he brought them to his nose again, feeling his cock thicken as the sharp smell hit his nostrils. He was tempted to wrap them around himself, to rub

94

himself into them, but drew back, afraid that she'd be able to tell what he'd done.

Christy's door was closed, and he didn't dare to open it, but Becky's was open. He looked in, and saw her lying on the bed, sleeping. Her leg was in a cast, and her skirt had ridden up to above her knee. She looked so vulnerable lying there that he had a sudden compulsion to protect her, to keep her away from the others, and moved towards her.

He could see where the cast ended on her thigh, the line showing under her skirt, and stared at the contrast between the hard white plaster and the soft creamy skin of the other leg. He touched the cast, experimentally, just to see what it felt like, then only half-consciously brushed his hand against her thigh, and felt a thrill, an electric charge run down his spine.

She was still asleep – she hadn't moved. His mouth was dry, and he knew he shouldn't be doing it, but he was thinking of excuses as he lifted the skirt: he was checking to see how comfortable she was; he needed to see if she wanted to be cleaned. It was dark between her thighs, and he pulled the skirt up to expose the top of the cast, then gasped as he saw it, dropping the skirt and moving back a step. Her inner thighs were marked with a delicate tracery of tattoos, Oriental images of waves, dragons and fish scales tumbling over each other and covering her bare crotch. She wasn't wearing any underwear, and Rob saw instantly that she was shaved down there, completely bare, the tattoos surrounding her pussy, framing it with dark swirling lines.

He couldn't stop himself. He ran a hand over the top of the cast, marvelling at the texture, then traced the line of one of the waves with his finger. He paused and looked at her face, to see if there was any change, but she looked exactly the same, so he moved his fingers higher up her thigh, gently stroking the marks and all the while staring at her bare sex lips.

He had to touch it. He licked a finger and ran it down the length of the slit, then sucked in his breath sharply as he realised that she was wet. He glanced at her face again – no change – then eased a finger inside her, groaning as he felt the moist warmth cling to his skin. The juice had pooled in her hole, and he moved it up to rub it over her clit, hardly caring now whether he was caught or not. It was hard, and he was rewarded with a sigh as he circled a finger over it then slid it back inside her.

Her sex was opening now, the lips puffy and swollen and a thin trickle of juice running down into her arse crease. He tried two fingers, which slid in easily, then pinched her clit, and heard her sigh. He moved back, scared now, and realised that she was awake, and watching him with languid eyes.

He couldn't think of what to say, but she made it easy for him. 'Don't stop now,' she said in a whisper, and with a choked sound he moved back and started to play with her slit again. She lay back and closed her eyes, whimpering as he started to flick her clit with hard, even strokes, trying to build her up to a peak then leave it alone, wanting to hear her beg for it; but her only response was to squeeze her thighs together, clamping his hand between her legs and pushing down on it.

She just lay there, a slight smile on her face, when he pulled up her top to expose her breasts. She hadn't been wearing a bra either, and her nipples were stiff and dark on the firm curves of her chest. He carried on rubbing her, and leaned down to take a nipple in his mouth, sucking and nibbling, then shifted to the other. He could hear her breathing getting faster, and bit into the flesh of one of the breasts as he flicked her clit harder, slowing down to feel every stroke as her chest and face flushed, then her whole body trembled and she let out a long, thin, high-pitched wail.

He took his hand away and sniffed at the slickness on his fingers. He needed release himself, but stared at the cast. With a sob he started to try to climb on top of her, but she stopped him.

'No. Look in my bag.' He knew what she wanted, but made a show of pulling out the clothes and looking quizzically at her. She just shook her head, smiling, and finally he pulled it out. She held out her hand, her eyes gleaming, and he gave it to her, then stared in rapt fascination as she trailed it down between her breasts and over the top of the tattoo to stroke the end against her slit, all the while watching his face.

'Come here,' she pointed to her side, reaching out for his bulge with her other hand and pulling him towards her. He helped her unzip his cock, and she pulled it out and licked the end, then slid the fat black dildo inside herself, groaning as it filled her to the hilt. He stared as her sex seemed to swell around it, the tattoos to either side bulging out, then groaned as she darted her head forwards, filling her mouth with cock and wrapping her tongue around it.

It didn't take him long to come, watching her fuck herself with the dildo as she sucked hard on his cock. She played with his balls too, and, when she felt them tighten, and knew that he was ready, she took it out of her mouth, wrapped her long silky red hair around it and started to pump it hard in her hand, fucking herself with the same strokes until he spurted, long streams of come jetting over her face, some landing on her cheek, some in her mouth, some dripping on to her chin. When he'd finished she squeezed his balls and licked the last drops off his cock, then pulled the dildo out with a wetly smacking sound.

He stared at her open hole, slowly closing on the wet pinkness, and stepped back, confused yet relieved at the same time. 'Becky, I –'

'Shhh.' She held a finger to her lips. 'Don't talk. It'll just be our secret; don't tell the others.' She reached over for a tissue. 'You can go now.'

He stumbled out in a daze, and made a half-hearted attempt to clean up, clearing away the worst of the mess and leaving the dishes to soak before leaving. He didn't know how he'd face the other girls, or Becky, again; he wasn't sure how he was meant to behave, having seen each of them behave that way, and didn't know whether their encounters together had been the start of something or the end.

As it happened he didn't have to make any decision about it. When he got back to his room there was a note on his door asking him to see the supervisor, Jules. Worried in case one of them had made a complaint – it would probably be easy for them, if they'd been unhappy with him, to prove that he'd been misbehaving – he approached the super's door with trepidation, and went over excuses and flat denials in his mind. His heart racing, he knocked on the door.

'Come in!'

Jules was typing something out on her computer as he walked in, and he waited in front of her desk, trying to look casual. When she finished, she nodded to the chair on the other side.

'Sit down, then.'

He sat.

'How's tricks? Is the chalet working out OK?'

Rob shrugged. 'Yeah, sure, everything's fine.'

Jules checked her notes, then leaned back in her chair and gave him a sympathetic smile. 'Don't take this personally; I don't think it's got anything to do with you, but the chalet's asked for a new person.'

Rob felt his face flush. 'Are you sure it's not anything I've done?' he blurted out, then mentally cursed himself for the stupid question.

But, if Jules noticed, she gave no sign. 'Probably not. They want a girl to start. We've got Liz free; she can take over this evening if you're ready to leave?'

It wasn't a question, but he nodded anyway.

'And we can start you on chalet six this evening – a new group arrives in –' she checked her watch '– an hour and a half. Here's their folder.' She pushed a file across the desk.

Rob opened it and his heart sank. Six men, all late twenties, probably minted, probably totally obnoxious. Still, at least he wasn't being sacked, and he looked up from the folder to try a smile out on Jules.

She surveyed him critically, then smiled back. 'Well, I'm glad you're not taking it too badly. As I say, I don't think it's anything personal, and there won't be any black marks against your work record. Good luck with the next lot; it looks like you'll need it.'

She turned back to her computer, and Rob nodded a mumbled 'thanks' then got up to leave. As he opened the door, she called him back.

'Oh, Rob? You *didn't* do anything, did you?'

He felt himself blush again, but managed a smile as he replied, 'No. But I understand if they want a girl around the place; that's fair enough.'

Jules smiled again and started typing.

As he'd expected, the next group of guests were a handful, and he didn't have much time to think about what might be happening with the girls. Some of his colleagues teased him about them, and one of them even joked that they'd caught him sniffing their knickers, and he'd gone red before he realised that it was only a joke; they couldn't possibly know that, and he tried to joke along with them, but his heart wasn't in it.

He only saw them once again, on the night before they were due to leave. They were leaving Tony's, the most expensive pizzeria in Verbier, well out of Rob's budget, and they were accompanied by three rich-looking young men, all arrogant swagger, immaculate hair and designer clothes. Rob stood on the pavement, watching, half-tempted to go over and say hello, but he knew that they must have noticed him, and Christy and Louise blanked him altogether, only marking his presence by throwing themselves into the arms of their respective beaus and laughing harder at their jokes. Becky, still in her cast and on crutches, was being helped down the steps by her companion, and, just when he thought she too would ignore him, she looked up, smiled and blew him a kiss. His heart melted, and when he saw her shaking her head in response to the man's questions about who he was, he turned to walk away, unable to watch her in the arms of another man any longer.

5

The Stewardess

The plane was almost ready. Just a couple more passengers to board, then the safety display and they'd be off. Emily had been late in getting there herself, and she took a couple of minutes to freshen up in the kitchen area, undoing her shirt to spray some perfume over her chest, checking in the mirror that her makeup hadn't smudged too much from when she'd started sweating as she ran through the terminal to get to the plane, and brushing her long red hair out. She thought it was one of her best features – it was certainly striking – even if the men she'd known had seemed more impressed by her milk-white skin, the pinkness of her nipples and her thin auburn floss.

She'd pulled the curtain to, but could feel someone's eyes on her back, and turned as she did her shirt up, to find a boy, probably just sixteen years old, staring at her. As she met his gaze he gulped and fished for the magazine in the seat pocket in front of him, and she smiled. Hopefully that'd be all the attention she'd get on this flight – shy boys.

It wasn't always like that. She wasn't sure whether it was the plane itself, or the uniform she wore – a thin, white, regulation cotton shirt that you could see the bra through, an A-line skirt that came to mid-thigh, stockings and medium leather heels. She'd felt game enough before to work without a bra, and enjoyed the stares she got from some of the men; a few had even seemed embarrassed, trying to cover bulges in their pants. And she'd even gone without knickers on one of the flights, teasing the co-pilot with a flash when she'd hoped he'd ask her out. It had worked, too, and she remembered his urgency when he'd confirmed his suspicions, the sharp intake of breath when he'd realised she was bare, wet and ready for him.

But this time she was tired. It was the last flight of her run, and she was looking forward to a couple of days off – in London, this time, rather than some foreign hellhole. The lure of travel, one of the main reasons she'd become a stewardess in the first place after leaving school six years ago, had long since worn off, although at least she was working the transatlantic run at the moment, rather than the long-haul flights to Nairobi or Delhi. But she still felt jetlagged all the time; all she wanted to do when she got back to London was sleep.

There was hardly anyone on the plane, which would make her life easier. She scanned the passengers quickly – a couple of children, some men and women sitting alone, one or two families, but, thank God, no groups. The worst were probably the bunches of drunk businessmen she had to deal with sometimes. She liked to look good, and she appreciated it if people noticed the efforts she'd gone to, but some of the men didn't know when to stop, pawing at her or asking her whether she had anything to suck on. Still, at least she wasn't working on one of the budget carriers, full of screaming kids, drunk people and shaven-headed yobs who thought nothing of hitting women. She shuddered.

It was her turn to make the announcements over the PA while Julie demonstrated the safety vest. She went through the lines mechanically, noting that few of the passengers were paying attention. Most of them were probably frequent flyers anyway, and some of them had even closed their eyes, ready to sleep; she felt a brief flash of annoyance – this was for their own good; they'd be sorry if anything went wrong – then relaxed. Sleeping passengers were the easiest to deal with, and it was always the ones who watched the safety demonstration most intently who were likely to be scared of flying. She revised her earlier opinion – *they* were probably the worst.

It was after they'd taken the tea and coffee round for refills that the buzzer flashed. Hoping it wasn't anything too serious – maybe a request for a spare pillow, or another blanket – she put on her calmest, most reassuring voice and walked towards the passenger. She'd noticed her before: a shy-looking woman with glasses and long brown hair, but pretty, probably early thirties, wearing a pair of jeans and a thin wool roll-neck. And nothing underneath it, which was why Emily had noticed her: the woman's nipples had been sticking straight out, although she'd looked embarrassed when she'd seen Emily staring at them, and had tried to cover them with her arms.

She looked even more sheepish now, and Emily gave her a professional smile. 'How can I help you, madam?'

The woman tried to smile back, but couldn't quite manage it. 'I'm afraid I've had a little accident.'

She pushed up the seat tray in front of her, and pointed to her crotch. Emily bent down, and could see a dark stain covering the front of her jeans, spreading to the sides of her thighs.

'Oh!' She straightened up. 'You've spilled some coffee. You didn't burn yourself, did you? Let me get a napkin to help you clear it up.'

The woman looked pained, and blushed deeply as she stammered, 'No, you don't understand. I had two cups of coffee, and, well, I don't normally drink coffee, because it makes me go to the toilet too much. But the toilet was busy, and I waited and waited, but I couldn't get out in time, and I –' She faltered, and bit her lip, looking anxiously at Emily, who felt her smile slip.

'You mean –? Oh dear.' It took a minute to sink in. Emily didn't know quite what to do; she'd never known it to happen before. This was a problem young children had, not adults. She tried to smile again. 'I'll just get some paper towels.'

She walked away, stunned. At least the woman was in a row of her own. But if she'd wet the seat – and Emily realised that there was no way she could have avoided doing so – she'd have to be reported. Suddenly Emily was angry – how dare she cause this kind of problem on her shift? There was no excuse for it: hardly anyone was on the plane, and she could easily have waited until a toilet was free. If she hadn't been able to handle the coffee, she shouldn't have had one cup, let alone two.

It was in this frame of mind, still shaking her head, that she returned to the woman, wearing a sterner expression than before. The woman noticed instantly, and looked down, again biting her lip.

Emily reached over with the napkins. 'If you could stand in the aisle for a second, please.'

She could tell that people around her were starting to pay attention, and the woman noticed as well. 'Do I have to?' She looked panicked, like a rabbit caught in headlights, and any sympathy Emily had had left for her predicament vanished.

'Now, please.' Emily glared at the woman until she moved.

It was worse than she'd thought: there was a damp patch covering most of the seat. Catching herself before she swore, she sighed and leaned over to spread the napkins over the damp patch.

'Excuse me?' she heard the woman's tentative voice behind her, and swung around. The woman was fidgeting, trying and failing to cover the front and back of her jeans with her hands at the same time. Emily could see some of the passengers looking over quizzically, staring at the dark patch.

'What now?' She didn't even try to keep the exasperation out of her voice.

'Could – could I have another seat?'

Emily's immediate response was to say no. The passenger had caused enough problems already, and might even do it again. But she paused and reconsidered: there were plenty of seats on the plane, and surely the woman would have learned her lesson by now.

'You can move one down.'

Bolder now, the woman's eyes brightened. 'Maybe I could move to a different row? You see –' her voice dropped '– it'll start to smell.'

Well, you shouldn't have bloody done it then, should you? Emily wanted to scream at her, but she relaxed and gave her best professional smile. 'I think it's best if you stay in this row, madam.'

The woman pouted and looked away, and Emily walked back down the aisle, angry again. Bloody cheek. She checked her watch – only another five hours to go: time to catch forty winks.

She was dreaming of a school exam she hadn't done any work for when the buzzer woke her. It took a second for her to work out where she was, and then she sat bolt upright. Julie was still fast asleep; she'd probably taken a sleeping pill so she wouldn't have to answer any calls, Emily thought bitterly. She felt groggy, and checked her watch: she'd only been asleep for an hour.

As she walked down the aisle she noted that everyone was asleep; almost all the passengers were reclining in their seats, covered by blankets and with an eyemask over their face; light flickered over the faces of a few insomniacs watching films or working on their laptops, but apart from the tinny sound of their headphones the plane was silent.

Her heart sank as she moved towards the back of the plane. Surely it wasn't that woman again? But there was only one light on in the rear, and it was her, sitting there as though under a spotlight. She looked up uncertainly as Emily approached.

'I thought maybe – the other stewardess –' she began, but Emily was only just registering where she'd moved to.

'I thought I told you to stay in your row?' Emily stared at the damp napkins on the seat in front of the woman, then glared at her.

She tried to look haughty, like she wasn't going to let Emily push her around, but her composure only lasted a second. 'I – I've paid for my seat and I think I should be allowed to sit where I like.' Her voice trailed away as she met Emily's glare.

'This flight has allocated seating!' Emily hissed, leaning towards her and trying to keep her voice down so that the other passengers didn't hear. 'And you've already ruined one seat! You're lucky I let you change seats at all! Anyway, what do you want this time?'

The woman flushed, and once again pushed up the tray in front of her. Emily stared and shook her head.

The jeans were dark again, even darker than before, but when she tried to peer between her legs to see how badly the seat had been soaked the woman squeezed her thighs together. That was it, Emily had had enough. The woman was looking at her with the plaintive expression she'd seen on the faces of the appalling spoiled brats that miserable parents took on flights sometimes; wretchedly behaved children who Emily had wanted badly to take in hand but had never been able to. Now she felt like one of these parents, but there *was* something she could do, and she suddenly had an idea.

'Come on, you.' She reached forwards and grabbed the woman's arm.

'What are you doing? Let me go!' She started to struggle, but Emily just gripped her arm more tightly.

'I know what to do with you. I won't have you spoiling any more of our seats. You're not four now; you've got to take responsibility for your actions.'

The woman went limp in Emily's arm, and allowed herself passively to be hauled through the aircraft towards the kitchen area.

Julie didn't look like she would be waking up any time soon. Emily cleared some papers off the counter, and told the woman to take off her jeans, wondering how far she could take it. But she did it, shivering slightly, then stood there trying to cover herself, a hand in front of her sodden panties.

'Take the knickers off too.'

At this the woman blanched. 'What are you going to do to me?'

'I'm going to make sure you don't have any more little accidents. Now take them off, or I'll report you at the other end. You might even get in the papers – pissed-up passenger wets two seats. I'll make sure they get a good picture, too.'

The woman flushed again. 'I'm not pissed!' But she turned away from Emily and pulled the knickers down, then tossed them in a wet pile on top of the jeans.

'Sit on the counter.'

The woman positioned herself, but kept her thighs pressed tightly together, and tried to cover her bush with a hand. Emily leaned forwards and pushed her legs apart, and the woman gave a small sob.

It was all wet, as Emily had expected, the woman's neat triangle matted, sodden and pressed down. But that wasn't the only wetness: Emily was stunned to see that her lips were swollen and open, and there was the unmistakable smell of sexual excitement. Surely she couldn't have been turned on by this?

Slightly shocked, Emily turned away, her mind racing. She'd only planned to make the woman a nappy, to put her in it and make her ashamed for what she'd done, but the sight of the woman's slit, all the hair pressed down and wet, had given her another idea.

'It'll help it stay on,' she muttered to herself, trying to justify what she was about to do.

She held a bowl under the hot-water machine, tested the water with her hand then reached into the flight accessories cabinet to fetch a small can of shaving foam, a razor and a flannel.

The woman had been watching her every move, but still sat there with her legs splayed, leaning back and displaying herself. 'Why are you going to do that?'

'It'll help your *nappy* stay on,' said Emily, stressing 'nappy' in the hopes of getting a response from the woman.

She was gratified to hear a moan, and the woman slumped back more, apparently entirely passive now.

Emily washed her crotch first, cleaning the inner thighs and down around her bumhole, then scrubbing around the hair and finally drawing the flannel over her slit. The woman gasped and sat up, then slumped back down as Emily started to spread the shaving foam over her bush.

The woman stayed silent as Emily pulled the razor over the top of her triangle, leaving it all bare, soft and white. When she came to the lips she pulled them out, grazing the woman's slit, and was disgusted to see a spurt of pee spill out.

'Can't you control yourself for one minute?' she asked, exasperated.

The woman just sobbed, and Emily pushed a towel under her bottom, then carried on shaving. With each stroke she could see more of her sex, the lips red and swollen, and she pretended to ignore the woman's cries as she stroked the skin, letting a thumb slip close to the greasy arsehole as she shifted from one side to the next, leaving no hair untouched. When she finally came to the wispy hairs at the bottom of her slit, just above her arsehole, she pinched the woman's mound, pushing the lips together, to make her slump further and give her better purchase. But juice was running from the woman's sex now, and pooling around her arsehole, some even trickling down on to the towel.

'Disgusting,' Emily muttered, but she couldn't help being fascinated by it.

The freshly shaved skin looked dry, and she thought for a moment of using some baby lotion to rub on to it, but realised she didn't need to, and reached down to push two fingers into the woman's oily hole and rub the cream over the newly bare skin. The woman gasped and squirmed, trying to rub her clit, which Emily could see, hard and bulging from its hood, against Emily's hand, but Emily wasn't ready for that, and stood back, confused by what had happened.

'Right.' She tried to snap out of her reverie, and looked around for nappy materials. They had normal-sized nappies, of course, but there was no way the woman would be able to fit into a pair of those, slim as she was; but they had bandages as well, plenty of them, and tape. Emily was confident she'd be able to do it. She'd seen enough mothers put nappies on their children to know how it worked, and gathered a roll of bandages, a nappy, some tape and a pair of scissors, then cut along the sides of the nappy and attached a length of bandage to each end.

'Lift your legs up.' She spread the puffy white material under the woman's bottom, then pulled it up between her legs. With the bandages it worked, and soon the woman was sitting with a giant nappy, which looked absurd as it circled her waist.

'Put your jeans on, then.' Emily motioned for the woman to get dressed again.

With a forlorn expression, she slid off the table, casting quick shy glances at Emily as she struggled to pull the jeans on. She was having trouble doing them up, the white material of the nappy bunching up and bulging ludicrously over the top, and she turned to Emily. 'I can't –'

Emily impatiently took the top of the jeans and pulled them roughly together, bringing a squeal from the woman, then wrenched up the zip. It only went halfway, and there was no way the button was going to close, but that was the woman's problem.

Emily smiled grimly at her, and nodded. 'There you go, that should keep you dry for a while. You can go and sit down again now, but I'll have to come and get you when we arrive, so that we can work out what to do about the mess you've made. Don't try and run away, now.' She smirked as the woman turned to waddle back down the aisle.

'Excuse me?' Emily called after her.

The woman turned back.

'You forgot these.' Emily held out her soaked knickers at arm's length, and the woman, making a sound halfway between a choke and a cough, took them from her.

Emily walked back to the kitchen area and cleared up the mess on the counter, reluctant to leave out anything that would force her to tell Julie what had happened, even though they normally shared everything. Then she sat down, kicked off her shoes and tried to relax, but her mind was still in a whirl, thinking about the way the woman had lain there so passively, letting her do whatever she wanted. She was still thinking about this, her mind halfway between desire and irritation, when she finally fell asleep.

She was dreaming that she was flying, and that the plane was shaking badly with turbulence, when she opened her eyes to find Julie shaking her. Her colleague smiled broadly. 'You're worse than me! Come on, get up. We're landing in twenty minutes.'

Emily yawned and stretched, her feet finding her shoes. Then she sat bolt upright, remembering. Had Julie dealt with the woman? She suddenly felt possessive, proprietary, and got up to walk down the aisle and take a look.

Some of the passengers were starting to wake up, the captain's first announcement about the descent having wormed its way into their dreams, or the first ear pops signalling the end of the journey. A few had raised their blinds, and were looking out into the fresh dawn light. But the woman still seemed to be asleep, a relaxed expression on her face, and Emily, half-disappointed, walked back to the front of the plane.

She told Julie she had to escort a passenger off the plane for special reasons, and Julie looked quizzical but didn't press her, probably keen not to get involved in any difficulties. Emily badly wanted to get back home as well, to finish her shift, lose the uniform and relax properly for the first time in weeks, but she also knew she had to see the woman again, to make her face what she'd done.

The woman was holding a blanket to her waist as she came towards the exit, and looking down, not meeting Emily's eyes, but Emily pulled her aside.

'That's company property, I'm afraid, madam,' she said as she tugged at the blanket, and the woman gave her such a pitiful look, still holding on to the edge, that she almost relented, but then the memory of the wet seats returned, and she pulled hard.

A few people stopped to watch, and even Julie turned, her farewell grin fixed on her lips, as the woman stumbled then tried to pull her top down over her waist. Her jeans were still half-undone, with rolls of white material bunched up, and Emily could see the realisation of what the woman was wearing dawning in the eyes of one or two of the passengers. The woman turned, trying to hide in the close confines of the exit area, and Emily, tempted though she was to keep her there, on display to all the passengers, realised it might get her in trouble, and escorted the woman off the plane, Julie's smile changing into a small O of astonishment as she too realised why the woman was walking in such a peculiar way.

Gripping the woman's arm to keep her from running, she asked in a conversational tone, 'Did the nappy work OK, then?'

The woman still didn't meet her eyes, but nodded, again red-faced. Emily steered her towards one of the nappy-changing rooms, and when the woman realised what she was doing she pulled against Emily's grip, but she just held tighter.

'Stop struggling or I'll call security.'

It was the last thing Emily was about to do – the woman was hers – but it worked, as she went limp in her arms, allowing herself to be pulled into the small room, and even sitting herself down on the counter without being asked. Emily undid the buttons of her jeans, pulled her shoes off and slid the jeans down her legs, then started to undo the makeshift nappy.

The woman clutched at her hands and stared at her, a wild expression in her face as she bit her lip and shook her head. 'No, don't –'

But it was too late. The front flap fell away, and the woman lay back and groaned. Just as Emily had expected, the front of the nappy was soaked, her bald, puffy sex glistening in the overhead light, but the smell should have alerted her to the other thing before she opened the nappy. It lay between the cheeks of her bum, small and brown, a dark stain spreading on the white material. Emily just stared at it in shock, then wrapped the nappy up and put it in the bin.

She reached for a tissue and began to wipe the woman clean, rubbing first the dampness away from her slit, which again responded to the attention by swelling and opening up, then pushing her legs up and wiping the brown smears away from the woman's bumhole. There was a choked sound of sobbing, and a spurt of yellow liquid landed on Emily's hand.

Emily felt her patience evaporate. She'd done so much for this woman, cleaned up after her, helped her not to make any more mess on the aircraft, and this is how she was repaid? All her rage at hundreds of unruly, impolite passengers came to a head, and suddenly the woman represented the yowling child, the drunk businessman and all the other fliers she'd come to hate over the years she'd been working for the airline; and, without even thinking about what she was doing, she pulled the woman off the counter, sat back on the toilet seat and wrenched her across her lap, her bare bum, still damp from the nappy, raised and her face down by the floor.

As Emily smacked her bum, laying fast, hard slaps across each cheek in turn, the woman's legs started to kick, and she yowled and tried to reach back to protect herself. Swearing, Emily grabbed her hands and held them, then carried on spanking her, watching the firm globes dance under her hand, exposing her arsehole and her puffy sex lips, greasy with more than just pee, the crimson handprints over the tender white skin joining until the whole area was a dark red.

But it wasn't enough – Emily wanted the woman to feel more pain, to suffer more – and she reached into her bag to pull out a hairbrush, then used the back of it to mark the swollen red cheeks more clearly, to feel the heat coming off them and hear the woman gasp with each blow, unable even to sob now, sucking in breath hard every time the hairbrush landed.

Emily started to place the blows with more care, slowing down to catch the sex lips with one, or moving down to mark the crease at the top of her thighs, and watching with satisfaction as her legs kicked harder. But the end of the hairbrush was now slick from where it had mashed against her pussy lips, and Emily paused to pull the cheeks apart. The lips parted wetly and Emily could see it all, bare, shaved and swollen, the slimy hole in the middle and the tight nub of the clit clearly visible, poking out. Cruelly she turned the hairbrush over and ran the

114

bristles over the pink wetness, and felt her own sex twitch as the woman gave a strangled yelp, then she pushed the fat hairbrush handle into the hole.

The woman seemed to slump, then to part her legs further. Emily let go of her hands, and the woman reached to the floor to brace herself as Emily flicked at her clit while alternately pulling the hairbrush out then plunging it in again, watching fascinated as the wet skin clung to the handle. Her legs weren't kicking any more, but she was pushing her hips up, trying to rub her clit against Emily's hand as she fucked her with the hairbrush handle, the slit oozing cream around each stroke.

'What – what are you doing to me?' the woman mumbled, but Emily just started to give her clit firmer flicks, rubbing it hard and fast as she plunged the hairbrush handle deeper in, fucking her harder. The woman's moans were faster and more urgent, and she was begging Emily, 'Fuck me! Harder!', pushing back on the hand, which slowed down for a series of hard, regular flicks until the woman was almost singing, a wail growing in pitch and hitting a high note as her body bucked under Emily's hands, the scarlet globes pressing together as Emily ground the hairbrush handle into her hole and pinched her clit.

And then it was over, and the woman slid to the ground, the hairbrush falling wetly from her pussy, and Emily had to touch herself, leaning back on the toilet seat and bracing her legs against the walls to hike her knickers to one side and feel her own wetness. She started to rub it, her eyes closed, then felt hands on her thighs and a tentative tongue darting in to taste her. She moved her hand and pushed her sex towards the woman's face, and sighed as she was held open by her hands, her tongue burrowing in deeply then sucking and nibbling on her clit.

When the woman eased the end of the hairbrush into her tight bumhole, after greasing it up in her slit, and held her clit sucked into her mouth, flicking it hard with her tongue, Emily felt herself boil over, and clutched at her nipples as she tried to keep back a wail, pushing herself on to the fat tube in her dirty hole, where she hardly ever let anyone play, and feeling it slide in as her ring clenched on it in spasms as she came hard. The woman was still flicking her clit as she was hit by the full force of it; everything that she'd done to the woman and everything the woman had done to her whirling in her mind and bringing her to the perfect come.

When Emily opened her eyes, she gazed languidly at the woman, whose face was wet with juice. The woman was still stroking herself slowly, rubbing the juice from her hole around the bare, swollen lips and pressing her red bum against the cool floor. She smiled shyly as she met Emily's gaze and said, 'You never told me your name?'

6

School Disco

I didn't really want to go. It wasn't by accident that I hadn't kept in touch with the other people from our year; I just hadn't been that interested in most of them. And then I'd gone to college, and met other people who were more my type, so I wasn't short of friends. Mel was the only one I'd stayed in contact with. However much later friends may be better suited to you, some of the ones you have when you're a bit younger have a special place in your heart; you've been through so much together, shared so many formative experiences. Mel was like that. I'd had my first cigarette with her, been to the first parties together; we'd both comforted each other when we'd been sick after drinking too much, and we'd both cried on each other's shoulders when we'd been having boy troubles, especially when the school had started taking boys in the sixth form.

We'd been inseparable at school, and, while I suppose I was the quiet one, Mel was brasher, more confident and sociable. It was only natural then that she'd been looking at one of those online sites that help old friends get together again. Apparently, a few of the girls from our year had been trying to arrange a reunion – not through the school, just an informal one – and they'd been using the site to recruit people. Mel thought it was a great idea, and told me about it one evening when I was round at her flat.

'Just think! You'll be able to see what everyone's been doing, catch up on all the goss.'

I must have grimaced, because she squealed and bounded over to me, turning on all her powers of persuasion. 'You'll love it! Look –' she unfolded a sheet that she'd printed out, with the details of the reunion on it '– everyone's got to wear school uniforms. And there'll be a disco and everything, free wine, beer . . .'

'I never liked school discos,' I pouted.

Mel pulled a long face, then pinched my arm, just under the shoulder. 'Don't be such a spoilsport. "I never liked school discos," ' she moaned, mocking me. 'That's because you never tried. Come on, I need you there. Moral support.' She got up and started to rearrange her hair in the mirror. 'Besides, I want to see what the boys are up to.'

I hadn't really thought about that. I had been a bit shy with boys at school, and, even though I'd snogged a few of them, I hadn't gone all the way. Not until my gap year. It wasn't that I hadn't liked them, just that the time had never seemed right. In fact, I felt slightly self-conscious about the way I'd been stand-offish at school, and maybe this would be a good opportunity to make up for lost time.

My eyes met Mel's in the mirror. 'OK,' I agreed.

She gave a little scream, clapped her hands and turned round to hug me.

The invitation had said strict school uniform, and Mel and I didn't want to be the ones to let the side down. I hadn't grown much since school, and I'd managed to borrow some of the clothes from my younger sister, who was at the same school. Mel still had her own clothes from school, but she'd fleshed out a little since, her tits and bum swelling out to some pretty impressive curves, so her outfit was especially tight. The skirts were pleated anyway, so that wasn't a problem, but her tits were almost bursting out of her top. When I pointed it out, she just grinned cheekily.

Well, if she didn't mind wandering around London like that, I didn't either. But we got a lot of attention on the tube, and I caught one man trying to look up my skirt. I think he did the same to Mel, but I could have sworn that, rather than ignore him, she slumped further down on the seat and parted her knees slightly, so that he could see her knickers. I didn't say anything to her about it, then or afterwards, but I did look at her while she was doing it. She was staring straight at him, biting her lip.

When we got to the venue, which was in Islington, we knew we'd done the right thing wearing our outfits. A girl I barely remembered was on the door, kitted out in full uniform, and was stopping anyone who was wearing casual clothes. An argument was in full flow when we arrived. It looked like John Duffy and Cathy Bell had arrived together, just wearing jeans and sweatshirts. The girl on the door was telling them they had to change, but that it wasn't too late, they had some school uniforms there. John and Cathy stepped aside for a second, and I saw him whisper something to her, and she nodded.

'OK, we'll change,' he said resignedly.

The girl on the door smiled, and ushered them in.

Mel and I followed, although we didn't go into the changing rooms. Instead we walked straight through to the main room. They'd gone to some effort. It wasn't huge, but everyone would fit in easily, and it looked exactly like a school disco. There was a PA at the far end of the room, with some appalling pop song blaring out. It was flanked by two sets of lights – the oldest, cheapest kind, with red, green and yellow lights flashing like some demented traffic warning – and there was bunting hanging down from the ceiling and balloons in the corners.

The walls were lined with orange plastic chairs, which instantly brought back memories of awkward moments waiting to be asked to dance. The wall by the door had one table covered in plates of sandwiches, all tuna mayonnaise and cheese and tomato in true school style, party-sized sausages, bowls of salad, surrounded by smaller bowls of salad cream and thousand-island dressing, and a few other plates of snacks and crisps. On another table stood plastic cups of white and red wine. There was also a keg of beer, and I could see under the table more cartons of wine, another couple of kegs and some containers full of plastic cups.

Mel and I helped ourselves to some wine. There were a few people there by now, huddled in small groups, but before going over to say hi I just wanted to look at everyone. There were more girls than boys, and the boys had made less of an effort than the girls. They were just wearing dark trousers, shirts and ties, and some of them had V-necked sweaters. Apart from the inept, oversized knots in their ties, they looked like they could have stepped out of any half-formal social engagement.

Not so the girls. A couple of them had really gone to town, putting their hair in pigtails and wearing shorter, flouncier skirts than we'd been allowed at school. And one of them had already undone the first few buttons of her shirt, showing off an ample creamy expanse of tit. I recognised her immediately; she'd always liked showing off. She saw me looking, and beckoned for me to go over. I sighed inwardly, drained my wine, took another full cup off the table and joined the throng.

But just as I was about to start talking to her, I noticed that her wide eyes were fixed on the entrance. The hubbub of conversation died down, to be replaced by a chorus of catcalls and wolf-whistles. I turned around, confused.

And then I saw it too. The couple we'd seen in casual clothes on their way in – John and Cathy – had changed into school clothes, but they weren't quite like what everyone else was wearing. Cathy was dressed for hockey, or one of the other games I'd studiously avoided playing in my school days. She was squeezed into a tight white T-shirt that left nothing to the imagination; at least she was wearing a bra, but it must have been thin, and she must have been cold or something, as her nipples were poking straight out. She was in a battered pair of plimsolls, and had white socks pulled all the way up to the knee.

But the worst of it was the skirt. It was tiny, and you could tell that she'd spent some time trying to tug it down so that it covered her, but if she pulled it down at the front it rode up at the back, and vice versa. She looked like she was about to cry, and quickly moved over to the drinks table to grab a cup of wine. But this just exposed her behind to us, and we all stared at her full bottom cheeks, the curves clearly visible under her hemline. We could even see a flash of white from the back of her knickers, but she must have felt us watching, as she abruptly tugged the back of the skirt down and turned to face us, her cheeks blazing.

It was difficult to know whether the jeers were reserved more for her outfit or for John's. While the other boys looked like the young adults they were, he had been dressed like some oversized schoolboy, in a scruffy blazer, a stained tie and a creased shirt. Worse still, he was wearing a pair of shorts. He managed a brave grin, but I could tell he was upset. Then another boy, one of his old friends, moved over to him and ruffled his hair. John smiled ruefully as he was led away to join their group.

I noticed that they hadn't come in alone. There was another girl standing by the entrance, a malicious smile on her cold face. She was wearing a prefect's badge, and holding a long wooden ruler. It was Alison Hayes, of course. She'd been a prefect at school, too, and she'd never been popular. I remembered that she'd bullied a few of the other girls when they'd been younger; lots of kids had been bullies for a while and had grown out of it, but she never had, and the way she'd done it meant that it had been hard to forgive. And she'd been a bad fighter, too, pulling hair hard, using her long fingernails to leave bright red weals on her victims' skin, and sometimes even biting. I'd never had any close dealings with her, thank God, but I knew girls who had. I'd heard other stories too, about what she used to make some of the other girls do. She had a real cheek, turning up here with her prefect's badge on. And what on earth was she doing holding a ruler?

A couple of hours later, I was having a great time. Mel had been right: it had been good to catch up with people, and everyone was downing the wine at a furious rate. The food had hardly been touched. I'd even managed to find a small bottle of whisky in the kitchen near the loos, and I'd had a couple of quick nips, which had gone down a treat. The music sounded hilarious now, even if I couldn't work out if its mixture of eighties hits – they'd already played both 'Lovecats' and 'Wishing Well' twice – was ironic or not. Nobody cared. They were just happy bopping around. Well, most of them were, anyway. A few had already taken to the dark corners for a snog, and I was sure that Dave Hewitt had his hand in Becky's knickers.

I'd danced with a couple of the boys myself, but there weren't any I really liked, and I hadn't snogged any of them – not yet. I thought I'd missed my chance when the PA suddenly went dead. A few people carried on dancing, or swaying rather, but even they stopped when the lights went on. We all turned to look at the entrance. And there the pair of them were. I knew who they were instantly. A couple of the prefects from our year – Alison and Vicky – both looking grim-faced and angry. Of course, it had been Vicky on the door; I hadn't recognised her properly. But I hadn't given much thought at all to who'd set up the whole event, and now the penny dropped. They had.

They'd been in the same group together: unpopular, clannish and a little scary. Alison was slightly built, with dark hair and a pinched face. Vicky was a giant by contrast, a six-foot blonde who was strong enough to be a serious menace both on the hockey pitch and off it; you wouldn't have called either of them pretty. As prefects they had been merciless, and took to their tasks with a bit too much relish, especially when they were administering discipline. Of course, they'd had to tell teachers if anything deserved a proper punishment, but they'd been allowed to punish minor infractions themselves – if a girl's room wasn't tidy, say, or if she hadn't finished her meal. These earned a rap on the knuckles with their rulers.

But I remembered the other stories, about what they'd done when they'd caught girls smoking. They were meant to tell the teachers then, but I'd heard that they'd let some girls off. Well, almost. The girls had had to pull their knickers down and take a few strokes on the bare bottom instead. The same thing happened if they caught girls rubbing themselves – or, worse still, each other. I don't think there were any strict rules and regulations over that kind of thing at school; everyone did it, touched themselves, I mean, and, as for the other, the school probably wanted to pretend it didn't happen.

But I heard that they'd threatened to send one girl they'd found doing it to herself with a candle to the matron, to report her for being a pervert. Apparently she'd agreed to take the ruler on her bare bum rather than be reported. I'd hardly been able to believe it was true, even though some of the girls swore to it; I couldn't see what the prefects would have got out of it. But I couldn't get the image out of my mind now.

It was silly, really. We were all grown up now, and still somehow the sight of these two prefects cowed everyone, evidently even the boys, into feeling like naughty teenagers again. It was partly the look of fury on their faces, partly the rulers they all carried, like a mark of authority, and partly their badges themselves. Still, someone giggled. But neither of the prefects was smiling. Vicky stepped forwards.

'OK, then. Who's been drinking the whisky?'

Nobody answered, as she glared around the room.

'Come on, own up.'

Still nobody spoke.

Then Alison piped up. 'We've locked the bathroom. Nobody will be able to go until the person who's been drinking the whisky owns up.'

At this there were gasps of disbelief and indignation, followed by a low murmuring. There was no way I was going to own up to it, though. They looked evil, standing there tapping their rulers on their thighs. Then the murmur died down, and in the silence that followed it became apparent that this new instruction was going to affect one of us much more than the others.

Cathy was hopping from one foot to the other, her hands tugging at the front of her skirt and her eyes glittering. Someone started to giggle nervously then stopped abruptly. I could see that Cathy was on the verge of tears.

'Please . . . I have to go,' she pleaded, but received only a slight shake of the head from Alison in reply. Then, evidently horrified to make the admission, she said, 'But I'm bursting! I'll have an accident if you don't let me go.'

Her cheeks reddened, and she looked down at the floor, her lower lip trembling. Still neither of the prefects relented.

Then John stepped forwards. 'Look, what is this? Let her go to the loo.'

He reached towards Vicky, as though to take her by the arm and move her away from the doorway, but she was too fast for him, and whipped the ruler across the back of his hand. He yelped and pulled his hand back, to stand rubbing it, looking for all the world like a penitent schoolboy. All that was missing was a cap. After that, nobody dared interfere.

I was sure the girls would have mercy on Cathy; it could have happened to any of us, although I remembered that she'd had a few problems with holding it in when we were at school. Still, I didn't think they'd let it go that far. But they did.

Everyone watched it, too. Hardly anyone had moved since the prefects had made their demands, but now all heads turned as Cathy started to sob, and a trickle of liquid made its way down her leg, gathering slowly into a pool by her feet. The trickle turned into a stream, and then she was weeping openly as it all came out. One of the other girls snorted in disgust. I flushed as I watched her, feeling that it was all my fault; if only I'd owned up then this would never have happened to her. But it was too late now – they had a victim, and they weren't about to let her go.

'Disgusting!' Vicky scoffed, and held up the front of Cathy's skimpy skirt for everyone to see. Her knickers were soaked right through, and we all stared at the darkness at the centre, the wet curls and the dark crease of her sex clearly visible through the translucent material.

'Take them off,' she ordered.

Cathy, still sobbing, bent over and pulled them down, stumbling slightly as she took first one then the other leg out. It was embarrassing to watch – we should really have given her her privacy – but I could see that at least two of the boys had distinct bulges at the front of their trousers as she exposed herself, and compassion wasn't the only emotion showing on some of the girls' faces. She'd trimmed it really nicely, so that there was a small square of bush at the top, but the lips themselves were hairless and shiny with wetness.

'Can I – can I go and wash now?' Cathy's eyes were cast to the ground, staring down into the pool that was still spreading around her feet.

'No. You'll stand there until somebody owns up. Then you can clean yourself up, and –' Vicky's nose wrinkled as she looked at it '– get rid of that mess.'

That was too much for me. The smell of the pee was quite strong now, and the game had gone far enough. I stepped forwards. 'Listen, this is stupid. It was me that drank the whisky, and I hardly had any of it. I'm sorry you've got so upset, but that's no excuse for what you've been doing. This is meant to be a party, for Christ's sake!'

Vicky and Alison exchanged glances then beckoned for me to join them. Nervous now, I walked across to join them, stepping gingerly around the pool of pee. Vicky took my upper arm, gripping it painfully hard, and turned me to face the others as Alison spoke.

'You have a choice of two punishments. Clean up that girl's mess – and that means all of it – or take twelve strokes with the ruler.'

'What the fuck do you mean?' I tried to wriggle out of Vicky's grip, but she was too strong. I stared at my audience. 'Come on, help me! There's only two of them here!'

But nobody moved. I looked at Mel, imploring her silently to come to my aid, but there was a strange gleam in her eye.

'So what's it to be? Cleaning or the ruler?' Vicky's fingers tightened as she prompted me.

I wasn't about to clean up Cathy's pee, especially not 'all of it'; that sounded a bit sinister. I'd never had the ruler when I'd been at school, but was sure it couldn't hurt that much. Not that I'd been a goody two-shoes; just that I hadn't been caught doing anything wrong. I decided to go for that, and mumbled out my decision.

'Speak up!'

'I'll take the ruler.'

'I'll take the ruler –?'

I knew what the bitch wanted me to say, and knew also that if I didn't play along it would just be worse for me. 'I'll take the ruler, please.'

I looked up, half-expecting Alison and Vicky to be smirking as I said this, but they just looked angry; but

127

then, when I looked at Mel, fully expecting my friend's sympathy, I was horrified to see an open expression of excitement on her face. And then I was turned around, Vicky tugging on my arm until I was facing the entrance.

'Go and get a chair.' Vicky gave me a push.

I could have run then, but I didn't. I don't know why. It was almost as though I wanted to see what would happen next; how bad the whole situation would get. So I fetched a chair, and carried it back to the prefects.

'No –' Alison allowed herself a prim, curt smile '– facing the door.'

I turned it around, and was then pushed over the back of it, forced into position so that I had to grab the sides of the seat to keep my balance. Then I felt the back of my skirt being pulled up and tucked into the waistband, and my knickers being pulled down. I whirled round, trying to protect myself with my hand, not wanting them all to see my naked bum out on display. It was the wrong thing to do. I felt a sharp pain in my hand, and a glancing blow to my bottom cheek, then Vicky was beside me, forcing my hand back down on to the seat and hissing into my ear. 'Do that again, you cow, and we'll double your marks.' And she left me.

I braced myself for the blow, clenching my cheeks as Alison touched them with the ruler. But when she didn't hit them this time it gave me a false sense of security, so that when it did come I was caught unawares. The pain sent white light splintering behind my eyes. I shot up, yowling, my hands instinctively going back to rub the burning mark – it felt huge, like I'd been branded – but on cue Vicky was there, pulling my hands away and pushing my head down.

I was sure that the second wouldn't be as bad as the first. I was wrong. The pain of the first had sensitised me to the point where it seemed that I was aware of everything – even the air pushed in front of the ruler as Alison brought it down again, viciously hard, turning it slightly so that an edge caught just in the swollen red area left by the first blow. Unable to move back, I started to sob, my breath catching in my throat as I shifted my weight from one foot to the other, hoping somehow to spread the pain. It didn't work.

And I didn't get used to it, either. The third was even worse than the first two, which had at least been on my bum. This one was just under the cheeks, the lower half of the ruler catching my upper thighs, and the middle dangerously close to my pussy lips. It was too much for me. I turned, sobbing, and begged them to stop, even as Vicky clutched my wrist and started to threaten me again.

'I'll clean it up! I'll clean it up!' I could barely get the words out, and paused to wipe my eyes and get some semblance of dignity back into my voice. 'I'll clean up all her pee.'

For a second there was the glimmer of a smile in Alison's eyes, then she nodded to Vicky, who strode off through the entrance.

I made to pull up my knickers, but Alison stopped me. 'You can take those off.'

Meek after my beating, I complied and stepped through them, then tried to tug my skirt down so that it hid everything I was showing. The material felt horribly rough on my ridged welts. I turned to the others, hoping to catch a wince of sympathy on someone's face, but if anything there was an air of anticipation, of excitement, as though this were vastly entertaining and they couldn't wait to see what came next.

When Vicky returned with a sponge and a bucket full of water, I was almost relieved. I'd thought for a second they might want me to . . . but no, even they weren't going to stoop so low. I took the bucket silently and moved over to Cathy, who seemed to look slightly less wan now that someone else was sharing her misery. I grimaced at her, happy at least that I was out of the reach of that wretched ruler, and kneeled on the floor to start mopping up the yellow pool. I was uncomfortably aware that in this position my skirt was riding up over my bum, and that they could all see my pussy, so I tried to keep my knees close together, so it wouldn't look too bad. But to keep my balance as I mopped, my knees automatically spread a little, and it didn't take long before I'd given up trying to hide myself. Anyway, the cool air felt wonderful on my poor bum.

I'd soon finished on the pool under Cathy's feet, and started to clean her legs. I wasn't too sure what I'd do when I got to her pussy – probably just mop it a bit with the sponge, then leave it for her to sort out later. But when I brought the sponge towards it I found that wasn't what Vicky and Alison had in mind at all.

'No. Not like that,' said Alison firmly.

I turned to face her, puzzled.

She gestured for me to put the sponge in the bucket. 'Lick it clean.'

'What?' The idea was preposterous. I'd never licked a girl before, and I wasn't about to start in front of an audience.

Alison's eyes narrowed. 'You'll be taking extra strokes with the ruler, then, for wasting our time.' She turned away from me and nodded to Vicky, who started to move towards me, flexing her hands.

'No – wait!' I couldn't face the ruler again. Perhaps it wouldn't be so bad, licking Cathy a little. It wasn't like I didn't know her, and it wouldn't be painful. I turned to her and tried to smile. She looked uneasy, as though she were about to start crying again.

'We'll put her on a table, so that you can get at her more easily,' Alison decided, and Vicky duly led her to one of the food tables, then cleared away a few plates of sandwiches with one sweep of her meaty hand.

Cathy sat down, her head hung low and her knees pressed firmly together. Vicky took hold of each knee and wrenched them apart, hard.

There was a gasp. Everyone had seen it. There was a tiny ball piercing nestled at the top of her pussy, through the clitoral hood. You couldn't miss it – she'd shaved the sides of her slit, which was now swollen and open, the inner lips pouting, and the white gleam of the metal ball stood out in stark contrast to the wet pinkness of her crease. I could see her shoulders shudder as she started to cry silently, her secret exposed.

Suddenly I wanted to make her feel better; to get it over with, so that she could put some clothes back on, so that she wasn't exposed any longer, so that she could return to some semblance of normality. So I walked over and kneeled between her legs, putting my hands under her thighs and muttering to her soothingly. And then I leaned forwards and started to lick.

I'd never tasted pee before, but Cathy's didn't taste too strong. After the initial shock it was fine, and I cleaned both sides of her pussy before testing the crease with my tongue. There the skin was softer and slicker, and I could taste something different mixed in with the pee, something sweeter and thicker. I dug my tongue deeper into her hole, experimentally, and found a well of the juice, which seemed to flow more readily as I licked. She was juicing up under my tongue.

A queasy wave of desire swept through me: a desire to comfort and please; a sense of revulsion at what I was doing; and an arousal I hadn't felt before, dark, dirty and forbidden. And, of the three feelings, the arousal was by far the strongest. I started to lap long strokes along the length of her slit, teasing her clit out from its studded hood, sucking on it and nibbling it. I ignored the giggles behind me, pretending not to hear when someone whispered 'Slut' loudly enough for me to hear.

I just concentrated on Cathy, the way her thighs tightened around my head, her moans growing more forceful; the way she started to grind her pelvis into my face, smearing my nose and cheeks with her juice. She squealed when I lifted her thighs and moved down, trailing her juices with my tongue down to her tight bottom hole, which I circled a couple of times before darting my tongue in, tasting its hot sourness. And then I worked on her clit again, rubbing my tongue hard over it then sucking it into my mouth and holding it there while I strummed the tip of my tongue against it.

That did it. She came with a scream, clenching her legs hard around my head and bucking her oily hole against my face. It was only when she relaxed her legs and let my face fall backwards that the full realisation of what I'd done hit me. The room was quiet, the only sounds Cathy's panting and the ringing in my ears from where she'd clamped my head with her thighs. My face was wet, and with a reflex of embarrassment I put up my forearm to wipe Cathy's juices away. I was covered in it. My cheeks crimson, and not daring to look at the others, I ran for the bathroom. The prefects let me through – I think even they realised enough was enough by now.

There I tried to take stock of what had happened. It seemed unreal, the kind of thing I'd never even fantasised about – as though it hadn't been me doing it. But I couldn't deny that I'd enjoyed it; that I had my own dampness between my legs. I stared at my shiny face in the mirror, then started to wash off the juices. Then the temptation sneaked into my head of touching myself here, where there was nobody else to see. I locked myself into one of the cubicles then rested my wealed bum on the cool seat and hiked up the front of my skirt.

I hadn't realised how wet it was. The lips were swollen and puffy, and there was a slow trickle of juice running from the end of my crease down towards my bottom hole. I sighed and smeared the juices along the length of it, circling my hard clit. But my reverie was broken when there was a loud rap on the door.

'What are you doing in there?' I recognised Mel's voice, and unlocked the door, all thoughts of my own pleasure temporarily gone. She stared at me, and the look on her face momentarily brought back all the shame of what had happened in the other room, then she repeated the question.

'Nothing,' I said, colouring. Then, to fill the awkward gap, I gripped her wrist, trying to forget how disloyal she'd looked earlier. 'We can't let them get away with this. We have to do something.'

She met my gaze steadily. 'What do you have in mind?'

When we went back in, things were starting to get back to normal. People were dancing and drinking again, and, if there was a more charged atmosphere, that was only to be expected. I watched as Mel moved around the room, spreading the word, and watched also as Vicky and Alison chatted by the food tables, their guard down, confident that they were in control here.

Whatever Mel had been telling everyone, it was working. We all started to move towards the food tables, slowly, so that the prefects wouldn't realise what was going on. I did see Vicky look up with a confused expression on her bovine face, but by then it was too late. Mel seized the moment and gave us our cue.

'Food fight!'

And we were all over the two prefects, at least five of us on each of them, pushing their heads down into the plates of sandwiches, pouring salad dressing into their hair and tearing at their clothes. They were fighting furiously, but now our fear had gone and we knew we were in control. Their rulers were the first things to be taken away from them, and, if Mel hadn't stepped in, years of bottled-up hatred on the parts of almost everyone there would have made the whole thing descend into a nasty free-for-all.

But she'd explained the plan to everyone, and we all stuck to it – near enough. First up was Vicky, who was held down by two of the boys as we pulled up her skirt and pulled down her knickers, ignoring her kicks and screams. I'd seen the funnel in the kitchen earlier, while I'd been drinking the whisky, and the idea for how to use it had popped into my head while I'd been talking to Mel.

We had to grease Vicky's bum first, so that it would fit in, but there was plenty of butter on the sandwiches, so we just smeared a couple of slices around her bottom hole, which opened and contracted rhythmically as she bucked in an attempt to get away. Then we pushed the end of the funnel in, and were rewarded with a high-pitched squeal as we did so. I glanced at Alison, and was gratified to see an expression of pure terror on her face.

'We're going to fill you up with thousand island dressing, and you're going to hold it in while you take twelve strokes with the ruler. If you let any of it spill out, we start the twelve strokes again.' Mel toyed with the funnel as she explained Vicky's predicament to her.

Vicky's response was to thrash around furiously, cursing all of us in inventively colourful invective.

Mel caught my eye and nodded towards Cathy's soiled knickers. I turned to fetch them, and, as I walked back, all thoughts of my own humiliation evaporated now in the desire for revenge, I saw Mel untying one of the boy's ties. She took the knickers from me, and rubbed them against Vicky's face, but the prefect wouldn't open her mouth, closing her eyes and wrinkling her nose in disgust, until Mel pinched her nose closed. After another brief struggle she opened her mouth to take in a deep breath of air, and Mel seized the opportunity to shove the knickers in, then quickly wound the tie round Vicky's head to keep it there.

'That'll shut her up,' Mel muttered as she moved over to the table to pick up one of the rulers.

Vicky's eyes, wide with terror, darted around the room. I could see trickles from the pee-soaked knickers running down her chin. Mel offered the ruler to Cathy, who shook her head, her eyes glancing towards Alison. Mel smiled, and turned to the group.

'Anyone want to give it a go? Twelve strokes, and more if she doesn't keep the dressing in.' She said it almost casually, as though she was offering the chance to play a game of backgammon rather than take revenge on this woman, who I knew had made so many of the girls' lives there a misery.

At first nobody moved, then one girl stepped forwards. I remembered her – short, slightly dumpy and bespectacled, her name was Jane. No, Jean, that was it, but I remembered that Vicky had started calling her Plain Jane at school, and the name had stuck. I hadn't really known her then, but I did know that I'd never seen her looking as determined as this.

Mel nodded and handed her the ruler, then turned back to the food tables and picked up the bowl of thousand-island dressing. Vicky started to buck and writhe again, making a high-pitched whining noise against the makeshift gag, and the boys holding her took a firmer grip. All eyes were on the funnel as Mel started to tip the bowl, slowly filling it with dressing. At first nothing happened, then with a glug a bubble rose to the top of the funnel, a muffled sob came from Vicky and the level of the dressing went down. Jubilant at the success of her scheme, Mel poured more of the dressing into the funnel, filling it. The level sank, slowly, until it was all gone.

'I'm taking the funnel out now, Vicky,' Mel said airily, before twisting it out.

I could see Vicky's bottom cheeks clenching, trying to hold in the dressing, but a tiny trickle of it had already escaped and was pooling around the top of her slit.

Mel nodded to Jean. 'She's all yours now.'

Jaw fixed in grim determination, Jean moved into position, and started to stroke the ruler across Vicky's raised cheeks. She teased the prefect, using all the techniques that had been used against her years before, lifting the ruler up as if about to strike, then lowering it gently again before suddenly, without any warning, delivering the first blow full across both cheeks.

Vicky whined like a terrified pig, her whole body tensing in the aftermath of the blow, which had left a scarlet mark across the whiteness of her bottom. Jean then laid down a flurry of strokes, Vicky's feet kicking up and down as a bright red criss-cross covered her cheeks.

Then she paused, running the end of the ruler across the marks she'd already made, now raised welts, before moving it down into Vicky's crease, parting the lips and putting her on full display. She was wet. There was no denying it, and there were giggles and exclamations from the audience.

Then someone piped up, 'Look, she's enjoying it!'

Vicky momentarily lost control. The shock of being exposed must have been too much for her, and she sobbed as her bumhole loosened then contracted again, sending another trickle of dressing down into her pussy.

Mel sighed. 'Looks like we'll have to start all over again, doesn't it?'

Vicky gave a muffled squeal and started to thrash around again, but was calmed with a tap to her bottom with the ruler. 'This time, we can all count together, then Vicky'll know how long she has to go.'

Jean smirked, raised the ruler, and laid it right over the last mark she'd made.

'One,' everyone chanted in unison.

Vicky's bum was now a mess of red marks from the first few blows she'd taken, and I could tell that Jean was trying to target the most bruised areas. She set up a regular rhythm, everyone chanting along in time, until she reached eight. Then she paused, and I could see Vicky tense up then relax.

Then Jean struck another blow, right under the bottom cheeks, grazing the tops of the thighs. Vicky bucked, but managed to keep control of her bumhole, and Jean followed through with a quick succession of strikes on the same area, Vicky's scarlet cheeks jumping with each blow. She'd stopped whining now, but her eyes were shut tight and her cheeks were streaked with tears. Finally, Jean finished, with a last blow across one cheek delivered full force, the end of the ruler just catching the edge of Vicky's crease. This got another muffled shriek out of Vicky, and Jean stepped back, smiling smugly.

Mel nodded to the boys. 'You can let her go now.'

Vicky slumped for a second without their support, then straightened and ran out of the room towards the bathroom, one hand to her red bum and the other clawing at the gag in her mouth.

Everyone's attention turned to Alison, but I had to go to the toilet to pee. I pushed open one of the cubicle doors, only to find Vicky sitting there, her skirt rucked up around her waist, crying softly to herself, as I'd expected. But she was also rubbing herself, her fingers stroking and pinching her swollen clit, her eyes closed and her legs splayed to give herself better access. She hadn't wasted any time.

When I pushed the door open, I'm not sure who was more shocked, Vicky or me. It was the last thing I'd expected to see and, when Vicky muttered, 'Fuck off,' and pushed the door closed again, I didn't interfere. Besides, I wanted to see what the others had in store for Alison.

On the way back to the main room I popped into the kitchen to finish off the whisky that had caused so much trouble – as far as I was concerned I deserved it, and it wasn't like the prefects were in any position to complain.

When I rejoined everyone, I found that Alison was lying spread-eagled on one of the tables, gagged, with her hands and knees pinned down and her skirt up around her waist, showing her pussy, open and glistening in the light.

Mel was facing the crowd. 'Any ideas on what to do with her, then?'

One of the boys piped up. 'How about some of us stand around and jerk off over her face then send her out into the street with come dripping off her chin?'

Mel smiled. 'No, the little slut would probably enjoy that,' she said, reaching back to pinch one of Alison's nipples. She was rewarded with a muffled squeal.

'How about I – we beat her with a ruler?' This came from Jean, whose brief experience wielding power had clearly left her hungry for more.

But Mel shook her head.

'Why don't we stuff her full of food? Not to eat, you know – up her hole.'

I turned to see who'd come up with this, and saw that Cathy was staring at Alison's open sex, with a dreamy expression that seemed at odds with her outrageous suggestion.

'You know, see what we can get inside her.'

A wide grin spread over Mel's face. 'Excellent. Why don't we all put something inside Alison – nothing too big, as it'll spoil it for anyone coming after you, so no cucumbers. But a drumstick is OK.' That got a few laughs.

And so we all took turns. Mel went first, stuffing a scotch egg in as far as it would go, Alison bucking in a desperate but futile attempt to get free. Some people put something small in, like a cherry tomato, while others took Mel at her word and used a drumstick. Some of the boys took their time over it, rubbing whatever they were going to use up and down Alison's slit before sliding it in. Cathy stopped one boy who was trying to stick a cocktail sausage up Alison's bum, telling him that that hole was being saved for something special.

When it came to my turn I realised that almost everyone else had been, and that her slit was already stuffed, so I just took a squeezy bottle of salad dressing and left a thick line of it around the opening to her hole, much to the amusement of the others;

she'd already had her sex soaked in vinaigrette, which must have stung if the twitching that accompanied it was anything to go by.

Finally, everyone had been, the last few improvising on what food was left, balling up bits of sandwich to add to the swollen mess already there. Bits of food had already started to fall out, slimy with Alison's juices and pulp from the cherry tomatoes, which had been crushed under the pressure.

Mel motioned to the boys and girls holding Alison down to flip her over, then picked up the funnel, greased the end again and slid it down into Alison's bumhole.

'And now for the grand finale,' she announced. 'Let's see how much wine Alison can take.'

A few people started clapping and cheering, as Mel took a carton of wine and held the tap over the mouth of the funnel. It filled quickly, and we all watched it drain down into Alison, the occasional bubble rising as her toes curled at the uncomfortable sensation.

Mel filled her up a few more times, occasionally shifting the funnel if progress was slow, until she was satisfied by how much her victim had taken. I knew it was a fair amount of wine, and that Alison would get drunk fast on it. Mel moved round to undo Alison's gag, and the first thing she did was giggle, proving me right. But her bottom hole was starting to twitch and spasm, leaking out trickles of wine each time.

'Hold it in, now, there's a good girl. We don't want to have an accident, do we?' Mel cautioned her as she helped her off the table.

Alison, unsteady on her feet, smoothed down her skirt, then made a quick dart for the toilet.

Mel grabbed her by the arm and pulled her back. 'Oh, no, you don't. You're going this way.' She beckoned to a few of the boys to help her, and they moved over to take her arms and hold her firmly, frogmarching her towards the exit with Mel leading.

As soon as Alison realised what was going to happen to her she panicked, screaming then babbling in fear, trying to persuade Mel not to do it. 'Please don't – I'll do anything; you can have my money, my jewellery, just don't –'

But by this time they were by the door. Mel opened it, and we could see out into the street. The pubs must have just closed, if the groups of young men and women staggering around were anything to go by.

Alison was a picture of terror now, her eyes huge and cheeks streaked with mascara. 'I'm begging you, please help –' she implored us, but it was too late.

She was shoved out on to the pavement, alone in the London night with one hole stuffed full of food and the other full of wine, and the door was slammed shut behind her. The last thing I saw of her was a trickle of red liquid running down her thigh.

Mel turned back to us, a huge, wicked smile breaking out on her lips.

7

This Little Piggy

There was no one else up on the ridge. She'd come up here when she was a kid, climbing the steep slope out of the dull estates, past fields of cows until the view opened out, gloriously showing the whole city, with Chew Magna lake behind. Then, it seemed, the summers had been endless, the mound a place of mystery and imagination, somewhere to let her mind wander free, surrounded by butterflies, old oaks and dandelions; now it was muggy and overcast, a storm threatening, and she'd been dismayed to see the sofas, old gym equipment and half-burned farm waste dumped by the site. Still, she hadn't come for a pastoral retreat this time: she had a far more specific task in mind.

She took the photo out and gazed at it. She remembered the woman, bright-eyed, pretty and overenthusiastic. A few of the others in the group thought she might have been an anthropologist, going native for some kind of scoop; nobody had guessed the truth, although it seemed glaringly obvious to her now. The paper had had a field day with the story, running the intro on the cover and a two-page spread about 'sick orgies', 'witches' and 'devil worship' a couple of pages on. But what made it worse was the fact that her job must have been the lure to the journalist, the point that made it worth running the story in the first place.

She'd just clammed up when she'd been called into the detective constable's office. He hadn't been unkind, had spoken about religious freedom, but when she wouldn't comment his tone changed, and words like 'public image', 'trust' and 'respectability' came up. She glimpsed the tiny gold cross on a chain around his neck for the very first time just before he told her about the suspension. Full pay, pending an internal investigation. She hadn't even had to hand anything in.

She knew some of the others would be trying to do something too, but she felt responsible for bringing it all down, and the photo was all any of them had – not even a scrap of clothing, much less a nail clipping. Still, that, along with the sigil she'd memorised, should be enough. She'd prepared the sigil earlier, taking pains to make sure it was a memorable image, whittling down the various options until only one remained, stark, clear and beautiful, which she'd concentrated on until it was burned into her mind.

She arranged the photo in front of her, surrounded herself with the other objects she'd brought down, and sat in the centre, willing her mind to calm, to focus. She could feel the first stirrings in her crotch, a familiar dampening, as she tried to work through her fantasies, bring herself up to the point where she could make it work. But the air seemed too close, her skin already covered in a sheen of sweat, and she couldn't get the sound of the insects buzzing lazily around her out of her head. She tried touching herself, tentatively at first, to see how wet she was, then giving herself long, languid strokes, pinching the hood of her clit, trying to let herself relax while still holding the sigil in her mind.

The distant crumple of thunder was followed by children's laughter. She opened her eyes. It wasn't going to work. She couldn't get herself in the mood; she needed help, and anyway the last thing she wanted was to be caught jerking off by some kids from the Whitchurch estates. Smiling to herself despite her disappointment, she gathered her materials, stood up and looked out over the city. She hadn't been out in town on a Friday for years, but she knew exactly where to go. She held her arms out and felt a tingle course down her neck and out through the tips of her fingers. The air was alive with energy. It would be a good night.

She parked under one of the flyovers near the floating harbour. The old greasy spoon that had been there before had been replaced by a swank harbourside eaterie, but the kids dealing pills out of their cars hadn't gone. Still, they revved up and sped off pretty fast when she got out of the car, opened the boot and started to change. It wouldn't do to have the full regulation kit, she supposed, and put on a pair of hold-ups rather than tights, but most of the rest of it would work: thick black starched cotton skirt and jacket, plain white shirt, handcuffs, truncheon, hat, sensible, low-heeled shoes. She considered a bra but decided against it – she didn't want to look too convincing once they'd got down to it, after all, and didn't have anything flouncy enough to suit the routine. The regulation white knickers didn't matter, though; once they'd got to that stage, they wouldn't have cared if she was wearing a pair of Y-fronts.

As she walked closer to the waterfront, she could hear the bars, all bassy rumbles, shouts and screams of laughter. The crowds were getting thicker down here too, built men with short hair, white shirts, black trousers and shoes, the girls teetering around on heels wearing tiny one-piece outfits. Some gave her strange looks, like she was crazy coming down here without her partner, but they turned away when she winked at them. She was relieved when a few gave her wolf whistles, clearly convinced that she was in fancy dress.

It took a couple of strolls along the parade before she saw what she was looking for. The bouncer said something into his lapel mike as she approached the bar door, then pulled himself up straight, staring at her with a grim expression as though daring her to pass him. She just grinned at him, gave a little shimmy and whispered 'Stripogram' in his ear, and was gratified to actually see him blush as he grinned sheepishly in turn and moved out of her way.

Inside it was dark and crowded, the music pumping and the bar four deep. People had noticed her but there wasn't anywhere for them to move, and as her eyes adjusted they turned back to their drinks or partners. She moved over to where the group she'd seen through the window was standing, four of them, all clutching bottles of beer in thick hands, with closely cropped hair and brutish expressions. Not her kind of man at all, really, but for now it was exactly what she needed. She moved closer, wanting to hear just enough to make her story convincing, and was soon rewarded when she heard one of them, a stocky one with a pierced eyebrow, call the tallest one Bruce. She just had to hope it wasn't a joke.

His head turned as she stroked his back and moved round to face him, and he flinched when he saw her uniform, then leered when he saw her face. She'd already undone the top few buttons of her shirt, and when his eyes dropped to her chest she let a hand rest lightly on his arse and asked, 'Bruce?'

His eyes darted around his mates, and she flashed each a sleazy grin in turn. 'One of you boys sort this out?' he asked.

In unison they shook their heads, their eyes shining. 'Didn't know it was your birthday, Bruce,' one said, slapping him on the back, and the others laughed.

He turned back to her. 'Who sent you, love?'

But she just smiled, put a finger to her lips and started her routine. She'd danced for boyfriends before, enjoyed putting on a show for them, brushing her hand against their cocks and feeling them get hard as they stared at her, and it always got her wet and ready. She knew this time would be no different, the danger of the environment, what she was doing there, even turning her on more easily and making her want to take it further.

She moved closer to the wall, making sure that they shielded her from the rest of the people at the bar, then took off her hat and shook her hair out so that it tumbled over her shoulders, and undid a few more buttons then leaned forwards, making sure they all got a good look at her tits, the nipples already stiff and straining against the cotton. She'd already started to hike up her skirt, one hand at either side inching it higher and higher until the tops of her hold-ups were visible and she was baring naked thigh flesh, then she turned and leaned over, bending right down until she was touching the floor. She could feel their eyes boring into her, staring at the white knickers all snug against her oily crease, and shifted her weight slowly from one foot to the other and back again, shimmying her arse back and forth to put on a good show for them.

When she turned back she could see the bulges in their pants. They weren't even talking now. She stared into Bruce's eyes, and, holding his gaze, reached into her knickers, then pulled her finger out, slick with juice, and rubbed it along his lips. She knew that they could mob her, here and now, but when he reached out for her she shook her head and indicated the gents, then moved away, pulling her skirt back down as she walked towards the door.

She could hear them behind her. 'That's no fucking stripper!'

'She's a fucking tart!'

'Like you give a shit?'

Their voices dwindled away, and then she was pushing the door open and she was inside. She'd never been in one of these before, and took in the features at a glance: the long aluminium trench along one side, a reek of stale piss and male hormones, a couple of boys jumping a little as she went in, turning to her with confused expressions then back to concentrate on what they were doing. Then Bruce and his lot were steaming in there, filling the tiny area between the cubicles and the sinks.

'Come on, you lot, out now.' One of the boys, panicked, turned from the trough before he was ready, zipping himself up with a dark stain and fleeing; the other followed just after.

The man with the pierced eyebrow pounded on the door of a locked cubicle. 'Oi! You! Get the fuck out!' Already another one of them was peering over the top, then looking back delightedly.

''E's only doing some lines!'

At this Bruce rammed the door with his shoulder. There was a squeak from inside, then a scrawny youth was pulled out bodily, powder spilling from his nose as his hand clutched a rolled-up note. 'At least let me get my fucking –' he protested as he was hauled bodily out the door.

'Sorry, pal, police business,' said the stocky one, and the others chuckled.

'Mind the door, mate,' Bruce told him, and then their attention was on her.

'You going to put on a show for us then, darling?'

One of the others made a grab for her arse, but Bruce pulled his hand off.

'Leave the lady be, all right? All in good time. She's not going to leave us before making sure we're all ready to go, is she now?' He leered at her, and she backed into one of the cubicles, sat on the seat and spread her legs.

They were all staring at her now, a couple of them holding their cocks through their pants, as she slid down on the seat and propped a foot against each side of the open door to keep her balance. She eyed each of them in turn, then ran a finger along her crease, letting her knickers soak up some of the juice. She could see Bruce's cock, bulging at the front of his pants, twitch, and she slowly began to pull off the knickers.

There were murmurs of appreciation from the men as it was exposed, the hairs pressed down flat against the sides from the oiliness, and the centre pink, hot and swollen. She took hold of the lips and pulled it open, flashing the pink at them. At this she could hear a groan, and looked up to see one of them unzipping himself and pulling his cock out, thick and veiny with an angry-looking purple head.

'If you're not going to go for her, Bruce, I'm –'

'Leave off, Don. You'll get your turn. First the lady's going to put on a show for us.'

Bruce turned back to her, and she nodded, then pulled her truncheon from her belt, put the tip of it to her mouth and rolled her tongue around it before letting it trail down over her chest and down to the creamy slit between her legs. She didn't have to pretend; their attention had got her all wet and ready, and as she circled her clit with the stick she couldn't help letting out a gasp. Then she eased the end in, and slid it up inside herself, then out, feeling the grooves of it rubbing against her, watching the one called Don tugging on his cock in the same rhythm. The others had got their cocks out as well now, pulling back on them as they gazed expectantly at her wanking herself off.

She wanted to taste them, have their cocks pressed up against her face, and she gave herself a final quick frig with the stick, then brought it to her lips again and licked it clean, looking each of the men in the eye. She peeled her knickers off her legs then stood up, walked out of the cubicle and kneeled in front of Bruce. He gave her a curious look, then turned to the others.

'We've got a real cock-hungry slut here this time, boys.'

As they laughed, he grabbed her hair and shoved his cock into her mouth. She closed her eyes and revelled in the taste of it, the slimy drop of pre-come dripping from the tip and the smell of the come coming from the tight balls. She dropped one hand to her slit, dipping the fingers in the hole then rubbing the juice around her clit, and cradled Bruce's balls with the other. He groaned and started back as she began to rock her head back and forth on it, running her tongue over the swollen end.

The others moved closer, and she could feel a cock nudging against her cheek. She opened her mouth wider, trying to fit them both in, but could only manage the heads, and licked both of them before swallowing the other, and reaching up to wank off first Bruce then the other man, feeling their cocks twitching as she worked them with her hand and mouth.

'Bend over, darling. I've got just the thing for you.'

As Bruce moved behind her, she took her mouth off the other man's cock and leaned forwards, propping herself up on her hands, trying to ignore the filth on the floor, and stuck her bum up, feeling the cool air on her hole. She was aching now, ready for it, and then he was in position, bending her over and pressing the end of his cock against her hole before sliding it in, filling her to the hilt so she could feel his balls bumping against her clit.

One of the men had taken his place in front of her, and had kneeled down with the other one, both with their hands on their cocks, bumping against her face. She took one in her mouth, and sucked hard on it as she pushed back on Bruce's cock, then she felt the cock in her mouth twitch and stiffen. She pulled it out, then watched the man's face as she rubbed the angry red head on her face, squeezing his balls quickly a couple of times and jerking on his cock.

'Oh, fuck –'

She could feel his cock pulsing then it jetted out, and she just managed to close her eyes before great arcs of it covered her face, landing in her hair, her cheeks and mouth, dripping down off her chin. As he pulled back she licked her lips, looking up at him.

'You fucking filthy tart,' he said, half-admiringly, as the other man took her hair and forced his cock into her mouth.

She heard a spitting sound, and felt something slimy land on her bumhole, then Bruce's finger was there, pushing in and stretching the hole. She wasn't sure if she was ready for this, and was turning back to tell him to slow down, but her head was pulled back, her mouth stuffed with cock again, and she resigned herself, focusing her attention on the cock in her mouth and letting it happen.

Bruce pulled his finger out but carried on toying with the hole. 'I'm not fucking that dirty arse of yours without a rubber.' She heard him tearing something open, then he was rubbing a couple of fingers in her slit and smearing the cream over her arse. She reached a hand back to stroke her clit, but the man in front pulled it back, and she stroked his balls, feeling their tight heaviness in her hand as she ran her tongue over his cock then bobbed her head hard and fast over the end. Then Bruce's fingers were pushing inside her again, and something bigger was pressing against the hole.

'You like it up the arse, don't you, you slag.'

She whimpered and pressed back on it, pushing out and hoping it wasn't too big to go in. Bruce's hand reached round to her slit and started rubbing her roughly, and she felt the end of it go in, filling her completely, then the rest slid in, each inch spearing her more fully. She reached back again and felt his balls, tight against her empty hole, then he pulled back and shoved it in again.

She closed her eyes and concentrated on the sensation of being used, being filled in the wrong hole, sucking cock and making men hard looking at her, putting on a display like some cheap tart, letting them use her. She pushed back harder on the cock, pumping her painfully now, willing him to fuck her with his fingers, to rub her clit, aching now for attention, as she let the other man rub his cock all over her face and pull roughly at her tits, bruising the nipples, pinching them and pulling them out.

Then she felt the cock inside her pulse, and Bruce groaned as he ground himself deep into her, his hand mashing against her wet pussy. The other man was coming now too, forcing his cock right to the back of her throat, not stopping even when she was gagging and trying to pull back as he flooded her mouth with come, not letting go of her hair until his cock had softened and he'd pulled out of her mouth.

As she fell to the floor, her arsehole closing slowly on air, she could dimly hear a banging on the door, and a thick, choked voice. 'For fuck's sake, boys, hurry up! I can't hold this door much longer.'

She lay back, not caring now about the dirt on the floor, and felt the men getting up, pulling their pants and trousers back on, panting heavily from their exertions.

Something slimy and foul-smelling hit her face, and she opened her eyes. It was the rubber, the one Bruce had used to stop his cock from getting dirty inside her. She could see the come inside it, great globs of it filling the end, and on a sudden impulse she sat up, put the end to her mouth and poured it on to her tongue, then looked up at the men, showing each of them the pool of it in her mouth, revelling in the expressions on their faces, before she swallowed it and licked her lips.

She was hitting the right spot now, getting the right energy, and she lay back again to start rubbing herself, holding her slit open with one hand, putting herself on display again, and flicking her clit with the other.

'She only wants fucking more! Come on, darling, finish up or you'll have the whole lot of them in here.'

A pair of strong male hands gripped her waist and pulled her up, but something fell out of her jacket and dropped to the floor with a clatter.

'What's this?'

She tried to shut the noise out of her head, her eyes closed, to concentrate on the mental image she'd generated, to use the power of the humiliation, the men's energy, but she could feel them all standing over her, quiet now.

'It's a fucking police badge! She's no stripper; she's a fucking copper!'

She recognised Bruce's voice, then one of the other men spoke, sounding scared now. 'For fuck's sake, Bruce, we'd better get out of here. It's probably a set-up, or something.'

'No, she loved it, the dirty tart,' he sneered. Then he was leaning over her, his voice thick with anger. 'You filthy slag bitch, I'll show you what we do to coppers!'

She heard a zip being pulled down, then felt a stream of warm, acrid fluid hit her, first on the thigh then moving over her hands, still working between her legs, then up over her chest and to her face. She instinctively screwed her eyes shut tight, then relaxed as it splashed over her, opening her mouth and revelling in the sensation, the taste, as she swallowed it.

That was enough. It hit her suddenly, a great wave bursting over her as her mind reeled from everything she'd done, letting these strangers fuck her, sucking their cocks, letting them come on her face, bugger her, even letting them piss on her while she rubbed herself, not caring about what a display she was making of herself, or the sheer rudeness of what she'd done. It was so powerful it almost obliterated the image she'd worked so hard to build up, almost distracted her from what she'd come here to do, but she managed to focus, to keep the image clear in her head, even as her legs twitched and shuddered on the piss-soaked floor.

The call had come a week later, and less than 24 hours after that she found herself in the station again, walking through the department to the detective constable's office. It felt strange going back in civvies, like she was one of the types about to be grilled in an interrogation room, perhaps one of the posh thieves they occasionally brought in, or a lawyer trying to get one of them out. She'd had a few people give her the nod, a couple of 'Nice to see you back's, and some glares, but nothing unexpected: she knew who her friends were.

She knocked on the door.

'Come!'

He looked up from his papers as she walked in and closed the door behind her, then beckoned to the chair in front of his desk. 'No point beating about the bush, Miss Sherman. You're back on – you've been cleared of any wrongdoing.' He waited for her reaction.

She tried not to grin. 'What did the investigation find then, sir?'

He snorted, and studied the papers in front of him. 'Never got that far. The paper's retracted the story – you'll find a couple of paragraphs on Wednesday. The journalist's lost the plot, totally made the whole thing up.' He looked up. 'I wish you'd told us you'd had nothing to do with it. Then the whole thing might not have gone so far.'

'Yes, sir.'

He looked down again. 'The girl who wrote the story's actually been committed now. For her own protection, really; started ranting about demons and magic, classic paranoid psychosis.'

She let her face stay blank. In the distance a siren wailed. She could feel the detective constable's eyes trying to read her face, and returned a level gaze. His phone rang, and she could have sworn he gave a little jump.

'Right – uh, thanks, Miss Sherman. You start again with immediate effect.' He picked up the phone and nodded to her.

She walked back down towards the exit. Her uniform was in her car, all neatly pressed and cleaned after the Bristol ritual. She smiled to herself as she imagined the faces of the others, their surprise and joy. They'd have to be more careful in the future, of course, set up some better kind of vetting procedure, not be so swayed by enthusiasm and beauty. And maybe she'd pay the journalist a trip too, show her there were no hard feelings. Perhaps she just needed a familiar face to reassure her, to show her that there was no such thing as magic.

8

Ballet School

The train was late, which didn't surprise Arabella at all. She barely managed to get all her bags on before it left the station, too, and glared at the conductor, who'd watched her with a blank expression and hadn't lifted a finger to help. But as soon as she was settled in her compartment she started to relax, watching the empty fields roll past and wondering, not for the first time, what delights the academy would hold for her.

She'd been training for years, of course, and been recommended for the position by her teachers. Apparently, the recommendation had been enough; no interview had been involved, and Arabella had barely been able to contain her excitement when the cream letter arrived in the post, with its ornate letterhead and impressive copperplate script. It was like a dream come true; a dream she'd cherished since putting on her first pair of dance shoes, or watching raptly as the ballerinas pirouetted around the stage during the one Christmas treat that would always remain with her.

It was only natural that she'd had doubts about taking it further – the other girls she knew were going to university, and a couple were already trying to start work – but what were dreams for, if not to be followed? Arabella knew she was good, and intended to shine at the academy; it was too good a chance to pass up.

Her reverie was broken by the opening of the door, and a flushed face peered in, piercing brown eyes framed by dark eyebrows and a long glossy pelt of brown hair.

'Oh! Sorry, I didn't think there was anyone in here.' The girl paused, clearly exhausted by struggling with two large suitcases and a handbag, then peered closely at Arabella. 'You're not the new student at the academy, are you?'

Arabella smiled back and nodded. Could this be her first new friend? She heard a loud 'excuse me', and realised that someone was trying to get past the girl. 'Don't stand there! Sit in here,' she offered.

The girl smiled again and pulled in her suitcases, groaning at the weight. 'Thanks. Could you help me put these in the rack? They're a bit heavy.'

Arabella stood up and together they hefted one of the cases up, but it snagged on the girl's handbag, knocking it to the floor and spilling its contents out. The girl flushed and hurriedly bent down, trying to cram the spillage back in, but her haste piqued Arabella's curiosity, and she couldn't help looking at the curious items the girl seemed so keen to hide. There was something made of shiny metal, looking like two clothes pegs attached by a chain, and something small and leather too, looking like some kind of floppy paintbrush. Arabella had no idea what they were, and didn't want to seem nosy, so didn't ask, and the girl certainly didn't seem to want to tell her.

After they'd lifted the other case, the girl sat down and took a hip flask out of her bag. She unscrewed it and offered it to Arabella, who took a sniff of the contents, wrinkled her nose and shook her head.

The girl shrugged and took a long swig, then almost burst out laughing and held out a hand. 'How rude of me! I'm Vania. I should have introduced myself before. You're Arabella, right?'

Surprised that the girl knew who she was, Arabella could only nod mutely.

The girl laughed again. 'Oh, I only know your name because we're going to be roomies.' Noticing Arabella's blank look, she went on, 'You know, living together! I do hope we'll be friends.'

She proffered the hip flask again, and this time Arabella took a swig, not wanting to get off on the wrong foot, and tried to hide a wince and a cough as the burning liquid went down.

After that they got on famously. Arabella warmed to Vania quickly: she was cheeky enough to be exciting, offering hints of a new world of experience, of a maturity Arabella hadn't met in her school-friends, but answered her questions about the academy seriously. Her descriptions of some of the teachers had Arabella in fits of giggles, and after a few more swigs of whisky Arabella felt bold enough to ask Vania about boys, wanting to sound daring herself, although in truth, despite the fact that she'd recently had her eighteenth birthday, her experience had been restricted to clumsy gropes at discos.

But a flicker of annoyance crossed Vania's face when she brought up the subject. 'You won't meet many *boys* at the academy. I suppose there's the delivery boys; some of the girls mix with them, but you don't want to do that.' She leaned forwards conspiratorially. 'They lack *class*. Of course –' she sat back again, a smile opening her face '– there are the porters too, but they're ancient. Best to stick with the rest of us girls.' She winked at Arabella, who found herself blushing, although she wasn't sure why. It must be the whisky; she wasn't used to it.

For the last half-hour of the journey she started to worry about her breath smelling of whisky for her arrival, but Vania had some mints, and bought her a coffee from the bar, which livened her up a little. She was slightly nervous about meeting the directress, and knew she would have to do it as soon as she arrived; it had been explained in her letter. The picture Vania painted of her was of some dragonish schoolmarm, and her jokes about the names the students called her did little to calm the butterflies in Arabella's stomach.

When they arrived at the station about twenty other girls piled out of the train, and a couple of burly, impassive porters loaded their cases on to a waiting minibus. Some of the girls greeted Vania warmly, and she introduced them to Arabella, but she couldn't help noticing that a few of the others kept their distance. She felt a little uncomfortable. Had she unwittingly taken sides in some battle she didn't understand?

But the academy was extraordinary, a huge Victorian structure that only came into full view with the final turn of the driveway. Arabella's misgivings were quickly forgotten in a rush of elation; she had made the right decision, she knew she had. This was the place for her.

The porters would carry her bags to her room; Vania gave her a bewildering set of directions for how to get there after her meeting, and pointed her in the direction of the directress's study. After wandering around the quadrangles and through endless stone corridors that seemed to Arabella identical, she finally found a discreet sign pointing the way; and when she arrived she found that she was clearly awaited, as the secretary ushered her in directly.

Rubbing her clammy palms against her dress, wondering how the directress would greet her, Arabella opened the door.

'You're late.' The woman sitting behind the desk didn't even look up, but just carried on writing on a pad.

'The train was delayed,' Arabella replied, sounding more confident than she felt.

The woman looked up and fixed her with a piercing stare over her half-moon glasses. Her smile was cold and her hair steely grey, fixed in two impeccable buns flanking her head. 'There are no excuses at the academy.'

Arabella was aware that she had started to sweat slightly. 'I'm sorry, Miss –'

'You may address me as Directress.' She put her pad down now. 'I trust you have your uniform?'

'Y-yes.'

The instructions had arrived with the letter of acceptance, directing Arabella to a bespoke tailor in Kensington; the skirt and blazer had taken a week to prepare, although the shirts and the regulation under-wear came ready-made. Arabella had been slightly flustered by the uniform – she had imagined hardly ever being out of her leotard – but had accepted it as part of her new conditions. Still, even though on reflection she realised that the letter might have been warning enough, Arabella had been so excited to be accepted that she hadn't paid that much attention to the tone; and she had hardly expected such a severe reception from the directress.

'You will wear your uniform at all times, except when in practice. You're rooming with Vania?'

Arabella nodded.

'She will provide you with a timetable.' The directress pushed her chair back, paused and smiled grimly, still holding Arabella's gaze, then went on. 'We are an isolated community here. While I expect that you will make friends, close fraternising – either with visitors or the other girls – has no place in this establishment. You come recommended; I don't doubt your dancing abilities. But you are here to perfect them. Do not be distracted.' She looked down and began to write again, then, seeing that Arabella stayed where she was, dismissed her with a wave of the hand.

Vania was already in her uniform when Arabella finally found the room. She couldn't help noticing that her new friend didn't seem to be wearing a bra, and the short flouncy skirt exposed almost all of her long, lithe legs. As Arabella unpacked, she could feel Vania's eyes on her clothes, which made her nervous for some reason. There was a shared bathroom at the end of the corridor, and Arabella briefly considered taking her uniform down there to get changed, but she quickly realised how inconvenient such coyness would prove. Still, Vania's stare was disconcerting, and Arabella stripped down as fast as possible, turning her bottom to her friend to peel off her frilly yellow knickers and replace them with the regulation thick white cotton panties, then tried to put on her uniform as quickly as she could.

Vania giggled when Arabella changed her knickers, and for a moment Arabella thought she'd gone too far, that she didn't really need to follow the regulations to the letter. She turned to look at her friend quizzically.

'You're a bit keen!' Vania was smirking.

Arabella bit her lip and considered taking them off again, even hooking her fingers around the waistband either side, ready to pull the tight fabric down again, but Vania stopped her.

'No, you're right,' her new friend assured her. 'Lots of newbies refuse to wear the proper underwear, but they're usually caught. They'll probably check over the next few days; it's a good idea to keep it on. You wouldn't want to get punished so early.'

Arabella wasn't sure what she meant: detention, perhaps, or extra ballet practice? But she hardly had time to think about it, as Vania eyed her critically and told her, in a different tone of voice, 'You've got a lovely figure, Arabella.'

Despite herself, she was flattered, and couldn't help looking appreciatively at her body in a mirror. She could see Vania in the reflection too, and watched as her friend ran her hands over her stomach and grimaced. 'Not like me. I've been eating too much recently. Don't you think I need to lose some weight?'

Arabella turned to her, ready with a reassuring word – Vania was, it had to be said, on the curvy side for a ballet dancer, but hardly fat – only to find her roommate cupping her breasts through her top, and looking directly at her. 'Do you think these are too big?'

Arabella blushed, and turned back to her dressing, acutely aware of her own breasts, hard and small as two apples. All she could manage was a strangled 'No', and her fingers seemed numb as she did up the buttons of her shirt. There was a heavy, pregnant silence, broken by a loud clanging bell.

Vania leaped to her feet. 'That's the dinner bell. You'd better hurry up; they don't like it if you're late.'

Arabella followed Vania out of the room, feeling horribly self-conscious in the uniform. She had tried it on before, both to check that it fitted and to get used to it, but it still felt awkward. She didn't usually wear such short skirts, and this one, almost revealing the curved underside of her buttocks, left her feeling uncomfortably vulnerable. The pants were made of thicker material than she usually wore, too, and felt somehow old-fashioned. She didn't wear her shirt as open-necked as Vania, who seemed to be flaunting herself in what Arabella considered a most inappropriate way, but with the jacket and shoes on she had a distinct feeling of déjà vu, of experiencing the first day at school all over again, the echoing sound of girls laughing and the smell of varnish bringing it all back.

The canteen was worse, reeking of boiled cabbage, and Vania and Arabella joined a long line of girls, all gossiping, giggling and casting furtive glances at each other as they waited to be served. A dull, squat woman sweating in a white coat doled out portions of a thin soup with what looked like stringy bits of meat in them, and there were rolls in a large basket at the end of the serving counter. Arabella, appalled by the meagre offering, tested some of them, but they all seemed to be stale. She was about to ask the server if there were others, but Vania dug an elbow into her ribs and shot her a warning glance, shaking her head.

Still, Arabella was glad to be with someone she knew, however little, and however ill-tempered Vania seemed just now – it looked like there were a few other new girls there too, but some of them clearly hadn't met anyone yet, and Arabella tried not to look at the fear on their faces as they peered wildly around, looking for a friendly space. She couldn't help noticing that some of them were having trouble with the food, too. The other girls on her table didn't seem to mind it too much; some of them were wolfing it down, dipping their stale bread in the watery fluid, but some of the girls elsewhere in the room were staring in shock at it.

Arabella felt the same way; she hadn't expected the food to be so bad. There must be shops nearby, some way of preparing her own food, she tried half-heartedly to convince herself. The meat, what little there was of it, tasted rancid; a few lumps of gristle had sunk to the bottom of her bowl. She toyed with it for a while, then pushed it away.

'Eat it!' hissed Vania.

Arabella made a moue of distaste, but she was disturbed by the look of panic on Vania's face. Her roommate nodded towards a heavy-set woman with a stern expression, sitting at the side of the room. Arabella followed her gaze, then looked up at the other staff members, who were eating with the directress at the top table; she felt a pang of hunger when she realised that they had real food, meat, greens, potatoes, and wondered why the other woman wasn't sitting with them. She wasn't eating at all, in fact, but was just watching the girls. Or, more precisely, watching *her*; she had caught Arabella's gaze, and looked like she was about to get up.

Arabella quickly looked away, and tried to follow the others' example, soaking the bread in the juice to soften it, and swallowing the stringy meat whole, trying to minimise the unpleasant taste. Out of the corner of her eye she saw the heavy-set woman rise and begin to walk towards her.

The girl sitting next to her said to her other neighbours, in an urgent whisper clearly audible to Arabella, 'Look out! It's Miss Mannaker!'

Arabella couldn't swallow, and froze in fear, intensely aware of the woman's clomping footsteps drawing closer; the rest of the room fell silent too, until suddenly a girl squealed directly behind her. She turned around, her heart in her throat.

'This girl,' boomed Miss Mannaker, looking at the

top table with her meaty fist clenched around the girl's upper arm – Arabella recognised her as one of the new girls, whose expression of anxiety earlier was nothing compared to the look of sheer panic now – 'has been throwing food on the floor.'

A shocked murmur passed through the room. Arabella could see the lumps of meat on the ground between the girl's feet; there were gaps in the floorboards, and she must have been trying to kick them in without being noticed. Unfortunately for her, it hadn't worked.

'Eat it.' The directress had risen, her strident voice echoing around the room.

The girl was squirming now, her face contorted as she tried to hold back the tears and babbled, 'No – no. I can't, please. Don't make me!'

But Miss Mannaker was already pushing her down, forcing her on to her knees. The girls either side of her had moved away, and the bench was pulled clear, offering everyone on Arabella's side of the room a clear view of the culprit. The room was silent now, except for the girl's sobs, but as she was bent down over the floor, still muttering 'No, no', her skirt pulled up, to reveal a silky pair of purple knickers stretched tight over the creamy white skin of her buttocks. Another murmur shot around the room.

'Silence!'

The directress's order stopped all talk dead, and every eye followed her as she stood and walked down towards the girl, who was quiet now as well, apart from the gagging noises that came as she hurriedly ate the lumps of gristle, as if aware that something far worse might come if she didn't obey now.

It was too late. The directress stared with an expression of horror at the offending purple knickers, then tore them off, exposing the girl's goosepimpled bottom, neatly trimmed pubic bush and shaved sex lips, tapering up to her dark ring. Arabella heard her give a sob, but she didn't – as Arabella was sure she would have done – try to cover herself up.

The directress gestured imperiously to Miss Mannaker, who nodded and walked to the side of the room. Arabella hadn't noticed the rack there, nor the row of crook-handled sticks, too thin to be used for walking, hanging there. But as Miss Mannaker returned to the directress and presented the stick, which the directress tested between her hands, flexing it slightly, Vania's fearful talk of punishment became far clearer to Arabella.

The directress looked up at the other girls, who were all craning their heads for a better view. 'Gather round, girls,' she said with a wave of her arm, and silently the girls from the far tables stood up and formed a semicircle around the table where Arabella was sitting. The directress then addressed the girl on her knees. 'Have you finished eating yet?'

There was a muffled 'Yes'.

'Then you'll be ready to take your punishment.'

Arabella realised that the girl hadn't seen the cane until now, but, on hearing the directress say the word 'punishment', the girl turned and tried to stand up, her mouth making an O of fear and her eyes widening at the sight of the springy wood being flexed between the directress's hands. Miss Mannaker crouched down to hold her in place by the neck, and she returned to her knees, slack-muscled now, although her body trembled as it was wracked with piteous sobs, her bare, exposed cheeks shaking from side to side.

'You'll take six strokes, and you'll count them out loud.'

The girl's nod was barely visible under Miss Mannaker's hand.

'You'll answer me – "Yes, Directress".'

'Yes, Directress,' she mumbled, but even as she finished the cane had whipped down, whistling through the air to land heavily on the white cheeks. The girl's buttocks leaped, and there was a sharp intake of breath, but she hadn't said anything by the time the second stroke landed, almost exactly on the place of the first, in quick succession. This time she squealed, and as the directress paused Arabella watched the white welt go slowly bright red.

In a voice choked with tears, the girl said, 'Two.'

'Two? You hadn't even counted one. We'll have to start again.' The directress was smiling, coldly, with a gleam in her eyes, but the girl had started to cry properly now, great heaving sobs making her body judder.

The next stroke was about an inch above the thick line left by the first, and the following one an inch below. The girl, clearly determined not to prolong her punishment any longer, managed to stammer out the numbers of the strokes between gasps, but then the tip of the cane lashed against her sex lips, and she snorted heavily. Even through her astonishment, Arabella couldn't help admiring the directress's accuracy as she alternated parallel stripes across the bottom cheeks with cracks to the tender flesh between them, pausing between each stroke to run the tip of the cane over the girl's tortured skin, at one point even dipping it between her sex lips, making her flinch. The directress raised an eyebrow at Miss Mannaker, who leaned over and peered at the slit, then looked up at her and nodded.

'Just as I thought,' the directress sneered. 'The kind of slut who wears purple knickers gets wet under the cane, too.'

The girl let out a louder sob now, and her whole body seemed to slump, only to arch in agony when the directress loosed the final blow, cutting her along the crease just under the buttocks. She managed a 'Six!' before being released and crumpling to the floor, unmindful of the soup stain beneath her, crying gently and rocking back and forth with her hands stroking her bottom. The other girls ignored her, and presently they returned to their seats, the few who still had soup taking care to finish their plates.

Arabella saw the girl who'd been caned later that evening, in the showers. The communal shower block had come as a surprise – she'd expected separate cubicles – although after what she'd seen earlier she was in a bit of a daze, and unsure what to expect. But if in the dining room the girls had been quiet, here, away from direct supervision, they were shrieking and running around, flicking towels at each other in the locker room, or languorously soaping themselves, oblivious to their nakedness in front of each other.

Or were they? Arabella watched in amazement as a lithe black girl using the shower next to hers had paid particular attention to her breasts and crotch, soaping her chest until the nipples stood out hard and long, then rubbing between her legs for far longer than Arabella imagined it took to clean herself down there. She was making cooing noises too, and when she caught Arabella staring at her she stuck out her tongue, looked at Arabella's pubic hair and grinned widely. Embarrassed, Arabella turned away and tried to see what was happening through the steam further along.

The girl who'd been caned was there, tenderly fingering her welts under the shower two away from Arabella. They looked far worse now than they'd done in the dining hall, angry red ridges making a blotchy mess of her bottom, and, as Arabella watched, the girl was approached by two others. She couldn't quite hear what they were saying to her, but she recognised the tone as one of concern, then curiosity, and watched as the girl nodded, and one of the others touched the welts. Then they were both feeling them, softly, and the girl seemed to have forgotten her shower under their ministrations, which quickly became less experimental touches than caresses. Arabella was embarrassed again, and left the shower.

Vania had already changed into her nightie by the time Arabella got back to the room, and seemed to be waiting for her, lying on top of her bed with a look of expectation. Arabella supposed that the way she stared was understandable if there were no boys here, but it still made her feel uncomfortable, and she let the towel slip to the floor and pulled her nightie on over her shoulders as quickly as she could.

Tucked up in bed, Arabella felt more secure, and even accepted a nip of the whisky Vania offered her, spluttering less now she was used to its fiery taste. She was bursting with questions, but wasn't sure where to start.

'Why is the food so bad, Vania?'

'Oh, that. I suppose the directress doesn't want us to put on any weight. There's treats as well – if you do anything to please the tutors they sometimes give you fruit, and a few of the girls have even sat on the top table. I wouldn't worry, though, it's perfectly nutritious.'

'But it tastes foul! And that poor girl . . .'

'It's just as well you saw that when you did. I didn't want you to end up like her, not on your first day. You have to watch Miss Mannaker; she's got eyes like a hawk.'

Arabella couldn't help noticing that Vania had slid down her bed, letting her nightie ride up over her thighs to expose some of the dark hair between them. She hurriedly averted her eyes, but Vania had noticed her looking.

'It's OK, you can look if you like. I don't mind. There's no point in us being shy with each other if we're going to be rooming together.'

Arabella turned back reluctantly, only to see that her roommate had pulled her nightie up further, and had even parted her legs a little, allowing a hand to trail down and stroke the curly hair in the dark cleft between them. Arabella was shocked, and turned away again.

'What's the matter? Haven't you ever touched yourself?' Vania asked in a gently mocking tone.

Arabella had, a few times, and the memory of those furtive nocturnal rubbings made her catch her breath; but she was too embarrassed to talk about it, especially with someone she'd only just met, and turned away from Vania. 'I'm tired. Let's turn out the light and go to sleep.'

Vania laughed. 'Don't be a spoilsport. Come on, let's take a look at yours.' And with that she swung her legs off the bed, padded over to Arabella and pulled back the covers, ignoring her feeble 'No' as she hung on to her duvet.

Arabella lay prone, listening to her heart thudding, as Vania lifted up the bottom of her nightie to peer beneath it then peeled it up over Arabella's thighs, exposing her sex. Arabella gulped and stared at the ceiling.

'You could do with a trim down here.' Vania surveyed Arabella's copious thatch critically. 'Look at mine.' She showed herself to Arabella again, rucking the nightie up around her waist, and Arabella could see that it was far neater, a t̶... above her sex lips, which were bare. 'M̶... other girls keep theirs like this. I know!' clapped her hands together. 'I've got all the equipment here; let me take care of it for you!'

Arabella knew that she was blushing, and was ashamed of herself. She'd promised herself she'd be bolder here; and she didn't want to stand out in the shower, showing a lack of experience, or sophistication. She was nervous, but she trusted Vania; even if she wasn't quite ready to talk about touching herself, her new friend had been so warm, so considerate, that she didn't want to let her down, or rebuff her again. If this was the way the girls acted here, she'd better join in; the idea of being friendless and alone at the academy filled her with an anxiety far stronger than any she felt over what Vania might do to her. 'OK,' she breathed, and let her thighs fall apart.

Vania's eyes widened as she took in the sight, then she squealed in delight, leaped up and began to rummage in a bag by the mirror. Arabella watched as she took out a can of shaving foam, a razor and a pair of scissors, then filled a bowl with warm water from the sink and came back.

She placed the bowl between Arabella's thighs, and took hold of one of her pillows. 'I'll need to prop you up with this.'

Meekly Arabella complied, raising her hips and allowing her friend to slide the pillow underneath her bottom. She'd never had anyone else pay so much attention to her sex before, and was aware that she was beginning to respond. She could feel a gooiness inside, a swelling of the lips, and prayed that Vania wouldn't notice.

But her friend was businesslike now, snipping away at the bushy hairs and marking off an area at the top of Arabella's pubis, then wetting her down and spraying shaving foam over the sides and top of her pussy. The foam tingled, and Arabella couldn't help sighing slightly when the razor first touched the sensitive skin. Her thighs were spread wide now, to allow Vania easier access, and she could feel her lips parting wetly as her friend busied herself with the shave.

If Vania noticed, she didn't say anything, but just continued to scrape away, pulling at the sex lips to make sure she removed all the hair, and grazing a little against the pink wetness inside each time she did it. Arabella groaned, and shifted her hips, but Vania just carried on, patting the finished areas down with warm water then washing the whole area once she'd shaved off the last lines of hair. 'I'll just rub some cream on it, so you don't get a rash,' Vania offered, gazing fondly at her.

Arabella flinched at the feel of the cold cream, then pushed herself towards Vania's hand as it warmed up. It felt lovely, rubbed into her skin, which had never felt so bare, so exposed. She peered down at it, delighted at the job Vania had done, but ashamed of her own wetness. Soon Vania would stop, and it would all be over. But her wetness wasn't going to go away so easily. Would she dare to touch herself in the same room with her friend?

As it happened, Vania didn't seem to want to stop. Where she'd shaved was already slick with cream, but still she rubbed it in, firmly, grazing her knuckles against the oily centre more now. It felt good, but Arabella was alarmed as well. She wondered if Vania was doing it deliberately, and what it would mean if she was, then her new friend did something that left no doubt in her mind, suddenly leaning forwards, peeling open Arabella's sex and licking it, a long stroke from base to tip, ending on her hard clit.

Arabella's body trembled, then she was pushing Vania away, excited but horrified at the same time, her thighs shutting tight and forcing her friend back.

'No! What are you doing?'

Vania looked shocked, then disappointed, and slid her hands along Arabella's thighs, gently trying to part them again. 'Come on, Arabella. We were having such a good time! And you can't pretend you weren't enjoying it. It'll be our little secret; nobody has to know,' she cajoled.

But Arabella was already mortified by her own responses, and pushed Vania away. 'I'm sorry, Vania, it's wrong. I won't do it. I'd like to go to bed now,' she said, feigning exhaustion by yawning elaborately and stretching her arms before pulling the covers over herself and turning away.

Clearly reluctant to leave her, Vania rose and gathered the shaving materials, emptied the bowl in the sink then turned the light off and climbed into bed herself.

Arabella pretended to have fallen asleep instantly, but she knew it would be some time before it could happen. She was too upset, too confused – by what Vania had done, and by the way her own body had responded. Had she done the right thing in rejecting Vania's advances? Worse still, she could hear Vania sighing softly to herself, her bed rocking and a wetly rhythmic sound coming from her. Arabella didn't dare turn to see what she was doing; she could imagine well enough, the picture of Vania touching herself burned more vividly into her mind than if she'd actually been watching it, and it wasn't long before the sound stopped, there was a long gasp, and a whispered but clearly audible 'Arabella' came from the other bed.

* * *

173

Arabella felt groggy the next day; it had taken her hours to fall asleep. Vania didn't talk to her, which she'd half-expected, but still it was upsetting. They dressed in silence, having to wear their uniforms even though they'd have ballet practice after breakfast, but, when Arabella had been served a bowl of thick, lumpy porridge, she found that there were no seats left on Vania's table.

Desperate, she stared around the room, trying to find a friendly face, but most either ignored her or scowled at her, and her vision was starting to blur with the tears building up behind her eyes when one girl looked up and smiled at her. Gratefully, Arabella walked towards the girl. She recognised her, the girl's blonde hair and blue eyes gave her almost exactly the opposite colouring from Vania; it was one of the ones who'd looked in such an unfriendly way at her roommate on the minibus. Maybe she'd switched sides on the battleground, Arabella thought ruefully, as she took her seat.

'Hi! I'm Tiffany,' the girl said, holding out her hand.

Arabella smiled, and shook the girl's hand. 'I'm Arabella. Thanks for letting me sit here.'

'No problem. You're sharing with Vania, right?'

Arabella nodded.

'I know she can be a bitch sometimes.'

Tiffany looked around the table, and the other girls murmured an assent, all smiling at Arabella. Tiffany then introduced her around, and Arabella, who knew she had no head for names, instantly forgot them, but warmed to the smiling faces. It looked as though she was right: these were all the girls Vania's group had looked down on. Arabella wondered why.

Whatever the reason, she was glad to have people to huddle around in the locker room as they changed into their leotards. Arabella noticed that these girls didn't stare as much as Vania; in fact, they seemed almost oblivious to each other's bodies. But they had some secret, something she wasn't yet privy to; they kept on whispering to each other, then looking at her and giggling, but the expressions on their faces were still kind, and Arabella felt confident that, whatever it was they were whispering about, she'd soon know about it.

The teacher for her first ballet class, Miss Carr, was younger than the other staff members she'd seen, and seemed kindlier, but she still put them through their paces. The piano teacher, a blind man called Peter – Arabella imagined that he'd been chosen for the job as he wouldn't spend any time ogling the girls – started slowly, but soon picked up the pace, until Arabella's mind was in a whirl. She was familiar with the exercises, standard *plies* followed by *battements* at the barre, stretching her legs so far out that it wasn't long before she'd worked up a sweat. The girl she'd seen being caned in the dining hall was in the class as well, and was clearly having trouble with some of the moves; Arabella imagined the markings on her bottom were still too painful for her to extend fully.

But Miss Carr didn't seem too sympathetic. She must have known the girl had been caned, but still barked orders at her, and, when the poor girl started to sob, the teacher took her legs and parted them forcibly, gripping her inner thigh to make sure one leg remained on the barre and ignoring the girl's wail of discomfort.

Arabella had been watching, glad it wasn't her, but she was aware that something was going on behind her, and turned to see what it was. One of the girls she'd been introduced to that morning was at the end of the room, facing the window with one leg on the barre, but her hands, rather than being stretched out to the side lying along her leg, as the other girls' were, seemed to be down between her legs. Arabella could see that the back of the leotard was askew, as though the girl was pulling the material to one side. And then she noticed it: a couple of faces, boys' faces, gleaming at the window. She realised that they must be the delivery boys Vania had talked about.

She was shocked, but she didn't say anything; and, as soon as the exercises continued, they vanished. The girl who'd been showing them something turned back to join in, looking flushed, but then they all did by now; it had been a hard morning's work.

Tiffany approached her after the class, before they'd gone through into the showers, and asked her if she could have a quick word. Arabella's heart raced.

'It's a little awkward talking to you about this, Arabella, but it's important,' Tiffany told her in a serious voice.

Arabella nodded, wide-eyed, yet the question, when it came, took her by surprise.

'Do you like boys?' asked Tiffany conspiratorially.

'Yes, of course.' Arabella was almost offended, and it didn't escape Tiffany's attention.

'I'm sorry. It's just that ... well, I know you've been sharing with Vania, and her and some of the other girls have different tastes. I just wasn't sure what yours were.'

'Well, I like boys.' Arabella wasn't about to admit that she'd barely known any, and she certainly wasn't going to mention how confused she'd felt at what had happened the night before. But she couldn't tell where this was leading. Tiffany leaned closer towards her, her voice little more than a whisper.

'I want to show you something, come on.'

She took Arabella's hand, and led her down the corridor away from the practice room, then stopped at a door before the shower room, knocked and listened, then went in.

Arabella was shocked to see Peter in there. He was sitting in a chair in the middle of the room, with some of Tiffany's friends seated on low benches around him. The girls looked up as Arabella came in, but Peter just stared straight ahead, smiling. She realised they'd interrupted something, that there was a tension in the atmosphere, so she sat down and tried to make herself as inconspicuous as possible. It didn't take her long to work out that whatever was going on had a distinctly sexual tone, and for a second she considered walking out again, but the thought of alienating another group of friends was too much for her to bear, so she tried to swallow her nervousness and watch what was going on.

The girl sitting directly in front of Peter ran her fingers over her chest, cupping her full breasts and staring at him. 'What am I doing now, Peter?'

It slowly dawned on Arabella that they seemed to be playing some kind of guessing game.

'You're touching yourself. Through your leotard.' He sounded excited, and Arabella could see a bulge in his crotch.

Was this the secret that the girls shared – that they teased this poor blind man, doing dirty things in front of him? Yet, despite her distaste, she was fascinated. She knew it happened, but she'd never seen the power a woman's sex could have over a man. She stared at his bulge.

The girl laughed at his answer. 'Peter, you're filthy. You think that's all a girl ever wants to do, rub herself.'

The other girls giggled.

'No, I'm touching my breasts.'

She'd pulled the leotard down over one breast now and was pinching the nipple into a full hardness. Peter reached down to his crotch, but an 'Ah-ah' from Tiffany stopped him. Arabella wondered why.

The girl had now slumped down on the bench and was pulling the leotard tight against her sex. Arabella could see the plump lips, and the dark line of the slit dividing them, then she peeled the material to one side, exposing the hairless pink folds beneath.

'What have I just done, Peter?' she asked breathlessly.

'You've stuck something inside yourself.' He was really excited now, rocking back and forth on his chair.

The girl giggled again. 'Peter! Always a step ahead of the game. No, I've just pulled my leotard to the side to get easier access. You like that, don't you?'

As Peter nodded, one of the other girls passed a bottle of baby oil to the girl displaying herself, who opened it and squeezed a line on to her crotch. Arabella watched, fascinated, as it rolled slowly down the slit, making it glisten in the light, to pool under her bottom.

'What's that?' Peter was sniffing the air now. 'That's baby oil, isn't it?' He sneered. 'You don't need that stuff; I know you're greasy enough.'

A few of the other girls giggled.

'I need it for what I'm doing now, Peter. Can you guess what that is?'

Cocking a leg up, she slid her hips further forwards and first circled her bumhole with a finger, oiling it up, then slid it in, up to the first knuckle, then further, sighing as she did it.

'You dirty bitch, I know what you're doing! You've stuck something up your arsehole, haven't you?' His hands had crept down to the bulge in his pants, now tenting straight up.

Tiffany turned to Arabella. 'Have you put one in your mouth before?'

It took a second for Arabella to work out what she meant. She shook her head, unable to even consider lying.

Tiffany smiled, not unkindly. 'Would you like to try?'

Arabella was wet; the sight of the man's arousal had turned her on, there was no denying it, and she felt a flood of juice at the idea of holding his cock, of rubbing it up against her face, even of tasting it. She hesitated, still uncertain how she should behave here, then, telling herself that it was OK, that it was normal for men and women to be attracted to each other, and that she needed the experience being offered, she nodded.

Tiffany stood up and took her by the hand, and they walked towards the centre of the room. The blonde unzipped Peter's trousers and pulled out a long, thick and veiny cock, already with a drop of liquid at the top. Arabella gasped. Surely she'd never be able to fit that in her mouth?

Tiffany, perhaps noticing her friend's alarm, took her hand again and squeezed it. 'It's easy. Just watch what I do.' And, bending down, she made an O with her red lips and dipped her head slowly over the stiff length.

Arabella watched in amazement as it disappeared into her mouth, Peter's legs stiffening and twitching, then relaxing as he let out a groan.

Tiffany brought her head back up and kissed the tip, then grinned at Arabella. Her lipstick was smeared, and Arabella saw that she'd left a ring of red around the base of his cock. 'Come on, just do the same thing. You'll enjoy the taste.'

179

She moved, and Arabella took her place, first curling a hand around the cock, testing its weight and firmness, then giving it an experimental lick. Encouraged by the shifting of Peter's hips and a low moan, she pushed her head over it, just as Tiffany had shown her, careful not to scrape it with her teeth.

She looked up, to see the other girls watching her. A couple of them had started to stroke themselves through their leotards, either toying with their nipples or mashing their fingers against their sex, rubbing in quick circular motions. Arabella could feel her own cream building up, and daringly reached a hand down to feel the hot wetness between her legs, not wanting to seem uptight in front of the other girls, then licked the cock head again.

'Suck it, go on.'

She felt Peter's hand grab the back of her head, pulling on the hair then pushing her on to it, and she tried to protest, but her mouth was full of cock, so she gave in and began to suck, as she'd been told.

She could hear Tiffany walking around her, and her voice as she talked to the girl who'd been fingering her bumhole. 'You're a filthy slut, Tasha. You deserve to be punished for teasing Peter like that.'

Arabella tried to look around, and saw Tiffany pulling the other girl's finger from her bottom, before the hand around her head pulled angrily on her hair, and she started to suck again, noisily slurping on the cock in her mouth.

'Clean it with your mouth.'

She heard Tiffany again, and a squeal of disapproval, then sucking sounds. She stole another glance at the girl and saw Tiffany rubbing a ballet shoe against the girl's slit, swollen, slick and gleaming in the light.

'Look at this! You're dripping down here. Looks like Peter was right, you've got so much slut juice you don't need any baby oil.' Tiffany's voice was full of scorn. 'Go on, take the position.'

But, every time Arabella tried to watch what was going on, her head was pulled back down, and she only caught quick flashes of Tiffany and the girl, or the others, sitting around and rubbing themselves more boldly now, before her head was pushed back down into Peter's crotch. His breathing was faster now, and Arabella reached down to cup his balls, which felt tight and heavy in her hand.

She could hear a new set of sounds, a whistle followed by a crack and a moan, and she saw that Tiffany was spanking the girl, upended now over the bench, her bum, greasy from the baby oil, reddening under the ballet shoe. Tiffany was raining blows all over the cheeks, then making the girl squeal by flicking the end against her sex, all the while murmuring disapprovingly of the girl's sluttishness, the wetness of her pussy, her lack of shame, the way she'd displayed herself like that.

But, if Arabella was getting excited, trying to watch what was happening and rubbing fast at her own slit, hot, wet and as swollen as she'd ever known it now, uncaring about anyone watching, enjoying the illicit thrill of showing off her excitement, Peter was responding too. She felt his balls pulse, and knew what was about to happen – she'd heard about it often enough from the girls at school – but, even though she pulled her head away, not wanting to taste it, as only the sluttiest girls liked the taste, she hadn't expected it to jet over her face, great gouts of it hitting her cheeks, landing ropily in her hair, one drop in her eye, and others on her mouth, firmly shut now even though Peter was trying to force her head back on to his cock, muttering, 'Slut, suck it,' as more of the thick come pulsed out.

Then she pulled away from him and stood up, distraught and half-blinded, the hot liquid covering her face and breaking the excitement of the moment. She had to get it off; it had all gone too far; she had to get out. With a squeal of despair, she rushed for the door and out, ignoring Tiffany's sharp 'Arabella, stop!' behind her, and ran down the corridor, blindly making for the shower room.

She knew she'd passed some girls on the way, some of Vania's friends in their uniform, one of whom called out after her, 'Filthy whore!' while another laughed delightedly, but she didn't care, she just had to clean herself up, wash the stringy liquid off her face, change out of the leotard, with its giveaway dampness between her legs. She hadn't wanted this – hadn't wanted to come to a school where everyone seemed obsessed by sex, and where anyone she ended up with seemed to have only one thing in mind. Before she reached the shower room, before she splashed the cold water on her face, then stepped into the shower, washing her hair in a frantic effort to clean it of the sticky fluid gumming it together, she'd already decided what she was going to do. If the directress didn't yet know about what kind of school she was running, she was going to now.

Vania wasn't in the bedroom when she came in to change, and she was grateful that her roommate wouldn't see her leotard. She eyed the stains on it guiltily, wondering how she could get it cleaned without rumours spreading, then bunched it up and flung it to the side. First things first.

In her uniform again she'd felt better, if still aware of a wetness between her thighs in the vulnerable short skirt, and she'd rushed to the directress's office and been shown in. The directress had watched her impassively as she'd described everything that had happened to her since she'd arrived: Vania's passes at her, the girls in the shower, the others playing with Peter, even the girl displaying herself to the delivery boys in the training session, although she neglected to mention her own part in any of the activities. She didn't tell the directress how she'd responded to being shaved, or how she'd sucked Peter's cock and liked it; the directress didn't need to know these things.

When she'd finished she was breathless, and waited for the directress to comfort her, to reassure her that she was right, that the other girls were wrong; that she welcomed Arabella's help in exposing the sordid goings-on in her academy. But instead the directress just stared at her. In the silence of the room, Arabella could feel her heart pounding.

'I detest sneaks.' The directress stood up, and Arabella impulsively took a step back. 'But you aren't even a sneak.'

Arabella was confused. What was going on?

'You come here with some tall tale and expect me to believe that everyone has approached you with some sexual offer or other? You've got sex on the brain, my girl, and there's only one remedy for that. Get into your sports clothes and run around the edge of the estate. It's five miles; that should give you time to mull over what you've been saying. And don't even think about trying to cut corners – I'll alert the groundspeople to your punishment; they'll keep an eye on you. Now get out, and don't come back with any more of this nonsense. If the academy isn't up to your exacting standards –' her voice was especially withering '– it shouldn't be difficult to arrange your departure.'

Trembling, her vision blurry from the tears she'd been holding back, Arabella didn't even dare try to speak, sure that she'd be in floods the moment she opened her mouth. Horribly upset, and barely able to believe the way she'd been treated, she ran back to her room to get changed. Surely she hadn't imagined everything? How could the directress refuse to believe her? By the time she'd finally pulled on the gymslip and shorts, the tears had started to roll down her cheeks, and she jogged, half-stumbling, to the front gate of the school, ignoring any of the girls who called out to her.

It had been raining, and the ground was muddy, splashing flecks of mud on to her bare thighs as she ran. At least it would be easy to follow the route the directress wanted: the academy grounds were encircled, and a track ran along the side, wide enough for the grounds staff vehicles, although their tyres had churned up the ground, so that her shoes were soon soaked.

If part of her had thought that at least a trip around the grounds would calm her, with its beautiful views, she was soon disappointed. The wall to her left was high and forbidding, and the forest that flanked the path to the right was obviously planted, in straight rows with a gloomy interior. She concentrated instead on the running, trying to centre herself around her breath; the directress couldn't have known that she'd enjoyed running, had almost become addicted to it, at school. She tried to focus on the positive side of what she'd been made to do: in a sense it was less punishment than refuge, somewhere to hide from the other girls, or at least to get the perspective she needed, to work out what she should do.

Which was why it was so dispiriting when the girls pounced on her after she'd cleared the brow of the first rise. It was totally unexpected, not least because Vania and Tiffany were together, in their uniforms, with a few other girls she recognised, as well as one of the boys she'd noticed earlier peering at them through the windows. She tried to dodge them at first, to run past them, but one of the girls tripped her up, and she landed heavily in a puddle, too winded to get up.

She felt a foot on her back, pressing her into the ground, and tried to struggle against it, the icy water already soaked through her thin top, her nipples stiff from the cold, grazing painfully against the rough ground, only to hear Vania's scornful voice.

'So, the little slut doesn't know what's good for her.'

'Running along to the directress like a sneak,' added Tiffany.

'And we all know what happens to sneaks.'

The girls began to chant, 'Sneak, sneak,' then one of them was pulling Arabella's shorts down. She kicked against the tugging hands, wailing in utter despair, but her bottom was exposed now to the cold air, and she felt something cold and gritty being pressed into the furrow of her sex and between her bottom cheeks, then her shorts were pulled up again.

'Look, the tart's had an accident,' one of them called out, and she could hear them all laughing. The foot was taken off her back now, and she pulled the shorts down, trying to scrape the mud from between the cheeks, sobbing gently into the ground as they all stared at her. Perhaps that was all; maybe they'd leave it at that.

But Vania pulled her to her feet, and Tiffany grabbed one of her arms; then, between them, they began to frogmarch her down the track.

'We've got just the punishment for you, you bitch,' snarled Vania.

Arabella looked around wildly, hoping for a sympathetic face, but they all seemed contorted with anger, or, in the case of the boy, lust. His grin was even worse than the others' scowls, and she turned quickly back to face the track.

'Where are you taking me?' she asked, but they were already pulling her off the track and leading her down a small path between the trees. She could hear laughter and an excited chatter behind her, then the path widened out into a clearing. The woods were older here, with more space between the trees, and the girls dragged her towards an old oak, the ground around the trunk littered with cigarette ends and beer cans. To one side there was an old, damp-looking mattress, and for a second Arabella thought they were going to lay her down on that and use her, but instead they raised her arms to one of the lower boughs of the tree, and the boy expertly tied her wrists together, pressing himself against her body.

She started to panic now, and babble, hoping that one of them would take pity on her. 'I won't tell the directress, I promise I won't. I'll suck your cock,' she offered, looking pleadingly at the boy, but he just laughed, and she turned to the others. 'I've got money. Please?'

To her horror she saw that Vania and one of the other girls had pulled on gardening gloves, and were gathering the nettles that had grown in clumps around the base of the trunk. Still unsure of what they might do, but terrified all the same, she started to struggle against the bonds, but they held tight, and her squirming and squealing only seemed to make the others laugh.

Finally, Vania held a large bunch of nettles, and nodded to one of the other girls, who came up to Arabella and, taking her top in both hands, tore it down the middle, exposing her breasts, the skin already goose-pimpled and bluish from the cold.

'You're going to take a nettling, slut,' said Tiffany.

Vania smiled grimly as she approached, then brushed the nettles softly against Arabella's chest, ignoring Arabella's desperate attempts to twist her body out of reach. She cried out as the stinging fire inflamed the skin; suddenly her breasts felt huge and swollen, the sharp pinpricks of the nettle leaving a burning rash across the bare flesh. Still she clung to the hope that that they would be satisfied with that, but then Vania raised her arm and brought the nettles down across her chest, hard.

The blow took her by surprise, and for a second she couldn't breathe, unable to believe the pain, then it came again, and again, Vania lashing the bunch against her until her chest was on fire. The pain seemed too much to bear, but still it continued, each stroke making her scream, until her chest was a heaving mottled mess, the flesh raised and swollen under the stings.

Then Vania stopped, and stepped back. Arabella was choking on her sobs, slumped in the rope around her wrists, aware only of the fiery stinging that seemed to cover her whole body. But then Tiffany took the nettles from Vania, pulled the front of Arabella's shorts away and stuffed them against her greasy slit, and she knew that the pain she'd felt before was nothing compared to this.

They left her there for a few minutes, bucking and writhing under the bonds, her shorts pulled back up tight so that with every movement she stung the tender flesh more, rubbing the swollen lips up against the poison leaves, unable to stop herself. She couldn't even see them now, her eyes blinded by tears of pain; but dimly, in the background, she could hear them laughing.

Just when Arabella thought something had to give, and she couldn't take it any more, her shorts were pulled down again and the nettles taken out. A finger burrowed experimentally between her legs and prodded at her, then pulled out again; Arabella no longer knew or cared whose it was.

'She's still wet, the little slut, and guess what?' Tiffany asked the others. 'She's a virgin.'

There was a gasp, then more laughter.

One of the girls sounded more sympathetic now. 'Maybe that's why she's a bit, you know –'

But Vania's voice had lost none of its hard edge. 'What's Tom going to do now, then?'

Tiffany laughed. 'Well, we don't want to spoil her, but where there's a will, there's a way.'

She felt herself being released from the bonds, and slumped into the boy's arms, then allowed herself to be half-carried, half-dragged across the ground to a log. One of the girls laid a blanket down in front of the log, and she let herself be draped face down over it, grateful for the softness of the blanket on her knees. The shorts were pulled down, and off, and her legs spread, the cool air soothing the burning between her thighs, then she felt someone lying on the blanket beneath her, and then there was something hot and wet burrowing against her aching slit.

Her whole body bucked at the contact, the fiery burn of the nettles, the cool air and the warm tongue too much of a contrast for her body to bear, but as it ran up and down her groove, dipping into her hole then spreading her juices along the length of her sex, she felt it soothing, licking away the pain, although she still felt a burning tickle all over the inflamed skin.

Then there was something cold and greasy being squirted over her bottom, and she heard one of the girls giggle, before a finger rubbed the oil around her bottom hole. She felt herself tighten up, then as the tongue continued to work against her, fast and nimble, flicking now over her clit, painfully hard, she relaxed and the finger slid in.

She gasped. She'd never let anything in there before, and it felt wrong, dirty, like she was being stretched too far. Then a second finger had joined the first, and was rotating, flexing the tight ring, and she sobbed as her arsehole contracted on the fingers. The mouth was nibbling on her clit now, sucking it in and flicking it fast with the tongue, and as she relaxed again the fingers slid further in and twisted round. They felt huge in there, painful and wrong, but she was distracted by the burning ache in her slit and the hot tongue busily exploring her hole.

'Better grease it up properly, Tom,' she heard one of the girls say. 'She's really tight up there.'

She heard a grunt, then the fingers were sliding slowly out of her, and her ring was closing on air. She felt almost disappointed at the empty feeling, then something bigger, hotter and smoother was pressing against her.

She closed up again, clenching her bumhole tight, but then there was someone beside her, one of the girls, she couldn't see which, stroking her hair and saying in a soothing voice, 'Relax, it's OK. Let yourself push back on it. It won't hurt you.'

She pushed out, and heard a gasp, then felt the bulbous end of the boy's cock inside her, stretching her impossibly wide. 'I can't take it; it's too much,' she moaned, but the girl next to her kissed her head, stroked her hair and murmured softly to her, so she pushed back again, only wanting to please them now, wanting the full feeling back, wanting the licking to go on, feeling the first tremors of something delicious running through her from head to toe.

Then more of it was in, and she heard a muttered 'Christ, that feels good' as it slid in, millimetre by millimetre, the boy's rough hands holding her bottom apart. She imagined his cock spreading her arseflesh, her ring taut against his stiff length, and felt a rush of juice at the thought that he was hers now; his cock was in her, the first she'd ever had, and she pushed back further on it.

The tongue left her, and she heard the boy groan again then push himself all the way in, then she was being licked again, and he was fucking her arse, slowly at first, relishing the tightness of her hot hole, his thumbs holding her sex lips apart as the girl nibbled on her clit. He pulled it all the way out, and she gasped in disappointment, her ring clenching on cold air, then he was pressing against her again, sliding in more easily this time, as she felt her clit being sucked into the girl's mouth again.

Then everything that had happened to her, everything she'd seen and experienced, from Vania lovingly shaving her to the taste of the cock in her mouth, boiled over in her mind, and she felt the first contractions buck her as her orgasm hit, hard and fast, her arsehole clenching on the boy's cock, painful now, with the burning of the nettle rash and the girl on her clit, sucking her hard, and she felt the boy's cock twitch and pulse, and something hot and wet inside her, making her more greasy, the boy moaning long and loud, then he was pulling out, her arsehole still clenching on nothing, and the girl released her clit, and she lay there, slumped over the log, sobbing at the intensity of it all.

They were around her in an instant, different now, caring and soothing, one of the girls rubbing her swollen chest with dock leaves, calming her as she flinched from the first contact, then rubbing a salve into her burning slit, kissing her and cuddling her, holding her in their arms, letting her cry and rock back and forth, stroking her hair and telling her they loved her.

'It's the same for all the new girls,' Vania was telling her, smoothing down her hair and kissing the tears from her cheeks. 'Everyone gets put through their paces.'

'But you're one of us now,' continued Tiffany. 'It won't always be like this, but sometimes it's better this way, don't you see?'

Arabella sobbed with relief, then gratitude, as someone wrapped a blanket around her, Tiffany and Vania alternating in kissing her and whispering soothingly in her ear. She felt like she'd just passed a test, something important that she'd had to go through, and for the first time since she'd stepped on the train, even though her breasts and her sex still stung, her bumhole aching painfully, she relaxed. Perhaps she could get used to life at the academy after all.

9

Up The Aisle

Emma often thought she was invisible to the students.
One librarian was much the same as another to them,
she imagined, and she had been forced to resort to
stern phrases once or twice on the library floor to
stop students braying on their mobiles, her disap-
proving gaze having been entirely ignored. It worked
both ways, of course: although some faces stuck in
Emma's mind, most of the students seemed like
minor variations on a theme. The fashions had
changed in the three years she'd been there – she'd
seen hair curly, straight, long and short, and had
noted with equanimity the transformation of the
scruffy male student through new grooming technol-
ogy – but the voices (Home Counties, arrogant), the
poses and the whole general feel of them had stayed
the same.

Which is why it was so strange that the girl had
stuck in Emma's mind. It was partly the circumstances of their first meeting; she understood that well
enough. A lot of students used the library to show off
– for whatever reason, it was a place to see and be
seen, and some of the girls seemed to treat the worn
carpets like a catwalk. Still, you didn't see students
kissing, or groping each other there very often; it
would have been inappropriate, to say the least.

That was one of the reasons Emma liked working here: it was an unchallenging atmosphere, with not much of a social life – nobody would ask her if she had a boyfriend, and she felt welcomed by the matronly older women who made up the bulk of the staff and had none of the brash sexuality that had terrified her so much in office girls she'd worked alongside before. She was aware that, at the rate she was going, this was her future – a reduced life of issuing, returning, cataloguing and filing books, with the occasional frisson of a lost book or a student haggling over a fine – and, although part of her resisted, occasionally overwhelming her with dreams terrifying in their fury and passion, another part accepted it as inevitable, an inescapable fate.

She'd been on the first floor, looking for a mislaid journal, when she saw the girl for the first time. She noticed a couple of things at once: the girl wasn't wearing a bra, her nipples sticking out through her thin woollen top; and, more strikingly, a boy had taken hold of the back of her thong, a black number with thin pink frills, and was tugging it up past the waistband of her tight jeans. Emma stopped and stared, transfixed. The boy looked like any other, in sportswear and with a cropped haircut, but there was something special about the girl. She wasn't beautiful, not in a classical sense, with glasses, curly hair and a slightly sharp nose, and she was bigger than was the fashion then, her bum looking like it had only just been able to squeeze into her jeans. They didn't seem to have seen her. It can't have been comfortable for the girl, Emma thought, and she was patting ineffectually against the boy's hand, wriggling as though she were trying to get away, but she didn't look too upset, and he seemed in no hurry to let go.

Emma coughed and walked past them, a little embarrassed, and was pleased to see the boy let go of the thong, even if he pulled it out even more before letting it flick back against the girl's flesh. The couple turned to the exit, and Emma watched the girl walk with a strange squirming movement, as though the thong were well up inside her, and she was enjoying rubbing her slick wetness against the material.

That night Emma couldn't get the girl out of her mind. She tried to concentrate on her book, but the image of what she'd seen kept flashing in front of her eyes. She couldn't understand how the girl could let a boy do something like that to her – in public, too. Emma was annoyed to find that she was jealous of the boy's attentions, of the girl's flaunting herself like that, and realised that it was futile trying to go on reading.

She put the book down, stood up and caught her reflection in the mirror. Would she dare to walk around without a bra? Her breasts were heavier than the girl's, but she reached back to unclasp the rear fastening, and tugged the straps down over her shoulders to let the full globes spill out into her hands. Experimentally she toyed with the nipples, pinching them and rolling them between her fingers to make them stand up, then rolled her top back down over them and gazed critically at her reflection. Not bad, she had to admit, and she poured herself a glass of wine, feeling pleased. If only she was this bold in front of men – she knew she wasn't unattractive, but she'd always found it distasteful to throw herself at men, or even to play the dim but cute card, as she'd seen so many of her friends doing; she'd always expected Mr Right to appear and sweep her off her feet, but somehow it had never happened. And now she was almost 35.

As she stared at herself in the mirror, she found herself absently stroking and tugging on her nipples, thinking about the girl. It was the first time she'd been turned on by anything in weeks, and when she felt the stickiness between her thighs she was embarrassed, hit by a wave of guilt and let her hands fall to her sides. She didn't want to touch herself, that was something only sad girls with no prospect of a man or fumbling teenagers did – she didn't like to think about the moments of weakness when she'd succumbed to the temptation herself – but her head was spinning, and she tried to salvage something of her good mood before it was overwhelmed by thoughts of her own lack of sex life, swearing to herself that she'd make more of an effort with her appearance the next day.

In the morning she tried letting her hair down in the mirror before walking to work. She normally wore it up in a bun, but today she felt more confident, and let it tumble over her shoulders, a cascade of auburn curls that seemed so rich she was usually embarrassed to let it show. But she felt good as she walked along the street, even aware that a couple of men were looking at her, and when she got to work she bounced up the steps before the realisation hit home: she was at the library again – grim, dim, dusty and airless. She paused on the threshold, tempted just to turn tail and go home again, then took a deep breath and wandered in.

Joanne, one of the counter librarians, was the first to notice, greeting her with the usual 'Morning, Emma' before doing a double take and exclaiming, 'Look at your hair! That looks lovely. Who did it for you?'

Aware that some of the other counter staff had paused and were watching, Emma felt the blood creep up her cheeks, and try as she might she couldn't meet Joanne's gaze as she answered, dropping her eyes to the floor, 'Nobody. It's just – I did it myself.'

She looked back up at Joanne, who was peering up at her curiously. 'No need to look so glum, dear. Special occasion, is it?' Then, conspiratorially, she leaned towards Emma and winked. 'Got a fella lined up for later on, have we?'

At this Emma's resolve broke, and she fled, dimly aware of Joanne muttering, 'Well – I only asked,' as Emma pushed past one of the library shelvers on her way to the toilet, her vision blurry with tears. Once safely inside, she quickly bundled her hair up into a bun again, desperate to escape once more into her invisibility, and dabbed at her moist eyes with a tissue before coming back out.

She'd been half-expecting to see the girl again, and volunteered for any work on the floors, searching for books for students and doing general stock-takes rather than counter work, and couldn't help feeling disappointed when the girl was nowhere to be seen.

But the following day she was sitting at the enquiry desk on the first floor, having resigned herself to not seeing the girl again, when her attentions were rewarded. Emma was trying to explain to a Japanese student why the theses couldn't be taken out of the library, when she suddenly spotted the girl out of the corner of her eye, emerging from one of the aisles and walking to the back of the floor. She faltered, staring after her, until the Japanese student's repeated 'Miss, miss' brought her back to reality.

If a librarian was on duty on the enquiry desk, she wasn't meant to leave, but Emma knew that in special circumstances, such as showing students how to use the microfiche machine, or helping disabled students navigate their way around the warren of aisles, it was not only acceptable but necessary. As soon as she'd finished talking to the Japanese student, she placed a CLOSED sign on the desk and walked to the back of the room.

She'd been half-hoping to find the girl alone, but, when she spotted her, a book open in front of her at a long desk behind the rear stalls, she was talking to the same boy she'd been with before. Worse, both looked up as she came round the corner, the girl gazing at her with a look of calm insolence. For a moment she thought of telling them off, wiping that cheeky grin off the boy's face by reminding them that the library was a place for quiet study, not socialising, and not in any way for anything dirty, like she'd seen the boy doing the other day; but she couldn't face them, and as she walked past and away they fell silent anyway, their eyes following her every step.

She hadn't been back at the enquiry desk five minutes, still flustered from seeing the girl again, when Emma saw her walk past the desk with the boy, up into one of the far aisles. The girl had turned round and caught Emma staring at her as she passed, and Emma had tried to busy herself at her desk, but it was too late: the girl knew Emma had been watching her.

Emma told herself not to be so foolish – she was in control here; this was her territory, and she was older as well, but her fragile self-assurance crumbled when she heard a moan from the aisle. Embarrassed, she first put it down to having sex on the brain, like some hormonal teen, but then she heard it again, faint yet unmistakable.

Maybe a student had fallen asleep, and was snoring, she tried half-heartedly to convince herself as she stood up and walked towards the oversized books, where the noise was coming from. But it was louder now, clearly a sound of sexual excitement, and she was confused, unsure as to how she should deal with the situation. Best to see exactly what was going on, she told herself, but she slowed down as she approached the row where they seemed to be, and tried to walk past quietly, afraid that they'd think she was trying to spy on them.

But when she saw them she realised they wouldn't be paying any attention to anything except each other, and she hurried past, shocked at the image they presented. They were kissing, fully tonguing each other, the first time she'd seen such behaviour in the library, but far worse than that was what the boy was doing with his hands. One had been pinching her nipple through her top, which was bad enough, but the other was down the back of her jeans, rummaging around with the front button undone and the zip half-down, so that she could see the sheer material of the girl's knickers. It looked a bit like he was just stroking the bare skin of her bottom, but he might have been doing something else, and with a lump in her throat she moved into the next aisle along, as quietly as she could, to see if she could work out exactly what he was up to.

Closer now, she could see his hand pushing rhythmically into the girl, and she imagined it rubbing against her wet slit, teasing her and making her excited, or, worse, probing her bottom hole, maybe even using the cream from her pussy to lube up the hole and make it easier for him to slide it in. She felt an unfamiliar twinge in her crotch again, as she saw the girl's hands rubbing at the front of the boy's jeans, tracing the outline of a stiff bulge.

She let her hands move down to her skirt, only half-consciously, feeling the goose-pimples rise on her skin as she watched the couple, then hooked the elasticated waistband of her skirt up with a fingernail and slid one hand down towards her pants, thick, sensible cotton, not like the tarty pair the slut girl had on, and felt through the bushy mat of hair for the swollen lips of her sex, already opening and juicy, and shuddered as she scraped a nail along the length of her slit.

The sensation felt fresh and new, as though it had been even longer than months since the last time she'd touched herself, and she kept her eyes fixed on the boy's hand as he finger-fucked the girl while she tugged on his cock, and matched his rhythm to her own, her surroundings melting into the background as she focused on the couple and the burning itch in her sex.

She leaned forwards and braced herself with one hand on a shelf as her legs began to shake, then dug her fingers deep inside herself, feeling the wet oiliness and rubbing it all over the engorged skin, revelling in the feel of it. She'd started to flick her clit, a hard nub now, fully emerged from its hood, when she saw the boy lift his finger and smear the end of it over the girl's lips. The girl opened her mouth to suck it in, then opened her eyes too, and Emma's hand froze in mid-stroke as she realised the girl was staring straight at her. Panicked, she just stood there, her hand still beneath her skirt, as she waited for the girl to tell her boyfriend, for the two of them to move off some-where else, somewhere private, away from her prying eyes, but she didn't.

Still staring into Emma's eyes, the girl slowly made an O of her lips and sucked the boy's finger into her mouth, cleaning it with her tongue as she rubbed harder in the boy's pants, until finally he shook and groaned, his body tensing, trembling then relaxing, his shoulders slumping. All the while she'd stared at Emma, and Emma, hardly daring to believe what was happening, had found herself stroking her slit again, feeling herself flood with juices as she stared back into the girl's eyes.

But the boy started giggling after he'd come, breaking the spell, and the girl had looked away, then both of them busied themselves with finding tissues and cleaning themselves up. Emma remained stock still, terrified the boy would see her, and pulled her hand slowly out of her pants while she waited for them to move away. Ashamed now of what she'd done, her mind reeling, she waited a few minutes after they'd gone, trying to look busy by tidying books with her left hand, her right still too wet to touch anything without leaving a telltale smear.

To her horror, Denise, another colleague, suddenly appeared at the end of the aisle. 'Oh, there you are!' she exclaimed, and walked towards her, as Emma turned and tried to hide her hand behind her back. But halfway down the aisle Denise paused. 'What's that smell?' She sniffed at the air, then looked quizzically at Emma. 'Can you smell that?'

Mute with fear, Emma could only shake her head.

Denise stared at her, then shrugged. 'Never mind. You're meant to be on duty at the enquiry desk, aren't you? There's been nobody there for a while now, and we didn't know where to find you.' She paused, clearly waiting for some kind of explanation.

Her mind racing, Emma stammered, 'I had to help a student. I thought I'd be back in a second, but it turned out to be more complicated than I'd expected. It's finished now, though. Can you hold the desk for me for a minute while I go to the toilet?' She was already pushing past her colleague, who said, 'Yes, of course,' as Emma fled to wash her hands.

That night Emma dressed up, for the first time in years. She searched through all her clothes, trying to find the tartiest thing she had, but could only come up with a black lacy bra and panties. Still, they were a bit flashier than what she normally wore, and, when she'd finished the bottle of wine she'd opened the night before, she felt pleasantly tipsy and bold enough to walk past the window in her underwear.

Perhaps there was a Peeping Tom hiding in the bushes, a panty thief lurking there in the hope of seeing a girl walk around half-naked. She hadn't washed down there since the afternoon, and had been amazed at how wet her knickers had been when she'd replaced them with the black pair, and at the thought of being watched she began to feel herself open up again. She imagined what he'd like to see, and brushed her hands over her bra, then pulled the cups down so that her nipples, stiff and long now, were peeping over the tops, then, giggling to herself, she bent over in full view of the window, giving anyone watching a full view of her lacy rear.

It felt good to show off, even to an imaginary audience, and she lay back on the sofa and tugged the crotch of her knickers to one side, burrowing her fingers into her moist pouch to finish what she'd started earlier. If a man had been watching, he wouldn't have been satisfied with just a glimpse of what she had to offer. He'd find his way into the flat, maybe waiting for someone to leave then sliding in after them. And he'd have worked out which one her flat was, and would come up and knock on the door, pretending to be a meter reader. She'd open it in her underwear, maybe even smelling of sex, and then he'd be unstoppable, demanding everything from her, pulling her bra down to make her nipples stick out again, then unzipping himself to tug on a long, fat cock.

He'd make her get on her knees and push it into her face, and he wouldn't take no for an answer, but would shove it into her mouth, not stopping even if she gagged, but holding her head there with a tight grip on her hair. It would be unwashed, a pervert's cock, tasting of pee and come from where he'd been rubbing himself in the bushes, and he'd laugh at her all exposed while he was still fully clothed.

But he wouldn't want to come in her face, or make her swallow it – he'd want to feel her hole, to see how juicy she was, what a dirty fuck slut she was, and he'd tell her that he was dripping, that he'd never seen anything like it, and he'd probably bend her over the back of the sofa, maybe slap her arse a couple of times, then he'd try fucking her hole. But it would be too wet for him, and he'd take her knickers off and rub them against her slit, trying to soak up some of the juices, all the while telling her what a whore she was, then he'd try again. She'd still be too juicy, though, ashamed of her body's responses, and, even though she'd try to stop, she'd feel herself flooding, the wetness oozing out; she couldn't help it, and eventually he'd stick his fingers in, right up, and rub them around, making her squeal, then he'd rub them over her tight ring, opening it up.

He'd spread her cheeks with both hands and display her, leering at the lewd sight as her sex opened wetly and her arsehole winked at him. She'd try to stop him, but he'd put a finger up her bum, stretching her and making her ready for what he was going to do next. She'd protest – she'd never let anyone up there; it was too small; she was scared he'd split her – but then she'd feel the end of it, all bulbous and hot, pressing against her tight virgin ring, and she'd try and relax and push back against it, until the end would pop in, and then . . . with a finger up her bum, and her other hand rubbing frantically at her clit, slapping it hard, she came violently, crying out, her legs shaking and her whole body trembling then locking as her arsehole contracted on her finger, once, vice, three times, and another wave of ecstasy hit er, but now the image of the girl sucking on the oy's finger, staring right into her eyes, filled her nind.

She came down slowly, and slumped on the sofa, nly half-satisfied. It had been good, the first time he'd really been able to let go and not feel guilty bout touching herself in ages, and the fantasy was n old one, one she'd had from her teens, but the mage of the girl, coming unbidden into her mind, larmed her. Was she becoming obsessed?

She kept an eye out for the girl over the next couple of days, but neither she nor her boyfriend seemed to come in. But she felt more confident now, as though vatching the girl had helped her to relax, and took to vearing her hair down regularly, riding high over any nide comments any of the counter staff made, and one day even wandered around for a couple of hours with her bra pulled down and her stiff nipples on full display, poking through her thin jumper. She delighted in the attention this gave her, where once it would have terrified her; the students seemed to pay her new attention too, some of them clearly fabricating excuses just so they could spend time with her. She even caught one of them adjusting a bulge in his pants as he followed her down an aisle. And, while some of her female colleagues looked slightly askance at her new appearance, others were more complimentary, telling her how her skin was glowing, and how well she looked, while most of the men, who'd seemed to ignore her up to that point, were casting approving glances her way.

She felt the excitement of being a teenager again, the thrill of making herself up to look beautiful, and she'd almost forgotten about the girl when she ran into the boyfriend in the open area on the first floor.

Students weren't allowed to use their mobile phone in the library, but Emma normally turned a blind eye so long as they weren't too obvious about it. But this student was far too loud – you could hear him from the other end of the aisles – and she went to ask him to be quiet, not realising who it was at first, only to stop when she saw his face. He noticed her, too, and a slow smile crept across his face; he made no effort to quieten his voice at all, but just watched her as he carried on talking.

Emma could feel herself going red, and her old sheepishness seemed to flood back – how much did he know? She thought frantically for a second that he might report her to some of the other staff members for spying, or not attending to her duties properly, then told herself that was stupid. What could he possibly say? Anything would sound ludicrous. But she had to say something to him – a small crowd of students had gathered, milling around the catalogue computers, and were clearly waiting for her to do something. She set her jaw and approached him.

'Excuse me? Could you be quiet, please?' Her voice started as a squeal, then dropped an octave as she pointed to a sign on the door clearly forbidding mobile phones. 'If you want to use your phone, you'll have to go outside.'

But he just stood there and carried on talking, watching her. He must have heard her; she felt her face flush again. 'Did you hear me? I can call Security if you like, and they'll confiscate your library card.'

He still didn't move, and when she turned and took a step towards the enquiry-desk phone, unsure whether she was ready to carry out her threat or not, she heard a 'Ciao', and turned back to see the boy putting his phone away, shrugging and saying, 'It was over anyway.' Then, obscenely, right in front of the other students, he grabbed his crotch, thrust it towards her, leering, then turned with a swagger and walked down the stairs.

Shaken by the encounter, Emma sat down at the enquiry desk and let out a long-held breath. She was still anxious, though – whenever she'd seen the boy before, the girl was always around as well. Where was she this time?

It didn't take long to find her. Patrolling the aisles, Emma found her sitting by the philosophy books. Emma tried at first to pretend she hadn't seen her, but the girl caught her eye straight away, and insolently, just like the boy, holding her gaze, she took a piece of chewing gum out of her mouth and squashed it under the table then sneered at her.

Emma knew she couldn't let this behaviour pass, even though she dreaded making direct contact with the girl. She walked towards her, repeating to herself that this was her territory; here she was in power; she couldn't be scared off by a student.

'You're not allowed to chew gum in here,' she began.

'I'm not,' said the girl with a trace of an accent, and opened her mouth, sticking out her full pink tongue to show Emma, who felt her temper rising again.

'You were chewing gum a minute ago. I saw you. You put it under the desk.' She folded her arms and glared at the girl. 'That's vandalism. I could report you for that.'

'Why do you keep following me around?' the girl asked suddenly.

Flustered by the change in direction, Emma could only gasp, her hands now fidgeting with each other, as the girl continued.

'I saw you the other day watching me and Paul. You know I did, too. I told Paul – he says you're maybe frustrated, like other English girls; you don't know how to *fuck*.' She said the last word with particular relish, watching as Emma took a step back, dumbfounded.

She couldn't think of anything to say.

'Anyway, we don't mind if you want to watch. It gets boring in the library, no? Paul is meeting me back here –' she waved to the rows of oversized books '– in an hour. Come along – maybe I'll let Paul teach you how to fuck, eh?'

Emma could only watch, aghast, as the girl gathered up her books and walked off. She'd left the gum as well, Emma realised, the mundane fact giving her something to focus on as she considered what the girl had said. The last thing she'd expected was a tirade like that, but there was something exciting about the girl's directness, she thought, as she took a tissue out of her pocket and scraped the gum off from under the desk.

She told herself that she wouldn't follow the girl's lead, even considering coming up with a ruse to send one of her colleagues to the oversized books aisle, having them caught in the act, but as the time drew closer she simply grew more nervous and distracted, unable to concentrate on her work. She'd seen the girl at three; four would be during her tea break, and nobody would notice if she didn't spend it in the staff room – she often went outside for it anyway.

But a few of the other staff members on the counter told her she looked a bit peaky, and Kate, their boss, even asked her if she wanted to go home, then suggested that they have a chat in the meeting room. It was the last thing Emma wanted to do, as it was nearly four, but she couldn't see any way out of it, and followed Kate into the room.

Kate sat down, and beckoned to the chair opposite. She saw Emma's eyes flicking to the clock anxiously, and said, 'Don't worry, Emma. I'm not going to be very long.' And then, leaning over with a broad grin on her face, 'And I'm not going to eat into your break, either. You can have one after this.'

Emma murmured a thank you and tried to smile, hoping her nervousness didn't show too badly.

'I'm worried about you, Emma. You seem to be having mood swings. A couple of weeks ago you seemed really happy, letting your hair down, and you looked lovely.' Emma made a show of gratitude for the compliment, and Kate went on. 'But I remember just before that you seemed very distracted, and today I can't help noticing that you're very anxious about something. Is everything all right at home?'

Emma felt herself slump into her chair. Clearly Kate wasn't going to let her go without a full discussion of her domestic life, and, even though she didn't want to miss the display going on upstairs, she braced herself for a searching interrogation. Perhaps it was for the best, she tried to convince herself, but part of her flashed obscene images into her head, of the girl sucking cock, or rubbing herself, or the boy spurting come on to her face; and every time she showed her distraction, Kate just took it as a sign of something more to wheedle out of her.

It was twenty past when she finally managed to extricate herself from the barrage of questions – no, she didn't want to talk about her boyfriend; she didn't have money problems, nothing was wrong with her family, except . . . She'd had to make up some story about being worried about her mother's health before Kate would let her go, and as she raced upstairs she mentally apologised to her mother for having used her in her ruse.

It was gloomy in the oversized books aisles, and it took her eyes a second to adjust to the murk. There was nobody there. Her heart sank, and she walked slowly down, trailing one finger along a shelf to build up a ridge of dust, then stopped when she got to the end. There was a strong and unmistakable smell of sex here. The girl must know her way round the library pretty well, if she knew that this was one of the quietest spots – hardly anyone ever came down here, but she imagined that the threat of being caught would probably appeal to her anyway.

She decided to walk round the floor once, to see if either of them were still there, and with every head of curly hair she spotted her heart raced, only to be let down as an unfamiliar face turned to her. She was about to give up and go back down to the counter when she spotted the girl, sitting watching Emma at a desk near where she'd begun her search.

Before she could think about what she was saying, Emma found herself apologising. 'I couldn't – my boss asked to see me, so I was late. I wanted to come up, but –'

As Emma spoke, the girl slowly hiked up her skirt, above her knees and higher, to expose soft white thighs with angry red marks where she'd been held, then higher still, to show her sex, still swollen, wet and open, freshly fucked and raw.

'Cover it up! Someone might see!' hissed Emma, starting to panic.

'No one will see. Paul fucked me in the place where I showed you, and nobody came then. Why will they come now? You can see he fucked me, eh?' She smiled, and dipped a finger into her hole, to pull out a glistening drop of come. 'He has a big cock, Paul. Maybe I'll let you try it sometime.' She pulled her skirt back down, breaking Emma's mesmerised gaze. 'But you missed the show – and I put on a good one for you, who likes to watch. But don't worry.' She smiled again, only there was a sneer in it now, and she reached into her bag. 'I saved you a souvenir. Here.'

She tossed a crumpled piece of thin material to Emma, who caught it and began to unfold it before dropping it in disgust when she saw what it was. The girl had thrown her knickers at her, her sex-soiled knickers. And she was laughing now, laughing at her.

'Maybe you like to give them a sniff. Or maybe, if you wear these, boys want to fuck you too. I bet you wear plain pants, eh? Granny pants?' And with this she lunged at Emma's skirt and pulled it up, exposing her ordinary white knickers, then sat back and laughed out loud.

All the frustration of the past few years, all of her self-doubt, anxiety and rage now boiled behind Emma's eyes, burning with tears, and she grabbed the girl's arm hard, ignoring her cries of 'Let go! You're hurting me!' and dragging her to her feet. She knew where to take her – the staff toilet on this floor was hardly ever used, and it locked from the inside. Half of her wanted to hurt the girl, to punish her for having teased her so much, but mixed in with her frustration was a powerful arousal, a realisation that here she could do what she wanted with the girl, get rid of the ache between her thighs.

'Where are you taking me?' the girl whimpered, scared now.

'You'll see,' replied Emma, her voice strangely thick, and, when they arrived at the room, the girl struggling in Emma's grip, Emma checked that the coast was clear, then swung the girl inside, followed her in, closed the door behind them and locked it.

The girl had regained some of her composure by now, and tried to get the upper hand, pushing at Emma and making a dive for the door. 'What the fuck do you think you're doing? Let me out now, or I tell your boss.'

Emma slapped her, hard, the sound echoing round the gleaming white tiles. The girl took a step back, astonished, her face pale apart from the scarlet handmark she now touched. Emma moved towards her and the girl stepped further back. 'Listen, you bitch,' Emma snarled, 'don't talk to me about my boss – I could make sure you don't even graduate, OK?'

The girl nodded mutely.

'I've had enough of your showing off, teasing me, fucking your boyfriend here.'

The girl started to speak but Emma silenced her with a glare.

'And now you're going to get what you deserve. Lie down on the floor.'

'No!' With a shriek the girl leaped forwards, pulling at Emma's hair. She caught her off-balance, and the two of them fell to the ground, tearing at each other's clothes and digging their nails into each other's skin. Emma ripped the girl's top open and pinched an exposed nipple, and as the girl cried out in pain she overpowered her, using her extra strength and weight to pin her down, driving a knee between her legs and feeling something give as a damp squishiness oozed on to her, and gripping the girl's wrists to hold her arms down.

The girl struggled, then relaxed, seemingly resigned to Emma's victory, so she turned around and lifted her skirt so that it fell around the girl's head, then sat slowly on her face, hiking the material of her knickers to one side to make sure the girl got a proper faceful. She was still wet, she knew, aroused from when the girl had been showing herself off, and she ground her slit against the girl's face, ignoring her squeals and her frantic attempts to kick herself out from underneath.

Emma raised herself a little, just so the girl would be sure to hear her. 'Lick me, or I won't let you go.'

When she heard a muffled 'No!' she sat back down on the face and waited until the girl banged her fist on the floor. She raised herself again and heard a dim 'Yes', then felt the first tentative dippings of the girl's tongue in her slit, and sat back down, mashing her sex on to the girl's face. It felt blissful to have the girl under her, controlled by her, with her bottom on the girl's face, making her lick it, and, as the short stabs were replaced by long licks from the tip of her slit down to the base near her bumhole, Emma let out a long moan.

The girl was licking hard now, flicking her tongue over the clit and even sucking it into her mouth, and the ticklish sensation made Emma shudder, but she didn't seem to be fighting any more, so Emma tried letting one of her hands go. It stayed where it was, the girl's whole body relaxed now, except for her legs, which had jerked up as the skirt was lifted, and now fell casually to each side, exposing her fully to Emma's gaze as her licking quickened and she felt the first shy probes of a tongue around her bumhole.

She gasped and shifted, to give the girl better access, and felt every move of the sharp tongue tip as it licked all around the hole before darting in, to penetrate the hole. Emma couldn't help it – she had to sit back and touch herself, and she braced herself with one hand on a chair while the tongue plunged in and out of her dirty bottom hole, teasing herself by stroking all the way down her slit and easing a couple of fingers inside herself to feel the juices welling up before she started to rub her clit, following the rhythm of the tongue jabbing inside her arsehole.

She could see the girl's hand snaking down to play with herself, gently laying a finger over the swollen slit then sliding it back and forth, picking up the pace as her tongue pressed deeper inside Emma. Emma could feel the pressure building up to a head, and flicked harder on her clit as her bumhole started to contract, squeezing the tongue out only for it to force its way back in for the second spasm, and she squealed as it hit her, wave after wave of urgent pleasure washing through her again and again, her slit burning, exposed to her busy fingers. She almost blacked out from the strength of it, her legs clamped around the girl's head, then released her and lay back, revelling in the feel of what she'd done.

The girl was still lying down too, panting with the exertion of licking Emma and making no effort to get up, her hand burrowing slowly into her slit, her face slick with Emma's juices. At the sight of her shiny features, Emma began to giggle, struck with an idea of what she could do next. Just queening the girl hadn't been enough; she'd seemed to enjoy it too much, and Emma was reminded of tricks that bullies had played on some of the girls at her school, something she never would have dared to do herself. Until now.

She stood up unsteadily, drawing her knickers back on, the cool dampness against her burning pussy making her shiver, then took one of the girl's hands. 'Come on, you, up you get.'

The girl opened her eyes, still rubbing herself with languid strokes. 'What are you doing now? You want to lick me?' She leered, and let her legs fall further apart, widening her sex with her fingers and showing Emma the pink wetness inside.

Emma felt a jolt course through her pussy at the sight, then shook her head and dragged the girl to her feet. 'You little slut, you think I'd be interested in licking you? Only filthy tarts lick other girls, filthy tarts like you, and you know what happens to filthy tarts? They get the punishment they deserve.'

She hauled the girl into the cubicle, while she was still too bewildered to fight, then gripped a hand round the back of her neck and forced her on to her knees over the bowl.

Emma could see a look of real fear on the girl's face now as she gazed wide-eyed into the bowl. Whoever had last been there had left a few sheets of toilet roll clinging to the sides, and Emma smiled grimly as she pushed on the back of the neck, until the girl's nose was almost touching the water, her hair already hanging down into the bowl.

'No, please! Stop! I'll do anything you want!' the girl babbled, trying to push back with her hands on either side of the bowl, her naked bottom up and exposed, her swollen pussy still wet and open. Emma ignored her pleas, and pushed harder on the neck until she heard the girl begin to splutter, then pushed on the flush and held firmly on to the girl's neck as her legs kicked and she let out a high-pitched wail that was barely audible over the flush.

The water jetted out over her head, soaking her hair completely, and, when the water had stopped churning and sucking, Emma released the girl's neck and let her fall back. She couldn't help giggling at the way she looked now, bedraggled and gasping, with thin streamers of pink tissue wrapped around her hair and falling off her cheeks. She was crying, too, sobbing gently, but while Emma had fully expected to be attacked, or to have the girl make a dash for the exit again – and she would have let her out this time, just to see her run through the library with the toilet paper in her hair – instead she sat back against the cubicle door, ignoring Emma completely, her hand going back to her slit and burrowing inside again, rubbing hard against her clit, one hand teasing and pinching a nipple.

Emma stared, transfixed, as the girl played with herself, building up a faster and faster rhythm until her legs kicked out and her whole body trembled then locked, and she let out a long, low groan. Emma, stunned, stepped past her and made for the door, to peer out and see if there was anyone around. Behind her she heard a tap being turned on, and looked back to see the girl standing in front of a sink, trying to clean the streamers out of her hair. She turned back to the corridor: to the left the coast was clear, but as her eyes swung to the right the figure of Kate loomed up suddenly, her eyes meeting Emma's and a smile breaking out on her face.

'There you are!' she boomed, and Emma ducked back inside, desperately confused as to what to do. She didn't even have the presence of mind to lock the door, so it swung open slowly, and Kate peered inquisitively around the frame. 'What's –?'she asked, then broke off as her eyes took in the scene: the soaked girl leaning over a basin pulling toilet paper from her hair; Emma, flushed and stammering in the corner; and the telltale smell of sex hanging heavily in the air.

10

The Waves

The first thing that struck me about New York was the size of the people. I'd become used, after months in South America, to being tall, but here I felt dwarfed. The second thing was how familiar it all looked. I'd seen the skyline before, in countless films and TV shows, but what it really reminded me of was the comics I'd read as a child, garishly coloured simple tales of vengeance, justice and a louder world than suburban London.

Manhattan was a walker's city, and, as I had the good fortune to be staying with a friend on the island, I'd cover vast swathes of ground, hiking through Central Park, up to Harlem, down through Little Italy and Chinatown, watching pigeons and junkies in Union Square or staring out at the grey Atlantic.

I only used the subway once, on a trip to see two of the places whose names had stuck in my imagination since I'd first heard them. I couldn't get close to Riker's Island, and was naïve to imagine that a visit was possible: it was a maximum-security prison, attached to the mainland by a heavily fortified bridge, and I contented myself with ambling through the blocks of wrecker's yards and auto spares dealers that flanked the entrance to the bridge. I still spent a while there, though, staring at the prison out on the water, and I'd underestimated how long it would take me to get to my second destination, so that it was four and the sun was low before I arrived.

I'd always loved fairgrounds, even if the actual experience of them rarely lived up to the promise: ghost trains promising pure terror provided nothing more than a loud blare in the dark, and the closest I'd come to a freakshow before was staring at my own distorted reflection in a house of mirrors.

This was different. Coney Island's reputation preceded it, and, if I'd been expecting a tatty seaside glamour, the hint of rain in the grey sky and the off-season emptiness only added to my sense of excitement. Most of the stalls along the boulevard were closed, although a few still sold hot dogs, and a couple of the rides flashed desultory lights. One wooden rollercoaster had been fenced off, and had returned in part to a state of nature, thick, tall weeds growing through the tracks, and most of the other rides had slumped too, abandoned to the elements and decaying fast under the harsh conditions.

But it wasn't the rides I'd come to see. The salt air had pockmarked the paint, but you could still see some of the designs, high up on wooden hoardings: a painting of some fishlike thing with a human head, bearing the title 'Barracuda Ape' and the legend 'Strange but True'; a picture of a girl with a snake, 'Mona'; 'Oddities of the World – Alive!', all in the energetic folksy style I'd only seen before on Indian painted adverts.

I wandered around the concessions, trying to make sure I didn't miss anything, the optimistic simplicity of the sideshow art in stark contrast to the ranks of liquor stores and pawn shops lining the back streets. The last thing I'd expected to find was an actual freakshow.

The tent was tiny, and set almost underneath the boulevard, on the sands, its thick red folds flapping in the wind. I would have missed it altogether if I hadn't walked the length of the stalls, and I descended the wooden steps to take a closer look at the banner. 'Maria the Mermaid', read the legend, 'Alive! Adults only', with a painting of a woman reclining on the sands, her head propped up on one hand and the other along her side. She was topless and, instead of legs, her body from the waist downwards was like the tail end of a fish, glistening with scales.

The tent looked tattier close up, the material riddled with holes, and I felt apprehensive, half-hoping it was closed; but a straw-haired boy emerged from the folds, and his eyes lit up when he saw me standing there.

'Five dollars to see the mermaid!'

It seemed a lot to look at what was probably some moth-eaten dummy, badly stitched together with sawdust spilling out; but then the banner did say 'Alive!', and I could see myself regretting my hesitance if I shied away.

The boy started to look bored. 'Five dollars to see the mermaid! You coming in, mister? The show's about to start; you're just in time.' He stood to one side to let me pass, and I fumbled a five-dollar note into his hand, nodded at his smirk then pushed through.

It was dark inside, and smelled musky, like a zoo. I'd half-expected the ground to be sand, but a tarpaulin had been laid down. When my eyes had adjusted to the gloom, I saw to my surprise that there were also metal chairs lined up, a dozen or so, in front of an inner curtain. About half of them were occupied, too, and all by men of varying ages. I followed their lead and took a seat, then gave a start

217

as tinny music crackled out through the tiny speakers set in the corners of the tent.

The front of the inner curtain was flooded with light, and a man emerged. He looked like the father of the boy outside, with straw-coloured hair too, but he had a far sterner expression, the redness of his face accentuated by a thin, tapering yellow moustache and beard. He looked like I'd imagined carny folk to look, proud yet dissipated, and was big enough to have been a circus strongman in his heyday; not that he didn't look impressive now, dressed in a red jacket with gold buttons and black trousers with something military about them. He surveyed the crowd. 'I see old faces, and I see new.' He seemed to look directly at me. 'Some of you have seen Maria before – for the rest of you, may I present for the very first time, the last mermaid left alive –' at this I couldn't repress a nervous grin '– Maria!'

With a flourish he stepped to one side, and the curtain twitched then jerkily opened, to reveal a large glass tank of water. It looked slightly translucent, a little murky, and seemed to be lit from within, but there was no mistaking the figure inside. A wave of excitement travelled through the men watching, and a few of us leaned forwards to get a better look. She clung to the side of the tank, her large, limpid eyes looking at each of us in turn as her tail swished back and forth in the water. It looked remarkably convincing, although I suppose in that light anything would have done. She was beautiful, too, in an otherworldly way, her face weirdly triangular, with widely spaced eyes and high cheekbones tapering down to full lips above a sharp chin. And, although she was topless, her breasts swaying in the water, she made no attempt to hide herself from us, or even to display herself; she was just there, and we were watching.

The host moved out of the shadows to stand in front of her. 'Who's first?' he boomed.

I had no idea what he meant. A couple of the other men fidgeted in their seats, but nobody moved.

The host's expression turned to scorn as he stared at us. 'Come on, then! You've paid your money; come up and have a go! We haven't got all day, you know.'

With that the man in front of me, about my age, with a look of grim determination on his face, leaped up and moved towards the tank. The host grinned and stepped back, and the young man took off his jacket and threw it to the floor, then walked to the back of the tank, rolled up his sleeves and put his hands into the water.

The girl made a cooing noise as his hands touched her skin. She faced us as his hands caressed her shoulders then moved down to her breasts, feeling the fullness of them then stroking the nipples. And she watched us, her eyes heavy lidded and drowsy, as his hands moved lower, over her belly and towards the scales.

Later I'd wonder what these men thought the girl was; why they came here. Surely they couldn't believe she was a mermaid; surely she was just some local girl hired for the event, with a fake tail fitted. But at the time I was mesmerised. I wasn't thinking about whether she was fake, or real, but rather about what he was doing to her, and how she was responding.

With one hand still stroking her breasts, the man reached the other round to the back of her tail, and was moving there. She was holding the front of the tank now, and began to moan. The sound was unmistakable, and clearly audible above the sloshing of the water in the tank, the only other sound in the tent. The wind outside was blocked by the thick tent fabric, and all the men seemed to be holding their breath, all except the man working his hand against her, or perhaps even into her, who stared down with a face of intense concentration and was breathing heavily. From time to time the girl's moans would raise in pitch, and she'd squeal and straighten, her mouth making an O and her eyes opening wide, then she'd push back on to his hand and relax again, her eyes half-closing and the pitch of her moaning so low it was almost a purr.

Suddenly the host stepped in. 'That's enough for you, now,' he addressed the young man, who flushed and stepped away awkwardly then shuffled back to his seat, either oblivious or uncaring that his front was soaked. The host turned to us. 'Maria is available for private hire, rates negotiable. Come and see me after the show.' I saw the man beside me pat his chest, presumably checking that his wallet was still there, maybe unconsciously imagining how much money he had, how much he would be willing to pay. The girl, meanwhile, who had looked disappointed when the man had stopped caressing her, had returned to her previous dreamy gaze, and stared around the room at the audience, a smile playing about the corner of her lips.

'Now who's next?'

This time a couple of the men got up, a short, stocky tattooed man and a taller man in a suit, who beckoned the other to go before him. The host laughed. The tattooed man had already taken off his coat, and was more direct and rough than the first man, taking his position behind the tank then grabbing the girl's hair with one hand and moving the other hard behind her. I still couldn't work out what he was doing, but the girl's squeal of alarm when he'd grabbed her hair had subsided into a low keening sound as she pushed back on his hand.

Suddenly the tent seemed unbearably close. I could feel my heart thudding in my chest, and realised that I was covered in sweat. The tattooed man looked ferocious as he rubbed at the girl, and I could see the host's broad grin as he looked on, and the girl's face, eyes closed and mouth open in pleasure. I didn't know what I'd do if I were called on to go up, and surely I would be: this was what I'd paid my money for; this was why it was 'Adults only', and if I didn't do it the host would mock me. I stood up abruptly, only just managing to catch the chair from falling to the ground behind me, and walked towards the exit. I could sense that the activity at the tank had paused, and couldn't resist a final glance back before I left. They were all looking at me, the tattooed man, the host and the girl, but it was the girl's gaze I returned, its secret promise almost stopping me in my tracks. I fled into the night air.

I didn't tell anyone about what had happened. What could I say? People would have told me that I was crazy, or naïve enough to fall for some cheap trick. I would have liked maybe to talk to one of the other men in the audience, but having left so suddenly I felt that I'd failed something, that I'd forfeited any sense of community with them. I travelled back to my friend's flat on the subway alone.

The rest of my stay in New York was uneventful. I did the tourist sights – the Statue of Liberty, Ellis Island, the museums and galleries – but soon tired of being jostled by obese tourists in primary colours, and looked for a different side of the city. It wasn't hard to find. The peepshows were still around then, and 42nd Street and Times Square hadn't been cleaned up yet. I wasn't sure whether I was trying to dull the memory of what I'd seen in Coney Island, or to recapture some of the uniquely sordid atmosphere of the tent, but, whichever it was, it didn't work. Hours spent in sleazy cinemas where the floor stuck to your feet and the punters always had one hand in their pants, watching an endless array of beautiful women being violated in every way imaginable, eye-popping enough to anyone raised in the censorious atmosphere of the UK, only recalled the ecstatic face of Maria; and any time I sat in a peepshow cubicle, watching a stripper grind away to the beat, my mind returned to the tent.

But gradually the memory drifted away. My holidays over, I returned to Britain, and immersed myself in efforts to try and find work. The trip soon felt like it had never happened, or it had happened to somebody else, and girlfriends and a new set of sexual obsessions pushed Maria out of my mind. If I thought about her at all, it was with a dim memory as of a dream; and not telling anybody, even those closest to me, meant that I was soon unsure that it had happened at all.

I hadn't been invited to the party. Jonno said it would be fine; nobody would mind, but I felt like a fraud wandering around drinking their champagne and eating their exquisite snacks. So how did I repay their generosity? By leaving the party and snooping around upstairs.

In my five years working as an interior designer I'd done well, although Jonno always said I'd do better if I played the game: flatter the right people, be seen at the right events, that kind of thing. But it wasn't something that came easily to me, and I tended to leave the schmoozing to Jonno, who was far more outgoing. We complemented each other well, which was probably one of the reasons our partnership had been successful; he loved the limelight, while I did the

222

hard work, I sometimes thought to myself, but that was unfair. Jonno's contribution was invaluable in securing the kinds of client that mattered.

Still, this wasn't my scene. The house was nice enough, worth far more than I'd ever earn: a fully detached mansion in Holland Park, the kind of property that simply isn't available any more. But I was bored to tears by the company, brittle, stick-thin women with insincere laughs firing daggers at each other, while their braying partners in blazers and chinos discussed golf and money. As I say, more Jonno's scene; I didn't even know whose party it was, let alone meet the host. But I'd made an effort, mingled a little, until a couple of my more colourful quips fell on stony ground, and I decided to go upstairs.

The chinking of glasses and waves of laughter subsided as I padded up to the first floor. Jonno would kill me if he knew what I was doing, but I'd never been one to resist when curiosity struck. I liked to know how people lived, and I usually got a much better idea of what lay under their masks by looking at their environments than blathering politely with a drink in my hand.

All the doors were closed except one, and I walked towards it to peer inside. There was nobody in there. It had to be the study: there was a desk at one end, with a computer monitor to one side, and the walls were lined with books. I crept inside, already scanning the titles. Whoever's study this was had a nautical leaning: the only fiction I could see was Conrad and Melville, and all the other books seemed to be about sailing, accounts of sea journeys and guides to marine biology, apart from the odd title on folklore and mythology. There were a couple of prints on the wall too: a slightly faded photograph of a boat, which looked like it was taken in the seventies, and several more recent photos, all of seascapes that had nothing, to my untrained eye, to distinguish one from another.

As I studied these, I noticed a drinks cabinet next to the computer and, with the thrill of a young boy who knows he's doing something he shouldn't, I poured myself a glass of Laphroaig.

It was only then that I noticed another door, set in a small alcove at the end of the room. There was a key in the lock, and, although I knew that I should leave it alone, that taking some whisky was more than enough of a liberty, I turned the lock and opened the door. Whatever I'd expected, it hadn't been that. It was dank and gloomy inside, but I could see two rows of trestle tables, reminding me of chemistry classes at school, all holding tanks of murky water, with tubes bubbling in them. Something about the look of the tanks – the milky opacity of the water, the algae clinging to the sides – reminded me of the tent I'd visited all that time ago, and as I stared, fascinated, something thumped against the side of the nearest tank.

I was so shocked I almost dropped my whisky, but that was nothing compared to the jump I gave when I heard a voice behind me.

'May I help you?'

I spun round, reddening and guiltily putting the drink down. A man had come in, wearing a tailored suit. He smiled icily, and moved towards the door I'd just opened, closing it, locking it and pocketing the key.

Flustered, I tried to make excuses for my presence. 'I'm terribly sorry. I was looking for the bathroom, and seem to have wandered in here by mistake.'

The man looked pointedly at my drink, then at the door to what I could only imagine was some kind of aquarium, or laboratory. 'The bathroom downstairs is clearly marked.'

I could only repeat myself. 'I'm sorry.'

The man looked irritated. 'Sorry? It's not enough, is it?' Then his face softened, and he beckoned to the whisky. 'You may drink it; I invite you. My name is Mark; this is my home.'

'It's a beautiful house. I'm afraid parties aren't really my thing.'

Now his smile was warmer. 'Nor mine.' He paused, and looked me up and down, then seemed to come to a decision. 'I want to introduce you to someone.' He turned and called clearly, but not too loudly, 'Maria!'

The initial wave of panic at having been caught up here had subsided, and I let the warm glow of the whisky fill me, relaxed again. But then Maria arrived, and my heart was in my throat once more. It had been ten years since I'd seen the girl in the tank – even if I hadn't thought about it recently, I could never have forgotten what had happened – but she looked exactly the same, even though it was impossible to think that they were the same woman. Her hair was dry, and flowed silkily over her shoulders, and she was dressed in some thin black confection that hung down to expose most of her chest; but the most important difference, of course, was that she had legs. I even looked to check, and she was wearing a pair of black heels, although she seemed to glide rather than stalk across the floor.

My astonishment must have been plain, as Mark eyed me quizzically. 'Have you met my wife before?'

I looked at him; I could tell she was staring into my eyes, with the same dreamy, faraway expression I remembered from all those years ago, but I couldn't face her gaze. Not yet. 'I – she reminds me of someone I used to know.'

'Good.' Mark beamed, and patted me on the back. 'I have something in mind, some small penalty you have to pay for this –' he searched for the word '– snooping.' His expression had changed again, and he glared at me.

I began to apologise, but he stopped me by holding up a hand. 'I want you to make love to my wife.' He smiled as I coughed, spluttering on the whisky. 'And I will watch, of course.'

My mind raced: I knew such practices were not uncommon, perhaps especially among the very rich. It seemed grubby, distasteful somehow, or at least it would have done if it hadn't been for Maria. She had already come closer to me, until finally her body was touching mine. I felt a jolt at the contact – she seemed cold, even through her dress – but she was pressing now, already starting to make the face I remembered, her eyelids drowsy and heavy, her lips full and moist.

'It would be no penalty at all,' I said, aware that my voice was choked with emotion.

Mark nodded. I still couldn't face her, although I was already powerfully aroused, and not a little frightened.

'You will do it in the pool. She likes it there.'

He turned, and walked out of the door. She took my hand and followed, pulling me along to another set of stairs at the far end of the floor from those leading down to the party. As we descended, I stupidly began to think about swimming pools, my internal chatter now a babble as my mind refused to accept what was happening, instead comparing the floor plan here to others I'd known, all the while keeping a professional eye on the furnishings.

The carpet on this flight of stairs had given out after the first dozen steps, and the sound of our feet on the stone steps that followed had a hollow ring, echoing in what was rapidly becoming less a stairway than a tunnel. There was a distinct change of atmosphere. The air smelled briny and damp, and there were wet patches and beads of condensation on the walls, the wallpaper peeling away or bulging, some furred with a slight mould. It seemed so incongruous given the state of the rest of the house that I was about to comment, when we reached a steel door.

Mark opened it, flicked on the lights inside and ushered us in, then closed the door with a resounding clang. The briny smell was much stronger here, and I was momentarily confused. There was nothing in the room but a compact swimming pool: no windows, no changing area, nothing else but a shower in the corner and a couple of towels hanging from a rail.

As if he'd noticed my confusion, Mark pointed to the pool. 'Chlorine hurts the eyes so, don't you find? And it does terrible things to Maria's skin. Salt water's just as hygienic. Don't worry, it's heated.'

He turned away, to seat himself by the side of the pool, and I finally faced her. Holding my gaze, she slid one shoulder then the other out of her dress, which slipped to the tiled floor. I stared at her body. She was exquisite, a jewel, perfect from head to toe, with full breasts, the nipples already jutting out, and a carefully trimmed mound, a small tuft of hair on the plump sex hinting of the pleasures within.

I could have stared at her forever, but she came towards me, her eyes never leaving mine, and kneeled down, her face in front of my crotch. She reached up to feel my cock, huge and stiff, and feeling ready to burst, then unzipped me, pulled it out and began to suck.

I wrapped my fingers through her hair, pulling her closer towards me. If her scalp was cold, her mouth was deliciously hot, her tongue working over my swollen cockhead then licking the whole length of it, her head bobbing quickly up and down. I almost stepped back when she cradled my balls in one cold hand, the iciness of her fingers going through me like a blade, but then I gave in to the contrast, letting her dig tenderly into the sac and scrape the sensitive furrowed skin with her long nails.

She had started to rub herself, too, burrowing in and flicking at her slit in time to the bobs of her head. When she started to rub the end of my cock over her lips, smearing her saliva all over her cheeks and chin as she covered her face with cock, her hand rubbing faster now in her sex, giving it little pinches and slaps, and moaning and cooing like I'd heard her – but it couldn't be her – doing so long ago, I felt my balls tighten, and knew that I'd finish too soon, come all over her face, if she didn't stop.

Bunching up her hair in one hand, I pulled her head back, and looked her full in the eyes.

She gazed back at me, looking drowsy and sluttish with her wet chin.

'I'm going to come if you don't stop.'

She squealed, looked delighted then turned and dived into the pool, only to surface a moment later and swim to the side, beaming. I was still wearing all my clothes, but I undressed as fast as I could, ending ludicrously in my shirt, socks and pants. I was barely aware of Mark now, sitting silently by the side of the pool; all my attention was on Maria, who giggled and held a hand out as I hopped from foot to foot, pulling each sock off, until I was finally naked, and dived in.

The water was colder than I'd expected, and I gasped on surfacing. But it was buoyant, far more than an ordinary swimming pool, and I followed Maria into the shallows, where she waited expectantly. I was still hard, my balls achingly full now, and she took me in her hand and guided me into her, wrapping her legs around me as I sank fully into her tight warmth.

She was pressed hard against me now, her arms around my neck, her mouth nibbling at my shoulder and her breasts firm on my chest, and she was cooing in my ear as I fucked her with long hard strokes, wanting to hear her moan and squeal as I pounded away. Her nails were digging into my arse, as though she were trying to claw me even deeper inside her, and I felt the smoothness of her own cheeks with my hands, pulling the globes apart then dipping a finger over her arsehole. She sobbed and ground herself against me, then moaned when I pushed it in, the tight hole creamy from where her sex juices must have oiled their way down earlier.

I alternated strokes of cock and finger, plunging one in and squeezing the other out, until this seemed too slow, and I cupped my arms under her shoulders and pumped her as hard as I could. She was trembling after that and I paused, hot despite the water; then I moved a hand down her back, to feel the weight of her arse cheek again. But this time my fingers grazed against something on her back, and she went berserk.

I don't know what it was. It seemed to be some kind of ridge, or fin, but whatever it was it was extra sensitive, even more so than her clit. I found it again and rubbed it, hard now, and she shook in my arms, grinding her sex against the base of my cock, whimpering now.

I couldn't hold back much longer, so I started to fuck her hard again, rubbing the ridge with one hand while supporting her with the other as my balls tightened. Her legs unhooked themselves from my back, and seemed to undulate in the water, a trick of the light, but I was past caring now, pumping hard inside her, my hand rubbing furiously on the ridge on her back, until with a long drawn-out squeal she came, her pussy clenching as waves of contractions ran up and down my cock, milking me into her as my balls emptied themselves.

All my feeling was in my cock when I came, but I noticed other things too, things I didn't pay too much attention to at the time, but remembered afterwards. The feel of the rough skin of her arse under my hand, hard, almost metallic, scaly; the sense of something inhumanly sinuous snaking itself around my legs as I hit my peak; and, when I opened my eyes, a glint of silver from the bottom of the pool, another trick of the light, of course.

Mark was kind afterwards. After Maria had detached herself and swum to the other end of the pool, where she watched us with those large eyes, I clung to the side, out of breath. I couldn't even pull myself out when Mark came over with a towel, but had to climb out of the steps at the shallow end.

Apart from thanking him for the towel, I couldn't think of anything to say; making polite conversation seemed ludicrous, and trying to talk about what had happened – or what I'd seen ten years before – impossible. Strangely, I wasn't nervous about being seen naked by another man, although it was the first time since school I'd been so exposed; but Mark's face, wistful, almost sorrowful but not at all judgemental, put me at my ease.

Most of the guests had gone when I finally returned to the party, and Jonno was so drunk he didn't ask me where I'd been. I drove him home, sober now, and I never told him about what had happened. He wouldn't believe me, of course; nobody would. I'm hardly sure exactly what happened myself. The house in Holland Park has been sold since then; I suppose it wouldn't be too hard to track Mark and Maria down, but there didn't seem to be any point. But even now, the smell of the sea brings her back to me, and whenever I see a girl with long black hair my heart leaps as I remember the secret promise of the ocean in her eyes.

NEXUS BACKLIST

To be published in July 2005

THE BOOK OF PUNISHMENT
Cat Scarlett

Indigo, bookseller and CP-loving submissive, is obsessed with an antiquarian work of sadomasochism which eluded her father all his life. Caned, roped and shamed through the fleshpots of Europe, she will suffer any indignity to prevent Dervil Badon and his transsexual slave Natasha from getting their hands on her prize. But Dervil has no intention of allowing a mere submissive to own the legendary *Book of Punishment*.

£6.99   ISBN 0 352 33975 6

NAUGHTY, NAUGHTY
Penny Birch

Gabrielle Salinger has been sent to track down Sabina, a voluptuous and dominant young women who has fallen under the influence of elderly sybarite David Anthony. Garielle soon discovers that the couple are already in France, getting up to all sorts of lewd mischief. Accompanied, but not really helped, by her girlfriend Poppy, Monty Hartle and the boys from the Razorback Paintball, Gabrielle is soon beginning to wonder if she's bitten off more than she can chew. By the time she's being hunted through the woods in an abbreviated bunny costume, she's sure that she has.

£6.99   ISBN 0 352 33976 4

THE BLACK MASQUE
Lisette Ashton

The ceremonies of the Black Masque are an erotic blend of vampires myth and fantasy. As they prepare to enact their greatest ceremony to date, passions run high among the perverse members. Eager virgins are prepared and the sacrificial altar is readied as the Masque anticipates its finest night. Unwittingly entangled in the twisted ceremony, private investigator Jo Valentine is drawn into their dark world of pleasure, pain and orgiastic excess.

£6.99   0 352 33977 2

If you would like more information about Nexus titles, please visit our website at www.nexus-books.co.uk, or send a stamped addressed envelope to:
  Nexus, Thames Wharf Studios,
  Rainville Road, London W6 9HA